T[illegible]NCE

. . . Not wanting to intrude in any way on the monks inside, nor to alarm them by his sudden appearance, Collier cautiously pulled the door open a little wider and peered round it . . .

Seated at the head of a long oak table laden with food was Helene, sensuously and delicately eating a peach. On her right sat Charalambos neatly cutting himself a slice of cheese and, on her left, Basileos, his face buried in a wine goblet.

Collier was utterly bewildered . . .

Had Helene and Charalambos been here all the time, he wondered, or had they just arrived? Not that that was important. They were here. With Basileos. That was enough. Why they were here and what they were up to was just one more mystery in the confusing maze from which there seemed no way out. But whatever their game was, Collier was in no doubt now that, in some way, he was part of it and that they were using him . . .

Also by Michael J. Bird in *Star*

WHO PAYS THE FERRYMAN?

THE APHRODITE INHERITANCE

Michael J. Bird

Based on the BBC television serial by Michael J. Bird

STAR

A STAR BOOK

published by

the Paperback Division of

W. H. ALLEN & Co. Ltd

A Star Book
Published in 1979
by the Paperback Division of
W. H. Allen & Co. Ltd
A Howard and Wyndham Company
44 Hill Street, London W1X 8LB

Printed in Great Britain by
Hazell Watson & Viney Ltd, Aylesbury, Bucks

ISBN 0 352 30274 7

To all those who believe it possible

CHAPTER ONE

The driver of the on-coming car flashed his headlights and Collier grinned but ignored the warning. All right, so there was a police trap up ahead. So what if they did come after him? He doubted if they would. Not on this stretch of the Paphos to Limassol road where, with a tarmacadamed ledge along the cliff face and with a sheer drop to one side, the main highway twisted and climbed to the British Base at Episkopi and then, beyond the garrison area, descended equally dramatically to the boredom and relative safety of the coastal plain once more. Not the safest spot on earth for a racing pursuit just to issue a summons for exceeding the speed limit. Collier's grin broadened. Not for the Cyprus police anyway he thought. He changed into third to keep the revs up and maintain the fifty miles an hour he was demanding from the Landrover.

And what if he was wrong and the law was feeling in an uncharacteristically reckless mood? So what? They still had to catch him and he wouldn't make that easy for them. And in the unlikely event of them nailing him, what then? Okay, so he'd slip them a fiver each and that would be the end of it. Or, if the chase had scared them sufficiently to make them bloody-minded enough to book him out of spite, the worst the court would hand down against a guilty plea with apologies would be a fine. And bribe or fine, the maximum even, he could afford either. He laughed out loud. There were many things he could afford. Now.

Collier swung the Landrover into a bend and entering the short straight on the far side of it he saw them; two constables, one a veteran and the other not long out of training school.

The older man, his arms folded across his chest, was leaning lazily against the offside of the car parked a few yards back from the road in the shade of a carob tree while his companion sat alert and with a purposely fierce and hopefully deterrent expression behind the steering wheel. The Englishman accelerated and the speedometer nudged sixty as he flashed past them, braked hard and, with a squeal of wasted rubber, took the tight left-hand curve fifty yards further up the road and roared away out of sight.

The young policeman frowned angrily. Such flagrant disregard for the law could not go unpunished. And what's more, to make it worse, the driver of the Landrover had been grinning as though taunting them, daring them to try and catch him. He reached forward, switched on the engine and gunned it, unnecessarily but resolutely.

His companion, however, did not move. He had seen the Kitson Neve sign stencilled on the side of the Landrover and he had recognised the face beneath the green safety helmet which the driver had been wearing. He was one of the Englishmen working on the big construction project up along the coast west of Peyia. This wasn't the first time he had seen him speeding to or from Limassol and more than once he'd been tempted to at least make an attempt to book him but he was well aware that Kitson Neve was an important and influential company and that the work they were doing was for the Cyprus Government. A mere constable had to be careful not to offend the wrong people.

Still perhaps one day he would take steps against this particular offender. But not today. Today it was too hot and this section of the road was far too dangerous for heroics. So if this fresh faced, know-nothing and over zealous kid his superiors had foisted on him imagined for one moment that he was going to risk his neck just to end up wasting a morning giving evidence in court, he was very much mistaken. The majority of drivers, forewarned of their presence by the customary and almost obligatory headlamp signal from fellow road users, slowed to the legal limit. For a while anyway. And surely on such a day as this, and here of all places, that was enough.

He glanced at the younger man who, revving the engine impatiently, was glaring up at him through the open window, raised his eyes in mock despair and shrugged, successfully dismissing any attempt to go after the Landrover as futile.

Scowling, his companion sulkily switched off the engine. It was then that they heard the crash.

The telescopic sight of the rifle had been zeroed in on the front, nearside tyre of the Landrover almost from the moment that it had appeared around the left-hand bend. When the tyre exploded under the impact of the bullet, almost tearing itself in two, the report covered the sound of the shot which came from high up on the cliff overlooking the road.

Desperately, Collier wrestled with the steering wheel and stamped on the brake as the vehicle skidded wildly but there was nothing he could do to save himself. The Landrover spun into the low barrier rail edging the right-hand side of the highway, ripped its way through it, hung in mid-air for a second and then plunged down the near vertical rock face, pitching its driver out into space. It struck the ground three hundred feet below, rolled over several times and then burst into flames.

The two policemen were on the scene in less than a minute. The Landrover was a blazing mass of twisted metal and, when they scrambled down to where he was lying like a bloody, broken doll among the scrub and rocks close to the spot where the vehicle had first hit the ground, Barry Collier was still alive.

But only just.

Martin Preece spotted his man the moment he came out from Customs and Immigration Control and approached the barrier.

He was in his late twenties, good-looking and well built with his fair hair cut in a neat, untrendy style. But then there was nothing trendy about him. His sports jacket and slacks were well cut and chosen with care and taste but they were conservative, even a little old-fashioned, in style. He was carrying a briefcase in one hand and a suitcase in the other. And tucked under his left arm was a copy of the *Daily Telegraph*.

The only photograph Preece had seen of him had been taken some years earlier but from what he had heard about him and from his general appearance he was in no doubt that this was David Collier. Slowly he edged forward through the throng to greet him.

It was hot. Hotter than Collier had imagined it would be in Cyprus in mid-September. Hot and humid and incredibly noisy. It seemed to him that practically the entire population of the island must have gathered at Larnaca Airport to welcome friends and relatives or late season tourists newly arrived from London. Beyond the barrier the terminal building was filled with a mass of jostling humanity, waving, laughing, shouting, crying.

Ordinarily Collier didn't like crowds and today more than any other the last thing he wanted was to be caught up in a surging, elbowing crush of people. The four hour flight had been bad enough with the ageing Boeing 727, on charter to Cyprus Airways, filled to capacity and ringing with the excited chatter of scores of Cypriots all of whom seemed to be either related in some way or to know one another and who, throughout the journey, had indulged in a gabble of gossip which at times had drowned even the throbbing resonance of the jets.

No, it hadn't been a comfortable flight. Nor a smooth one. Not that that had apparently worried his fellow passengers, with the exception of the two middle-aged women in black dresses and Marks and Spencer's cardigans shoe-horned in alongside him who, every time the plane had plummeted in an air pocket, had clutched one another, crossed themselves furiously and then leant forward threateningly over the sick bag which each had held open on her lap from the moment the aircraft had taxied for take-off.

For the rest, the turbulence seemed to have passed unnoticed or been taken for granted. And no one, including the two women, had seemed at all concerned when, as the Boeing lost altitude on the approach to Larnaca, water began to drip from the roof of the cabin. No one, that is, except Collier who, as the occasional drip developed into something resembling the onset of a spring shower, took shelter under an umbrella improvised from the grubby, plastic-covered sheet of safety instructions snatched from the seat pocket in front of him. And Collier was not so disturbed as he might otherwise have been. But then he had a lot on his mind and at that moment it wasn't his safety and well-being that were of paramount importance to him. It hadn't been throughout the flight during which he had re-read the telegram at least a dozen times.

Collier squeezed his way through the crowd, past a bulging and tearful family reunion, and into the scrum beyond.

'Mr Collier? Mr David Collier?'

The voice had come from just behind him and to his left. Collier swung round to find a broad shouldered, sun tanned man regarding him with shrewd, intelligent eyes and a polite, welcoming smile. He had a pleasant, open face and Collier judged him to be around thirty-five.

Collier nodded.

'My name's Preece.'

The name rang a bell with Collier but only distantly and it showed. He regarded the stranger blankly.

'Martin Preece,' the man continued. 'Resident engineer, Kitson Neve.'

Now Collier had him placed, an echo from one of his brother's letters.

'Oh yes, of course,' he said with a hint of apology. 'Good of you to meet me.'

Preece's smile warmed and broadened a little. He reached out and took Collier's suitcase from him.

'How is Barry?' Collier asked anxiously.

The cloying, sickly smell in the windowless, white-tiled room was beginning to make David Collier's head swim.

Barry's body lay on a trolley covered with a white sheet, one corner of which the orderly had lifted to reveal the dead man's face.

It had seemed a long drive from Larnaca to Limassol and throughout Martin Preece had remained silent while Collier struggled with the shock and tried desperately to come to terms with it. But even now, though, staring down at his brother, he still found it difficult to accept. He felt that he had only to reach out and shake Barry's shoulder and he would wake as if from a deep sleep and smile at him. But then, suddenly, he knew it was true, that Barry was dead and that the heavy stench hanging in the air was formalin. He felt sick and he gagged.

He glanced across at the doctor standing on the other side of the trolley and saw the official, enquiring look on the man's face. Collier nodded. The doctor made a sign to the orderly who lowered the sheet.

'I'm sorry,' the doctor said quietly. 'But he didn't really have a chance, I'm afraid. Multiple injuries. Frankly I'm surprised that he hung on as long as he did.' He shrugged and spread his hands in an apologetic gesture of helplessness. 'There will have to be a post-mortem of course. Merely as a matter of routine. You understand.'

Collier nodded.

'He never regained consciousness so he didn't suffer,' the doctor assured him. 'Pain I mean. If that helps.'

Half way to the door Collier turned and looked back.

'It doesn't. Much,' he said flatly.

Preece had waited outside the hospital and when Collier came through the doors and back into the sunlight again he was at his side in an instant.

'What can I say.' He shrugged impotently. 'And I'm sorry that you had to walk straight into it like this. A hell of a shock for you.'

Collier, lost and confused, looked at him enquiringly.

'The man who telephoned me from your London office just said that Barry was critically ill.'

Preece nodded. 'Yes. Well that was the situation at the time,' he explained. 'But then . . .' He sighed. 'It was very sudden, I understand. While you were on your way. And you couldn't have got here any quicker.'

Collier shook his head and gave a helpless shrug. Slowly the two men moved down the steps to the waiting Audi.

'A bloody awful business,' said Preece. 'Awful. Goes without saying that everyone's very cut up about it. Your brother was a good man. One of the best.'

He opened the nearside rear door of the car and Collier got into it. Preece settled himself beside him.

'The Project Director wants to pay his respects personally of course,' he continued, and then signalled to the driver.

The car pulled smoothly away from the steps, circled the drive and then glided out of the hospital gateway and into the early afternoon traffic.

Less than ten minutes later Collier, still numbed with shock and clutching a cup of tea which had been thrust on him and which he hadn't had the heart to refuse, was sitting opposite Leonard Wyndham in Kitson Neve's Limassol office.

'A damn shame! Damn shame!'

Wyndham, a short, dapper man in his fifties, sighed deeply and then spooned sugar into his tea from a bowl standing on his desk. He stared down into his cup.

'A first class chap, Barry.' The Project Director's tone was sympathetic but brisk. 'Right spirit. Kept the work moving I can tell you.' He looked up at Preece. 'You can testify to that, eh Martin?'

'Yes, I certainly can,' murmured Preece.

Wyndham picked up his eulogy once more. 'And he got on so well with everyone. The men under him thought the world of him. We all did. We could do with more like Barry and that's the truth.' He gestured to the confused neatness of plans drawing-pinned to the wall behind him. 'An important project, this, you know,' he went on. 'The biggest desalination plant in the eastern Med. A power station, service roads, the lot. Three years' work. Quite a coup Kitson Neve getting the contract, believe me.' Again he sighed. 'Oh yes, your brother'll be missed. And not easy to replace. Section Managers of his calibre are thin on the ground.' He nodded sagely. 'Yes indeed. A great loss to his friends, a credit to the firm and a credit to his family. And that's not a bad way to be remembered, is it?'

'No, I suppose not,' replied Collier, unconvinced.

The official sympathies over, Wyndham now adopted an even brisker and more businesslike tone. 'Now, what about accommodation?' He glanced at Preece. 'We've fixed up something of course.'

'Well, we had made arrangements,' confirmed Preece. 'But Mr Collier tells me that he's already booked into the Curium Palace.'

'Oh!' The Project Director seemed surprised, even a little put out.

Collier nodded. 'Yes. The company I work for made a reservation there. They've been very good about everything.'

'I see. Well you'll be all right at the Curium. A comfortable billet, eh Martin?'

'Very,' agreed Preece.

Wyndham leant forward and, slightly lowering his voice, introduced a reverential note into his businesslike approach. 'Now I know this must all be very painful for you,' he said. 'But there are certain arrangements which have to be made.'

He picked up a cigarette box from his desk, opened it and offered it to Collier. Collier shook his head.

Without taking a cigarette for himself or offering one to Preece, Wyndham closed the box again and set it down once more.

'It goes without saying that Kitson Neve will fly your brother back to the U.K. At their expense.'

'That's good of them,' replied Collier listlessly.

Wyndham dismissed the company's generosity with a wave of his hand. 'The very least we can do,' he said.

Collier hesitated, turning the thought over in his mind. Then he asked, 'Tell me, is there a British cemetery anywhere on the island?'

The Project Director looked surprised. 'Well yes, there is. But naturally I assumed . . .' He frowned slightly. 'And surely your parents . . .'

'They're dead,' interrupted Collier. 'And there isn't anyone else. Only an aunt and uncle and some cousins. But they're in New Zealand.'

Wyndham gave a little shrug. 'Well of course in that case it's up to you then. Naturally we'll go along with your wishes.'

Collier would willingly have left it at that but he could see from Wyndham's expression that some further explanation was called for.

'It's not as if Barry had any real roots back in England,' he said quietly. 'His job took him all over the place. So there's nowhere he could really call home. Nowhere he belongs. And he liked Cyprus. He told me so in his letters. And he'd been here quite a while.'

Wyndham nodded. 'Indeed. Well over a year.' Again he looked at Preece. 'He was with you on the first survey, wasn't he, Martin?'

Preece nodded. 'Yes. Barry was in on the project from the very beginning.'

'And he has friends here,' said Collier.

'Many,' agreed Wyndham. Collier's argument seemed eminently reasonable to him. 'Very well then,' he said. 'Leave it to me.' He opened his desk diary and flicked through the pages. 'The day after tomorrow?'

Collier was a little taken aback. 'But what about the inquest?' he asked.

'A formality,' Wyndham assured him. 'Just a formality. Day after tomorrow then?'

Collier nodded.

'C of E was he?' queried Wyndham.

Collier shrugged. 'He wasn't anything really.'

'Quite so. Quite so. I understand,' murmured the Project Director. 'But I think that counts as C of E.'

He picked up his pen and made a note in his diary. Now, as far as he was concerned, with his condolences expressed and the question of the burial decided, the painful interview was over.

He lay down his pen and gave Collier a final, consoling look. Once more he shook his head sadly and sighed. 'Again my deepest sympathy, Mr Collier. A tragedy. A tragedy.'

Wyndham slowly began to rise from his chair.

'What happened exactly?' asked Collier quietly.

Half way to his feet and nonplussed by the question, Wyndham shot a puzzled look at Preece and then lowered himself down into his seat again.

'I'm sorry, but I'm not sure that I understand.'

'My brother,' said Collier. 'How did it happen? Exactly.'

The Project Director frowned. 'You don't know?' he exclaimed. Visibly annoyed, he turned his attention to Preece. 'You didn't tell him?' he challenged testily.

'No,' replied Preece levelly and holding his gaze. 'I thought it might be best if Mr Collier had a word with . . .'

Wyndham nodded, relieved to be let off the hook. 'Yes, you're right,' he said, cutting in on him. 'Best person.' He picked up one of the telephones on his desk and dialled. Collier could hear the number ringing out and then it was answered.

Wyndham adopted an over polite and slightly patronising tone of voice. 'Oh, Leonard Wyndham here,' he announced. 'Project Director, Kitson Neve. I'd like to speak to Inspector Mitsides.'

CHAPTER TWO

'It was an accident,' Mitsides shouted above the din of a passing lorry. He waited while the sound receded and the dust settled and then he said it again. 'It was an accident. Or anyway that will be the coroner's verdict. He will have no alternative.'

The Chief Inspector had been waiting for Collier and Preece when they had driven up to the spot where the Landrover had plunged off the road. Now the three men stood close to the edge of the cliff just beyond the twisted gap in the barrier rail.

Mitsides stared down at the rocks far below them, scowled and shook his head. 'Accidental death,' he added as a postscript and his tone was scathing.

Frowning, Collier shot a worried look at the policeman. 'You doubt it?' he asked. The policeman raised his head and held his questioning gaze.

Giorgios Mitsides had been in the Cyprus Police for thirty years. He had joined when he was eighteen and when the British ran the country. And on the day when he had heard that his application had been successful he had bought himself his first pipe. From the beginning he had been a good policeman but the briar, bought to impress his Englishness on his superiors, his dedication and his consistently good reports had had little effect on his career. For too long he had remained a constable, first with the uniformed branch and then, at last, with the C.I.D. Many a young and less experienced man from the Home Counties had come and gone before he'd made Detective Sergeant. And it wasn't until the 17th August 1960, the day after independence, that he'd been promoted to Inspector. But Mitsides wasn't bitter. He'd been well trained. There was no denying that. And the frustration and disappointments of those early years were behind him now and almost forgotten. Almost. Today the British horizon in Cyprus was limited to the boundaries of the two small Sovereign Base Areas. Now it was Cypriot who exploited Cypriot. But little else had changed. Everywhere 'highly desirable', red roofed, bijou residences which wouldn't have looked too much out of place in Surbiton and tower blocks and hotels aping the City and the West End had sprung up to replace older, traditional buildings and dispossess those uncaring of their heritage and hungry for a car. The traffic continued to flow on the left-hand side of the road – legally anyway – and many of the pillar-boxes still bore the royal cypher while, as in the past, the rich, the influential and the rulers of the land aspired to send their sons to British public schools and to have their gallstones removed in the London Clinic. And as for Giorgios Mitsides? Well the Chief Inspector still smoked a pipe. And he held it, unlit, in his hand as, coolly, he studied David Collier. He sighed.

'This stretch of road is a death trap,' he said. 'Your brother knew that. He had to. There has been enough publicity about it. And there are warning signs. But still he was driving recklessly. Showing off. And, as far as I am concerned, that is closer to suicide than to an accident.'

Collier flushed angrily. 'Barry wasn't like that,' he bridled. 'Reckless, I mean.'

'No? You have seen the skid marks. What would you say he was doing? Fifty? Sixty? And with bends such as these.'

'He was a good driver,' protested Collier. 'Experienced. He knew how to handle a car. Any car.'

'Oh really!' Mitsides shook his head wearily. 'So will that be his epitaph then?' Reaching into his pocket he took out a lighter and lit his pipe.

'A tyre blew, you said.'

The Chief Inspector nodded. 'Which, if he had not been speeding, would have been no problem. I'm sorry, Mr Collier. I'm a policeman. I have been for many years. I deal in realities. And stupidity is one of them. As is death.'

Collier groped wildly in his mind for further arguments, more excuses but he could come up with neither. He had seen the tyre tracks on the road and he knew that Mitsides had to be right. He stared down at the steep fall only a foot away from where he was standing.

Mitsides drew on his pipe. He studied the Englishman. He felt sorry for him but there would be others to sympathise, others to console. That was not his job.

'I have some of your brother's personal effects,' he said. 'If you come to my office I will give them to you. Would tomorrow morning be convenient?'

Collier looked up at him miserably and nodded. The policeman glanced at Preece and inclined his head. 'Mr Preece.'

'Chief Inspector.'

Mitsides turned and started to move towards his car which was parked on the verge on the opposite side of the road. Then he paused and turned back to look at Collier again.

'It is not that I do not sympathise,' he said curtly. 'It is just that I've seen too much of this. And it is all such a waste. Of living. And waste makes me angry.'

Swinging round on his heel once more he walked briskly over to the police car and got into it.

Collier and Preece watched as the car pulled on to the road and then, gathering speed, headed back for Limassol.

'He's a good man,' murmured Preece as if by way of apology. 'Knows what he's about.'

Collier looked at him. 'If you say so,' he said stonily.

The two men drove back into town and Preece dropped Collier at the Curium Palace. At eight thirty Preece was back at the hotel and, despite Collier's protestations that he wasn't hungry, insisted that he must eat and took him to a *taverna* overlooking the sea.

They sat at a table outside close to the water's edge and under a black velvet sky dusted with stars. The sound of *bouzoukis* drifted across to them from within the *taverna* but the music did nothing to lift the air of depression and unease which they had brought with them to the meal.

Collier picked at his food politely but disinterestedly and declined Preece's offer of wine, explaining that he did not drink.

'Something non-alcoholic then,' suggested his companion.

Collier gave him a weak smile, shook his head and then went back to toying with the *kebab* which he had ordered but didn't want.

Valiantly Preece tried to make conversation but it was an uphill struggle and he finally gave up the attempt. He picked up his glass, sipped his wine and studied Collier who, head down and gazing at his plate, was clearly lost in a desert of grief in which he could not be reached.

By ten they were back at the hotel. At the foot of the steps to the entrance Preece said, 'Well, goodnight then.'

Collier conjured up another faint smile. 'Goodnight. And thank you.'

Preece shrugged off his gratitude. 'For what? Sure there's nothing else I can do?'

'Positive. You've been very kind.'

Preece put out his hand. 'Can't say how sorry I am to have met you like this. So very sorry.'

Collier shook hands with him. 'Thank you,' he said. And then he moved away up the steps and into the hotel.

He slept badly that night and it showed the following morning when he was ushered into Chief Inspector Mitsides' office.

The policeman looked up at him from his desk, frowned slightly and then got to his feet and shook hands.

'A coffee?' he enquired solicitously.

'No thanks,' said Collier dully and then moved over to the window and gazed down into the street.

Mitsides regarded him sympathetically for a few moments and then, with an almost imperceptible shrug, crossed to a row of metal filing cabinets, opened one of the drawers and took out a large and bulky brown manila envelope. Stapled to the envelope was an inventory of its contents.

'These are the things which your brother had on him when he was admitted to hospital,' he said briskly, returning to his desk. He read from the inventory. 'Wristwatch, wallet containing eleven pounds, diary, pen, cheque book, eight hundred and sixty-two mil in coins, his car keys and the key to his flat in Paphos.'

Collier turned to look at him and then crossed to the desk. 'Thank you.'

Mitsides handed him the package. 'Do you want to check the items against the list?'

Collier shook his head. 'I'm sure that's not necessary.'

The Chief Inspector removed the inventory from the envelope. 'Well then if you will just sign here.' He indicated the spot.

Collier made no move to comply. He stood weighing the envelope in his hand and staring at it disconsolately. 'So little to show really,' he said bitterly. 'And much of it in one envelope.'

Mitsides' official manner softened momentarily. 'Yes,' he replied quietly. 'But then it is only the possessions we acquire in a lifetime which can be weighed and valued. And things should never be seen as any man's true legacy or worth.'

Collier studied him for a moment and then, picking up a pen from the desk, signed the receipt.

'Did you know my brother?' he asked.

The Chief Inspector nodded. 'I met him once. Officially.' Collier frowned. 'Three months ago,' Mitsides went on. 'A man in his section fell from a cliff while working and was killed. It was an accident.'

Collier regarded him sourly remembering their first meeting. 'Oh,' he retorted with heavy sarcasm. 'I thought you didn't believe in accidents, Chief Inspector.'

The policeman accepted the sally with a faint smile.

'Of course I do, Mr Collier,' he said. 'In that which is truly accidental. But then I have to, don't I? You see I come from a very large family.'

Back in his hotel room Collier emptied the contents of the envelope on to the bed and examined them.

The glass in the face of Barry's wristwatch was broken and the watch had stopped at 11.27. Collier laid it to one side and then picked up his brother's diary and idly turned the pages.

Most of them were blank but occasionally there was a hastily scrawled telephone number and an odd entry such as

'Pick up cleaning', 'Anna!', '8.30. Dance. Limassol', 'Crystalla!!!', 'Barbecue Mike's place. 7 o'clock' and 'Ruth!! Swimming'.

Collier discarded the diary and reached for the wallet.

In addition to the eleven pounds in Cyprus money it contained a U.K. driving licence, membership cards of one or two discotheques and nightclubs and a receipt for some cleaning.

In the centre-fold of the wallet there were a number of clear plastic photograph and credit card holders and Collier leafed through them. In the first of them was his brother's company identity card and in the second a snapshot of Barry and David Collier taken in England during one of Barry's trips home.

Collier studied the snapshot and smiled sadly at the memory it stirred.

The third plastic envelope contained another snapshot; a colour photograph of Barry and a fair haired man of medium height and build standing on a beach somewhere. Both men were wearing swimming trunks and grinning hugely and each had one arm around a girl, Cypriots from the look of them and both wearing the briefest of bikinis.

Collier turned to the next photograph and reacted with a start of surprise tinged with shock.

The girl standing next to his brother in the previous snap smiled up at him provocatively. She was seated on a rock, posing archly, and she was naked.

Recovering from his surprise, Collier gave a faint, wry smile. Was this Crystalla or Anna he wondered.

But if the naked girl had been a surprise to Collier the last photograph in the wallet was an even bigger one for him. It had obviously been taken by flashlight and it was of two blocks of hieroglyphics carved in stone.

Intrigued and interested, Collier studied the symbols for a while but he could make nothing whatever of them. With a sigh he dropped the wallet back on to the bed, stood up and took off his jacket. He'd walked back to the hotel from police headquarters and he was sticky with perspiration and in need of a shower.

Removing his tie, he crossed to the bathroom. He frowned slightly. The girl he could understand. Barry had always been a devil with the girls and had frequently boasted of his conquests. But why the photograph of the stone carvings? That was way out of character. As far as Collier was aware his brother had never shown any interest in archaeology.

But it was only a passing puzzle and minutes later, revelling in the cooling shower, he had dismissed it from his mind.

It was that night that Collier first met Eugene Hellman.

CHAPTER THREE

'Mr Collier.'

The accent was faint but unmistakably American.

Collier had eaten dinner alone in the hotel restaurant and was crossing the foyer to the lifts when he was intercepted.

Everything about Eugene Hellman spelled power; power and money. He was suntanned and athletic looking, handsomely groomed and impeccably dressed. He had about him an air of easy assurance, even arrogance. Collier found it almost impossible to put any precise age to him. He certainly wasn't young but then again he wasn't old. Nor, with his sinewy body and glowing aura of general fitness and health, did he show any of the signs which would immediately classify him as middle-aged. His voice was cultivated and together with his expensive suit he was also wearing a gleaming, friendly but sympathetic smile.

He was flanked by two men in their early thirties who, at first glance, could have been taken for twins. It was only on closer study that it became clear that this was a mistaken impression. They just looked alike, uncannily so. But it wasn't a family resemblance, more the fact that they were of an age, of the same height and muscular build, both blond and both wearing identical, lightweight suits of sober, charcoal grey. And they were both very neat in that clean cut, ivy league way so unmistakably American and assiduously cultivated by junior executives in the more prestigious U.S. multinational corporations. But then, by their appearance and general demeanour, standing off respectfully at a discreet distance from Hellman, hands crossed below their waists, they could equally well have been taken for Mormon missionaries, except for the fact that there was something about them which struck Collier as faintly sinister. Neither of them was smiling and both held the Englishman in a steady, searching and watchful gaze.

'My name is Hellman.'

The American, his smile unwavering, produced a slim, leather wallet from his inside jacket pocket, extracted a visiting card and handed it to Collier. 'Eugene Hellman. Can you spare me a moment?'

Collier hesitated. He glanced at the card and then shot a look at Hellman's companions.

'My . . . business associates,' said Hellman without turning his head. 'Mr Travis and Mr Olsen.'

Responding to the introduction the two men gave Collier a curt nod of greeting.

'I won't keep you, Mr Collier,' continued Hellman. 'But I would very much like to talk to you though. You see I knew your brother.' Placing an arm around Collier's shoulders, he guided him over towards the bar. Travis and Olsen followed.

'Shall we sit here?' suggested the American, choosing a table in a quiet corner and not really offering Collier any alternative.

Travis and Olsen settled themselves by the door, out of earshot but within sight and call should the need arise.

There were less than a dozen other customers in the dimly lit bar and the barman, standing behind the counter polishing glasses, noted the entrance of the quartet with interest.

He was a wiry man of medium height and, like Hellman, of indeterminate age. He had a swarthy, wordly-wise face not unlike that of a good-natured gipsy thief. His sharp eyes missed nothing and the hands which held the glass and the tea towel were sensitive but strong.

He grinned to himself, put down the towel and the glass and moved out from behind the counter.

'You knew Barry?' Collier said, making no attempt to conceal his surprise.

'I sure did,' smiled Hellman. 'And more than just an acquaintance. I like to think that we were friends. That's why I cannot tell you how deeply grieved I am by what has happened. That's why I had to speak to you. To offer my condolences. A great loss.' He sighed deeply. 'Yes indeed.' He looked up at the barman now standing by the table and then across at Collier again. 'What'll you have?' he asked.

'A tomato juice?' suggested Collier tentatively.

Hellman shot a look of surprise and then shrugged. 'Whatever.'

'A tomato juice,' confirmed Collier.

'Right.' Hellman glanced up at the barman and when he gave his order it was just that, an order. 'A tomato juice and a bourbon on the rocks.'

The barman flashed him a wicked, mischievous smile. 'One tomato juice. One bourbon on the rocks,' he acknowledged. 'In an instant, sir.' He turned as if to cross to Travis and Olsen but, without looking up at him and still unsmiling, Hellman checked him brusquely. 'Leave it. They're not drinking.'

'Oh really,' exclaimed the barman. 'Nuts.'

Hellman shot him a look but if the remark had been a jibe then the barman covered it well. His smile was not disarming. 'They would like some you think?' he said innocently, the epitome of the perfect barman. 'Or some olives perhaps?'

Hellman scowled. 'Nothing,' he said.

'I see.' The barman nodded. 'Well in that case, sir, they will be served even quicker than this gentleman and yourself.' He moved away from the table.

Hellman leaned forward. His tone was again solicitous. 'Now this is a very sad time for you. And a difficult one. Is there anything I can do?'

'That's very kind of you, Mr. Hellman, but I don't think so.'

'Anything. You've only got to say,' the American assured him.

Behind the counter the barman poured a short measure of bourbon and topped it up with a lot of ice. Then he opened a tin of tomato juice, tipped it into a glass and stirred in a liberal shot of Worcester sauce. His eyes on Collier and Hellman, he reached in under the counter and surreptitiously produced an unlabelled bottle of clear liquid. Uncorking the bottle he sniffed its contents, recoiling a little from the heady fumes. Ah yes, he mused to himself, there is no doubt the best *zivenia* is made in the mountains. But even so he still doubted the claims of those who said that you could run a car on it.

He topped up the tomato juice with the *zivenia*, stirred the drink again briskly and then added ice and decoration. The concoction looked magnificent. The barman grinned to himself. And it will taste even better he thought.

'You were with Barry at the end?' queried Hellman in a slightly funereal tone.

Collier shook his head. 'No, unfortunately. I was too late.'

The American's expression could have been taken as either one of sadness or slight disappointment. 'I'm sorry,' he said. 'That's sad.'

'Yes.'

'One bourbon on the rocks,' announced the barman returning to the table and putting the glass down in front of Hellman. 'And a tomato juice.'

'Thank you,' said Collier. The barman gave him another flashing smile and withdrew.

'So you don't know if Barry said anything,' Hellman said casually, picking up his glass. 'I mean, any last wishes. That kind of thing.'

'I'm told that he never regained consciousness.'

The American shook his head sadly. 'Tough. Still maybe better that way, uh?' He lifted his glass in salute. 'To Barry. A great guy.'

'Thank you.' Collier lifted his glass to join the toast and sipped his tomato juice. It was unlike any tomato juice he'd ever tasted before, but very pleasant. Very pleasant indeed. He took another sip from his glass. A longer one this time and then he said, 'How did you come to know my brother, Mr Hellman?'

'Oh, we met casually one day. I don't remember exactly where. Water skiing I think. Yeah. That's right. Water skiing.'

'You live on Cyprus?'

'No, just visiting. But I've been here a while. My yacht's moored off Cape Aspro.' Hellman swallowed some more bourbon flavoured ice water. 'Barry never mentioned me when he wrote to you?'

Collier shook his head. 'But then he wasn't a great one for writing letters. And when he did write it was usually just a few lines.'

Hellman smiled, man-to-man style. 'So you don't know what he got up to out here, uh?'

Collier frowned. 'I'm sorry?' he said, not understanding.

The American grinned. 'Well, the happy bachelor bit. Wine, women and song. All that.'

'Well I knew he was having a good time. He liked Cyprus.'

Hellman nodded. 'He sure did. And, hell, why not? He had every reason to. It's a great spot.' He took another sip from his glass. 'Kitson Neve treating you okay?'

'Yes. Very well. With every consideration.'

'Good. That's the way it should be. But if you run into any problems you let me know, uh?'

'Thank you. But I don't really thing there will be any.'

'I guess not,' agreed Hellman. 'But still you never know. And just in case I'll give you a number where you can reach me.' He took a leather covered memo pad from his pocket and opened it.

'I should imagine I've already got it,' said Collier. 'In Barry's diary.'

Hellman, his head down over the memo pad and busily writing the telephone number, seemed to stiffen. But then he tore the page from the pad and when he looked up again he was smiling once more. 'His diary,' he said casually. 'You have it?'

'Yes.'

Hellman studied him. 'Of course,' he murmured quietly. 'Personal effects.'

Collier nodded. 'It was among the things the police gave me.'

'Well maybe you'll get a better idea of his life out here from that.'

'It's not that kind of diary,' Collier assured him. 'Just appointments, telephone numbers. Not much else.'

'Oh, I see,' said Hellman with a smile. 'The kind of diary I keep. Well just in case my number shouldn't happen to be in it, here.' He handed Collier the page from the memo pad.

'Thank you,' said Collier and then drank the rest of his tomato juice.

'Say, why don't you come on board one evening for dinner,' suggested Hellman. 'You'd be very welcome. We could talk some more.'

'That's kind of you, Mr Hellman. I'd like to but I won't be here very long. And what with the funeral tomorrow and then all the formalities and settling up everything.' He broke off and shrugged.

'Sure. Sure,' said Hellman sympathetically. 'I understand.' He drained the rest of his drink and stood up. Collier noticed that Travis and Olsen were instantly on their feet. Slowly he stood up himself.

'Well I'm grateful to you for giving me some of your time,' said the American. 'And again . . .' He made a helpless gesture. 'Well what can one say. A great guy.'

'It's nice to know that Barry had such good friends.'

'Well he was very important to me,' Hellman confirmed. 'And that's for sure.' He put out his hand and Collier took it. 'Maybe we'll meet again some time.'

'I hope so,' said Collier.

The American checked the bill, put some money down on the table to settle it and then, with a parting smile, turned and moved away from the table and out of the room with his two associates not more than a pace behind him.

Collier watched them go and then idly he picked up his glass and stared into it. That really had been a most unusual tomato juice. And he was feeling better, more relaxed. Maybe talking to Hellman had taken some of the grief out of him, he thought.

'You liked it, sir?' The barman was standing alongside him and looking at the glass in his hand.

'Very much,' said Collier with a smile. 'It was . . . Well, different.'

The barman nodded. 'It's the herbs,' he said gravely.

'The herbs?'

'Those that I put in with the Worcester sauce.' The barman made a crumbling gesture with his fingers. 'Just a sprinkling you understand. But it is that which makes it a Charalambos special.'

Collier gave him a questioning look.

'Charalambos,' exclaimed the barman. 'That is how I am called, sir.'

'Oh, I see,' said Collier, putting the glass back down on the table. 'Well it was very good. Thank you. Goodnight.'

Charalambos gave him another flashing smile. 'Goodnight, Mr Collier,' he said.

And it was only while he was waiting for the lift that Collier wondered how it was that the barman knew his name.

The *zivenia* had done all that was required of it and Collier was sleeping soundly when, some three hours later, Charalambos, having expertly picked the automatic lock on the door, slipped quietly into the room.

He closed the door carefully, glanced across at Collier, grinned and crossed to the chest-of-drawers standing against the wall opposite the end of the bed.

Cautiously the barman opened the top drawer. Lying in it were all the things belonging to Barry Collier which Chief Inspector Mitsides had handed over to his brother.

Charalambos picked up the wallet and looked through it. Pausing briefly to admire the photograph of the naked girl posing on the rock, he turned to the last of the photographs. The hieroglyphics had been nothing but a puzzle to Collier but, from his expression, they clearly made a great deal of sense to the barman. Gazing at the snapshot he nodded and smiled to himself.

It was then that he heard a faint scraping sound outside the window which opened on to a balcony overlooking the gardens to one side of the hotel.

Putting the wallet back where he found it and closing the drawer again, Charalambos slipped quickly into the deep shadows to one side of the window.

There was a click as the window was successfully forced and then, very slowly, it was pushed open and Travis stepped off the balcony and into the room.

From the safety of the shadows, Charalambos, with a faint smile, watched as the American, having first checked that Collier was asleep, began systematically to search the room, starting with the drawers in the bedside table.

But it was not until he reached the chest-of-drawers that Travis eventually found what he was looking for, Barry Collier's diary. With a look of triumph, he lifted it out of the drawer and he was still flipping through its pages when Charalambos crept up silently behind him and delivered a short but powerful karate chop to the side of his neck.

Travis went out like a Greek match, instantly on being struck and with only a brief splutter. Charalambos caught him as he crumpled and, at the same time, retrieved the diary from the victim's slack fingers before it fell from his hand.

With one arm around the American to support him, Charalambos put the diary back into the drawer and then, taking Barry's wallet, closed the drawer once more. Staring at the wallet as if uncertain as to what to do with it, the barman hesitated for a few seconds. Then, effortlessly hoisting Travis into a fireman's lift across his shoulders, he carried him over to the wardrobe, opened it and slipped the wallet into the inside pocket of a sports jacket which was slung over the third hanger.

Closing the wardobe again, Charalambos, with Travis draped over him like a cloak, crossed to the bedroom door, opened it a little and peered out into the corridor.

There was no one about. Glancing back at the bed Charalambos grinned once more and this time broadly as if enjoying some huge joke. And then he carried Travis out into the corridor and closed the door quietly.

'You're certain it was Collier who hit you?' challenged Hellman as he neatly sliced off the top of a boiled egg with his knife.

The American was having breakfast on the sun deck of his yacht, sitting at a table set with excellent china, a silver coffee pot and a crystal jug containing freshly squeezed and chilled orange juice.

Slumped in a chair across from him was Travis. He was unshaven, his clothes were unkempt and he was very nervous because he knew from experience that Hellman could be very intolerant of failure. Standing to one side of him was Olsen.

Carefully avoiding looking at his employer, Travis rubbed the back of his neck which was bruised and painful. 'It had to be,' he mumbled. 'There was no one else in the room. I thought he was asleep. He came up behind me.'

'And then dumped you in your car,' sniggered Olsen.

Scowling, Travis shot a look at him.

Hellman dipped a soldier of toast into his egg. 'And that's very interesting, isn't it?' he said thoughtfully. He bit into the toast. 'I mean, he wakes up, finds friend Travis giving his room a good going over and turns out the lights on him. Still that's natural enough provided you have the nerve and the muscle.' He looked across at Travis and Olsen. 'But what doesn't he do?' he asked.

Travis and Olsen returned his gaze blankly.

Hellman sighed, irritated by their stupidity. 'Well what would you expect any law abiding citizen to do under those circumstances?' he prompted.

'Call the police,' exclaimed Travis, suddenly catching on.

Hellman nodded. 'Exactly. So it would seem that I misjudged him.' He plunged another soldier into the yolk of his egg. 'The innocent Mr David Collier *is* sitting in on the game.' He popped the toast into his mouth and then dabbed at his lips with his linen serviette. 'And maybe holding a pretty good hand.'

CHAPTER FOUR

'As you said. It's what Barry would have wanted. I'm sure of that,' affirmed Preece.

Collier nodded and wondered why Eugene Hellman had not been at the graveside. After all the American had claimed that he and Barry had been more than just acquaintances. Mentally Collier shrugged. 'It was a good turn out,' he remarked, slicing into his steak.

'Just about everyone was there,' said Preece. 'We closed the site down for the day. Out of respect.'

Collier nodded. 'Good of you.'

Preece shook his head. 'Wyndham's idea. He's the boss. But only right and fitting anyway.'

And who was the man who looked as though he wanted to talk to me but either didn't get the chance or was too embarrassed to, pondered Collier. He'd been standing in the forefront of the group opposite him across the grave. And there had been something familiar about him. It was a face that Collier thought he'd seen somewhere before but which he hadn't been able to place. He toyed with the idea of asking Preece to identify him but then decided against it. Whatever the man wanted it couldn't have been important or he would have approached him. Probably just another workmate of Barry's full of hesitant sympathy and stammered condolences. And Collier had had enough of that for one day to go looking for more.

What he had really wanted after the funeral was to be alone, but Leonard Wyndham wouldn't hear of it and had insisted on taking him to lunch, a meal which seemed to have gone on for hours. He had managed to snatch some time to himself during the late afternoon and early evening and he had shut himself away in his room. From choice he would have eaten on his own that night but in view of Martin Preece's kindness and support since he'd arrived in Cyprus an invitation to have dinner with him at the Curium Palace had seemed almost obligatory on his part. And in fact he was glad that he had asked him and that Preece had accepted. Collier liked the man and now he had recovered from the first numbing shock of Barry's death he found him good company.

'What time are you planning on going over to Barry's place tomorrow?' enquired Preece.

'Early. Straight after breakfast. How far is Paphos?'

'Takes about an hour to get there. I'll call for you, shall I? Drive you over.'

'No, please don't bother. I'll take a taxi.'

'Sure? No trouble.'

'Positive,' Collier assured him. 'I'll probably stay there for a while. Overnight anyway. There'll be quite a bit to sort out I expect.'

'Well if there's anything I can do give me a call,' said Preece. 'Right?'

'Right.'

'And I'll see you again before you go back to England?'

'Of course.'

The two men finished their meal and then lingered at their table, Preece nursing a large brandy and Collier pouring himself several cups of coffee and reminiscing about Barry and their childhood together.

It was close to midnight when they finally left the restaurant. Collier escorted Preece to his car.

'Well, goodnight,' he said.

'Goodnight.'

The two men shook hands and Preece slid in behind the wheel of the Kitson Neve Audi and Collier watched him drive away.

It was as he was re-crossing the foyer, heading for the lifts, that Collier was suddenly seized with the idea that he had to go into the bar for a nightcap. The very thought was ridiculous and he tried to dismiss it from his mind. Why the bar? He didn't drink and what kind of nightcap was a tomato juice or a tonic water. But try as he might to shake it off the impulse proved irresistible. Well why not, mused

Collier, as he surrendered to it and changed direction. After all that coffee I probably won't sleep anyway.

The bar was practically empty, just two couples each in a world of their own and on opposite sides of the room. Collier paused in the doorway, looked around and then slowly crossed to the bar counter. And as he did so Charalambos turned to him, smiled warmly, reached down and then placed a frosted and decorated glass of tomato juice on the counter before him, giving it a final stir with a swizzle stick as he did so.

It was almost as if the barman had been expecting him, but Collier knew that that was impossible. He must have seen me in the mirror as I came through the door, he reasoned. But even so he still wouldn't have had time to prepare the drink that quickly. Collier shrugged. The tomato juice had probably been poured earlier for a customer who had then changed his mind and Charalambos had kept it and simply freshened it up when he had seen Collier walk in.

Collier picked up the glass and sipped the juice. It was good. If anything even better than the last one the barman had mixed for him.

'The herbs?' said Collier with a smile and relishing the taste.

'The herbs,' confirmed Charalambos, and then he added quietly. 'This is not a happy time for you, Mr Collier.'

Collier frowned. He had not come into the bar to be reminded of that. 'No,' he said.

Charalambos busied himself wiping down the gleaming surface of the counter. 'It is strange, is it not?' he went on. 'Death is a journey which is so much harder for the living to bear than for those who have to embark on it. But then perhaps that is because the dead do not look back. And why should they? For them there is no longer any past. Charon waits to ferry them to a new future.' He looked up and smiled. 'And to such interesting company.'

Collier gave him a hard, searching look. 'You're a philosopher,' he said.

Charalambos laughed. 'No, sir. A realist. Believe me.'

Collier made a move to settle himself on one of the bar

stools but Charalambos raised a hand and checked him. He pointed to one of the small alcoves set into the far wall of the bar. 'May I suggest, Mr Collier, that you enjoy your drink over there.'

Collier turned his head and gazed across at the shadowy alcove which appeared to be empty. Then he looked back at Charalambos and gave him a questioning look.

'There is someone who wishes to speak to you,' the barman explained.

'Oh!' said Collier, visibly surprised. 'Who?'

'Someone you should listen to.'

Collier frowned deeply and hesitated. He stared at Charalambos. What was this all about? What was he up to? The barman held his gaze.

'Someone who has been waiting for you for quite a long time,' he continued. He put out a hand to pick up Collier's glass. 'May I?'

Mystified and with a vague feeling of annoyance, Collier shook his head. 'No thank you,' he said a trifle huffily. 'I'll take it.' He picked up his glass and, turning from the counter, slowly crossed to the alcove.

There was a glass of champagne on the table and a figure was sitting on the bench against the wall swathed in shadow. Collier tried to make out who it was but he couldn't.

'David Collier,' he announced awkwardly. 'You wanted to speak to me?'

'Yes. Please sit down.' The woman's voice was husky and only slightly accented. The fact that the stranger was a woman only served to increase Collier's sense of awkwardness and unease. Again he hesitated and then he sat down on one of the chairs across the table from her.

Although he could not see her face Collier was aware that the woman was studying him closely and this made him feel even more uncomfortable.

'What can I do for you?' he asked.

'You are a man I think who values the truth.'

Collier nodded. 'I like to think so.'

'Then it is more a question of what I can do for you,' said

the woman as she leaned forward into the soft light given out by the table lamp.

It was only with some difficulty that Collier just managed to stifle the gasp which would have been audible across the bar. She was beautiful, breathtakingly so. Fair haired, almost blonde and with brilliant, pale blue eyes. The dress she was wearing was simple but clearly an exclusive product of one of the top fashion houses and it set off to perfection the lines of a very desirable body. There hung about her an air of charm, wit and intelligence with more than a dash of feminine guile added for good measure. Collier had never been face-to-face with quite such a woman before in his life and this only added to his confusion.

Seeing his reaction the woman smiled gently in an attempt to put him at his ease. 'There is something I have to tell you about your brother,' she said.

Collier frowned. 'Barry! Did you know him then?'

The woman looked down into her champagne glass and toyed with the stem of it. 'You could say that there was a very special relationship between us,' she murmured.

'I see,' said Collier lamely. But he didn't see. It just didn't fit. How did Barry even get close to a woman like this, he thought. All right, so he was attractive and good-looking enough to take his pick. But somehow he'd never imagined his brother becoming involved in any way with someone like this. One night stands, out for a few drinks and a bit of fun, yes. A three month affair perhaps. But always with a body, never with a mind. Well this beautiful creature sitting across the table from him clearly had the body but she certainly looked as though she also had a mind. And that was something Barry would never have been able to satisfy. He remembered his brother telling him once with a grin, 'The only time a woman says anything interesting is when she says yes. And after that there shouldn't be much conversation.' No, there was nothing subtle about Barry. Not in his relationships with the opposite sex anyway. And nothing deep. Ever. So the whole idea was crazy. Impossible. But she had said it herself, 'A very special relationship.' So either he'd been under-selling his brother or he was overselling her. So which one was she then? Crystalla? Anna? Ruth, perhaps?

The woman looked up from her glass to meet his gaze. 'What's your name?' he asked.

She hesitated, stared for a moment down into her champagne again and smiled a little smile as if enjoying a private joke. 'Helene,' she said lifting her head once more. 'Call me Helene.'

Collier's eyes met hers but only momentarily. To cover his confusion he picked up his glass and drank from it. 'What do you have to tell me?' he asked, lowering his glass again. A sudden thought struck him and it horrified him. Oh my God, she's pregnant. He shot a worried look at her. 'If it's very personal,' he stammered. 'If . . . Of course I'll do what I can but . . .'

Helene shook her head. 'It concerns his death,' she said.

'His death?' Collier frowned once more.

Helene nodded solemnly. 'Yes. You have to know that it was not an accident. Your brother was murdered.'

It took a few seconds for what she had said to sink in.

'Murdered!' exclaimed Collier. 'But that's ridiculous. It was an accident. Chief Inspector Mitsides told me so himself. He's quite certain of that.'

'Perhaps. But just the same what I have said is the truth.'

Shocked and bewildered, Collier studied her for a moment and then he shook his head. 'I don't believe it,' he said. 'It can't be.'

'But it is,' Helene assured him quietly.

Again David studied her closely. She has to be out of her mind, he thought. Grief perhaps. Yes that's it, grief. She's distraught and suffering from some kind of delusion. Reason with her, that's the only thing to do. He gave her a faint, sympathetic smile.

'Look, you said yourself that you were close. Barry and you. Well perhaps . . . Well, isn't it possible . . .'

Helene sighed. 'Mr Collier, do I strike you as being an hysterical woman?' she asked. 'In any way unbalanced?'

She didn't. Outwardly anyway. 'No,' countered Collier floundering. 'But what you are suggesting . . .'

Helene interrupted. 'It is not a suggestion. It is a fact.'

Again Collier shook his head. 'No, it's not possible. Barry! Murdered! Why? For what possible motive? Tell me that. And who did it?'

'Someone may wish to see another dead for many reasons. And I only said he was killed. Not that I knew who killed him.'

'So you've no idea, is that it?'

'Your brother was murdered. That is all I am saying.'

'And you can prove it?' challenged Collier.

Helene shook her head. 'No. Not at this moment.'

Collier was beginning to get angry. 'So it's not a fact,' he snapped. 'At best it's a theory. And a fantastic one at that.'

'It's the truth,' she said simply.

'And what did the police say when you went to them with this truth of yours?'

'I have not been to the police.'

'Oh!' countered Collier on a rising note of triumph. 'Why not?'

Helene hesitated. 'Because before doing anything else I wanted to talk to you.'

'Really!' Collier's voice was scathing. 'Or was it because you knew that without any evidence they'd . . .'

Again Helene interrupted him. 'But there is evidence,' she said.

Collier was stopped in his tracks by this. He frowned. 'But just a second ago you said . . .'

'That I could not prove it.' Helene nodded. 'And that is so. But there is evidence. Evidence which I think will do much to convince you. And if you will come with me I will show it to you.'

Still frowning, Collier gazed at her searchingly. Her story was absurd of course. It couldn't be true. And yet there was something about her. And now with this talk of evidence. Nevertheless he hesitated.

'Mr Collier,' she went on. 'Just allow for the possibility, however far-fetched it may seem to you, that what I have told you is the truth. Would you not then want your brother's murderer punished?'

'Of course.'

'Then come with me.'

It took a few seconds longer for Collier to make up his mind. Then he nodded. If nothing else it was probably kinder to humour her and have done with this nonsense once and for all. 'All right,' he said.

Helene stood up. 'Wait for two minutes and then follow me,' she instructed him. 'Come out of the hotel, turn left and walk along the road. Presently I will pick you up.'

She moved out from behind the table and away from the alcove. Collier watched her go and then stared moodily and angrily into his glass. What kind of a fool does she take him for? What kind of fool am I? He checked his wristwatch. One minute and fifty-two seconds to go. He picked up his glass, emptied it in one swallow and then stood up. As he was crossing the bar he looked over at the counter. There was no sign of Charalambos.

He hadn't walked more than twenty yards before an Alfetta GT 1.6 drew up alongside him and Helene leaned across and opened the front nearside door for him. Collier got into the car. Without even glancing at him, Helene accelerated away down the road again.

They travelled in silence making for Larnaca but a few miles outside Limassol Helene turned off the main road on to a narrower one signposted to Aghios Georgios.

The Alfa Romeo purred sweetly, it's suspension absorbing most of the ruts in the uneven surface of the secondary road. Further and further they drove into the interior until finally they were climbing into the foothills of the central mountain range. Collier checked his watch and then looked across at Helene.

'How much longer?' he grunted irritably. 'We've been driving for almost an hour.'

'Not far now,' Helene assured him.

Ten minutes later she swung the Alfetta off the road and onto a rough track. Collier was beginning to worry. They were miles from anywhere and as far as he could see there was no sign of habitation in any direction. But then they turned a corner and the track led the way to a small village, ghost-like in the intermittent moonlight.

Helene parked the Alfetta in the shadow of one of the buildings and got out of the car. Collier followed her and looked around. His anxiety was in no way allayed by what he saw. What had looked like a village as they had approached it was nothing more than a cluster of houses, all in various stages of decay and the place was clearly deserted.

'What the hell!' he exclaimed.

Helene ignored him. She moved away from the car and across the road. In the gaping doorway of one of the houses she paused and looked back at Collier and then she entered the building. Puzzled but curious, Collier followed her.

What had once presumably been the living room of the house was now a mass of rubble. Only three of the walls were still standing and most of the roof had long since caved in.

As Collier came in through the front door Helene was stooping by a fireplace set in the far wall. She glanced at him and then, reaching up into the chimney, pulled from it a battered, Samsonite, executive-style briefcase. Straightening up, she held the briefcase out to Collier.

'Your brother gave me this the night before he had his "accident",' she said. 'He was very nervous and he told me not to say anything to anybody about it. Open it.'

Collier hesitated for a second and then shrugged. Crossing to her, he took the briefcase, stood it down on a pile of rubble, undid the catches and lifted the lid.

Collier was stunned by what he saw. The briefcase was filled with money, bundles of notes of various denominations.

'Swiss francs,' Helene informed him. 'In Sterling a little over fifty thousand pounds. Now how do you suppose that a section manager on a construction project came by that kind of money? And in foreign currency.'

There was no answer to this and Collier knew it. 'I can't imagine,' he said quietly. 'Just the same, there could be a perfectly acceptable explanation.'

'Such as?' Helene challenged.

Collier shrugged helplessly and then went on to the defensive again. 'Anyway this still doesn't prove that Barry was murdered,' he growled.

'But you no longer find the possibility quite so fantastic. Is that not so?'

Despite his doubts Collier was deeply disturbed. He could come up with no explanation as to how Barry had come by such a sum of money. And what if she was telling the truth.

'We must take this to Chief Inspector Mitsides,' he said decisively.

'Yes,' replied Helene. 'Do that.' She tossed her car keys down on to the money in the briefcase. 'Here, take my car.' Then she moved away quickly from him towards the door of the house.

Taken entirely off guard and very surprised, Collier called after her in protest. 'No, wait! You must come with me.'

By now Helene had reached the front door. She did not look back. 'No, I cannot,' she shouted. 'I cannot become involved.' And with that she ran from the house.

Collier scooped up the car keys and slammed the briefcase shut again but he had difficulty closing the catches. Fumbling with them and cursing silently he at last managed to get them shut and then, snatching up the briefcase, he ran off in pursuit.

Outside in the deserted, moonlit street there was no sign of Helene. Collier called out to her.

'Helene! Helene, where are you?'

There was no reply. No sound of any kind. Crossing the street, Collier peered into the ruined house opposite. Nothing. Then he called again. 'Helene!' Still there was no response. The woman had disappeared.

Totally bewildered, Collier crossed to the Alfa Romeo and opened the door on the driver's side. Then, scanning the desolate, ruined buildings around him once more, he made one last appeal.

'Helene!' he shouted. 'For God's sake! Answer me. You can't stay here all night.'

He waited, desperately hoping that whatever game she was playing she would tire of it and, realising that if he did drive off she would be stranded in the middle of nowhere, re-appear. But he was disappointed.

Collier's anger overcame his concern. All right then if that's what she wants, he muttered to himself, what the hell! It's her look out. Stupid bitch. Tossing the briefcase on to the passenger seat, he got into the car and started the engine.

It was not without some difficulty that he turned the Alfetta in the narrow road but once this was accomplished he accelerated back in the direction from which they had come, still hoping that as he drove he would pick up the figure of Helene in the headlights. But there was no sign of her.

Coming off the track and on to the secondary road once more Collier was able to make better speed. It was then that he was ambushed.

The second car must have been waiting for him with its lights off some yards up from the turn off and he neither heard nor saw it until it was almost level with him. The two cars touched momentarily.

'Damn fool!' Collier screamed angrily and, stamping on the brake, he spun the steering wheel. The Alfetta lurched up on to the grass verge and then nosedived into a shallow ditch. The second car pulled up sharply less than twenty feet away. Three men leapt out of it and ran towards the Alfa Romeo. One of them wrenched open the door, the other two grabbed Collier and pulled him out of the car.

'What do you think you're doing?' Collier shouted, confused and afraid. 'Let go of me. What do you want?'

He struggled wildly but then one of the men hit him on the back of the head with a cosh and he collapsed unconscious on to the grass.

The man with the cosh reached into the Alfetta and switched off the engine and the lights. Then, with the briefcase in his hand, he and his two companions ran back to their car, the rear window of which was lowered at their approach.

The man with the briefcase handed it through the open window to a figure sitting in the back seat of the car. It was Charalambos.

‘You didn’t hit him too hard?’ he asked the man in Greek and with more than a touch of concern in his voice.

The man shook his head. ‘No. Just a tap as you said.’

The three assailants got into the car. Charalambos looked across at Collier slumped on the ground and smiled. But there was no menace or malice in his smile, only a strange kind of amusement. Then he settled back in his seat and the car moved off down the road.

CHAPTER FIVE

The scent of crushed lemons percolated gradually into Collier's disordered senses. For a moment he thought this must be another of Charalambos' specials. Then a stab of pain in the nape of his neck reminded him forcefully that this hangover had not come out of a bottle. He winced as his exploring fingers found the bruise but the localised pain helped to bring his vision back into focus.

What the hell was he doing lying in a patch of herbs at the roadside in the middle of the night? Memory followed his other faculties back into rank and he knew for certain that it would be a waste of time checking to see if the briefcase was still in the back of the car. Hold-up artists don't force you off the road, belt you on the head and leave empty handed. He rolled over onto his back and a wave of nausea swept over him and he wished he hadn't. He got up with difficulty and stood swaying on his feet.

Getting behind the wheel of the Alfetta would be more of a challenge but one which would have to be met unless he fancied a long walk. He didn't, but it soon became apparent that was what he was going to get. The engine fired without hesitation but, with its bonnet at an angle in the ditch, the car's wheels only spun helplessly on the grass verge whatever gear or speed he selected. He eased himself out of the car and looked around. He was in the middle of nowhere.

Cursing quietly he began to walk slowly and uncertainly down the road in the direction in which he had been driving.

Two hours later he limped into a village. The constable who eventually opened the door of the shuttered and locked police station did not look pleased to see his visitor. Grumbling continuously and fighting a losing battle to pin his elusive shirt tail in his over large trousers, he led Collier into what passed for an office.

When, at last, Chief Inspector Mitsides arrived, his

sergeant in close attendance, Collier looked testily at his watch.

'It is a long drive from Limassol,' Mitsides reminded him patiently.

Collier was not to be placated. '. . . Even so.'

'I was at home, Mr Collier. Asleep. But, according to Sergeant Karaolis here, you insisted that I come in person.'

'Yes,' bristled Collier surlily.

'And when it was explained to you that I was off duty that made no difference. I am told that you even became somewhat offensive.'

Collier had the grace to be a little embarrassed but only a little. 'I lost my temper.'

'So I believe,' acknowledged the Chief Inspector. 'Well I am sure that the sergeant will accept your apology.'

Though scarcely contrite Collier felt that it might be as well to make a gesture. 'I'm sorry,' he mumbled.

Karaolis did not respond in any way to this somewhat reluctant apology and Mitsides was disinclined to let the matter rest.

'He is a very able police officer,' he stated.

'No doubt,' conceded Collier. 'But I wanted you here.'

'Clearly. But why?'

'Because, Chief Inspector, you were so sure, so confident, about the way my brother died.'

This time Mitsides could not keep a trace of exasperation out of his voice. 'I had no reason not to be. It was an accident. Regrettable, but one of those accidents with which life is fraught.'

Collier was not to be denied. 'Well there's a good chance you're wrong. What I heard and saw tonight and then what happened to me just may make you think again.'

Mitsides did not reply at once but studied the Englishman intently, trying to determine whether he was simply obsessed by his brother's death or might have a genuine case. His training told him to keep an open mind so he proceeded cautiously. 'On the telephone you said you had been attacked I understand.'

'Yes.'

'And robbed?'

Collier nodded, pouncing eagerly on his opportunity to convince the Chief Inspector.

'Of evidence. Evidence that suggests Barry could have been murdered.'

Mitsides was clearly astonished by the turn the conversation had taken. 'Murdered! Oh come now, Mr Collier.'

'Yes, I know. I didn't believe it either. Not at first. But then . . . well.' Collier shrugged.

Mitsides studied him and then, with a sigh of resignation, settled himself on the edge of the constable's desk. He nodded to Karaolis who took a notebook from his pocket.

'So then,' said the Chief Inspector, trying his best to control the note of irritation in his voice. 'As it happened. What, when and where.'

CHAPTER SIX

Collier had never imagined for a moment that he would have any difficulty in retracing his steps to the car. After all he had walked every damn centimetre of the way. Yet the road was completely empty. Not a sign of a vehicle of any kind. He wondered if he had been concussed and lost track of his movements. Perhaps there had been another turn off to Aghios Georgios. The police car slowed down and the driver looked at him enquiringly.

'An Alfa Romeo you said.' Mitsides regarded him suspiciously, the annoyance increasingly apparent with every sentence he uttered.

Collier was quite emphatic. 'A red Alfetta. Just here. I'm sure of it.'

Somewhat pointlessly the four men got out of the car to look around, though even a Dinky toy would have been conspicuous in these bare and arid surroundings. Sergeant Karaolis and the driver wandered up each side of the road, heads bent in close scrutiny as Mitsides turned enquiringly to Collier.

Collier's uncertainty increased. 'This can't be the right road.'

Mitsides looked at him pityingly. 'Towards Larnaca you said. A turning on the left. Signposted to Aghios Georgios.'

'Yes.'

'Well this is it. Only no car.'

Collier gazed about him in bewilderment. 'But that's ridiculous! I told you. It nosedived into the ditch. I couldn't budge it. It would have taken a breakdown truck or a tractor to bring it out.'

The Chief Inspector's reply was now undisguisedly sarcastic. 'And there aren't many of those about this early in the day. Certainly not on this road. And, anyway, anyone finding a car like that would have reported it, don't you think?'

Collier grudgingly conceded the point. 'I suppose so.'

'And we have just come from the nearest police station. No report.' Mitsides turned enquiringly towards his two men but they both shook their heads with a shrug for accompaniment which eloquently said, 'What did you expect?'

Without much success the Chief Inspector tried to remain polite. 'So, no car, Mr Collier and, what is more, no skid marks. No sign of any kind of struggle. Anywhere along the road. Now how do you explain that?'

Collier was totally nonplussed. 'I can't. If this *is* the right road.'

'It has to be. You see it is the only one to Aghios Georgios.'

Collier snapped back at him irritably. 'Well then this is where it happened. Just after I turned off the track from the ruined village.'

With a patient sigh one reserves for lunatics and small children, Mitsides climbed back into the car. 'Ah yes. Of course. The ruined village.'

He waved the driver on and in a few minutes they had drawn up in the street of the village which looked even more deserted without the soft make-up of night to hide the ravages of neglect.

Collier and the Chief Inspector climbed out and began to walk slowly down the centre of the village street while Karaolis and the constable, determined to be drawn into no more wild goose chases, leaned against the car. As befitted a worldly-wise sergeant, Karaolis offered his companion a cigarette, sure sign that there would be time to kill. When they had lit up the young constable grimaced enquiringly at his superior who lightly tapped his own forehead as he gazed after the retreating figures of their boss and the mad Englishman.

Collier felt unnerved by the disappearance of the car and this made him tentative in identifying the cache to which the mysterious Helene had led him. 'I think this is the house. But I can't be sure. They all look alike and it was dark.'

Mitsides was unimpressed by the excuses. 'Bright moonlight. According to your statement.'

'Just the same. Things, places, they look different in the daylight.' Even as he spoke Collier recognised a house further down the street and grabbed the Chief Inspector's arm excitedly. 'But yes, this is the one. I'm positive now. Over there.'

He crossed quickly to the house, almost dragging Mitsides behind him, and led him through the gaping front door and crumbling living room to the far wall and the fireplace.

'This is where we were,' he exclaimed, pointing. 'The woman got the briefcase from in there.'

'The mysterious Helene,' sighed Mitsides.

'Well that's what she *said* her name was.'

'Such a pity she ran off the way she did.' The Chief Inspector paused to rub his point in. 'Your one and only witness.'

Collier refused to be put off by the innuendo. 'It shouldn't be difficult to trace her. Not someone you'd miss in a crowd. She's . . .' As he groped for the right word to describe the otherworldly vision that was Helene the Chief Inspector chipped in.

'A dream, Mr Collier.' Before Collier could take offence Mitsides gave him a guileless smile. 'Isn't that the expression?'

'It may well be but it isn't the right one. Helene is real.'

'And where do you suggest we should start looking for her?' enquired the Chief Inspector who had long given up expecting rational discourse.

'God knows. You're the policeman. But she's around somewhere,' Collier added lamely.

'Keeping out of sight.' Mitsides looked provocatively into a cupboard from which the door had long fallen.

Collier was not to be put off. 'Presumably. Not drawing attention to herself anyway.'

The Chief Inspector refrained from comment but his brisk return to the street was expressive enough to make Collier angry.

'You don't believe me, do you?' challenged Collier,

following him. 'You don't believe any of it. You think I made it all up.'

Mitsides turned to look at him. 'No,' he said quietly.

'What then?'

'These past few days will have been difficult for you. You have been under a strain. The accident. Your brother's death. The funeral. It must all have been a considerable shock.'

Collier's anger did not abate. 'Oh I see. It was some kind of mental aberration. Is that it?'

'Well that's one possibility.'

'Then what was I doing out in the middle of nowhere? Miles from Limassol. And how did I get there?' challenged Collier.

'Heaven only knows,' the Chief Inspector replied. 'But admit it, Mr Collier, your story is not an easy one to accept, is it? A rendezvous with an exotic woman in an hotel bar, talk of murder, a briefcase with . . . How much money in it?'

Collier fell into the trap. 'Fifty thousand pounds. Plus. In Swiss francs . . .'

Mitsides studied him closely and nodded. 'Yes. It always is. And then an ambush on a lonely road. Tell me, do you read a lot of thrillers?'

Collier's indignant denial was instantly tempered by the recognition that in the absence of an atom of evidence his tale was indeed fantastic. He had better try a less bullheaded approach.

'All right, yes I agree, it's pretty wild. But it is the truth.'

The Chief Inspector tried to sound more patient than he felt. 'So where's the car? And what happened to the skid marks? With two cars braking the way you said they did there would have to be skid marks, wouldn't there?'

'There were. I saw them.'

'Only now they've vanished. Just like the beautiful Helene did, eh?' Mitsides shook his head sadly. 'There's not a single piece of evidence to support any part of your statement.'

Collier knew all too well that the Chief Inspector was right. In fact so little evidence that for a moment he began to wonder if he had dreamed it all, confused image and reality and succumbed to the perpetual magic in the Cyprus air. There must be some way to check. Then it came to him.

'The barman! Charalambos,' he exclaimed in triumph. 'He can confirm some of it. My meeting with the woman for instance. And if nothing else that will, at least, prove that she existed. Then maybe you'll stop thinking this is all some kind of hallucination and take it seriously. Talk to him.'

The Chief Inspector frowned and Collier felt his chance slipping from him.

'Talk to him. Please,' he begged.

'*Kalimera*,' said the short, fat and balding man behind the bar, ignoring the obvious foreignness of the Chief Inspector's companion.

'*Kalimera*,' responded Mitsides, flipping open his police pass and returning it to his top pocket in a single sweeping movement. 'Police. Chief Inspector Mitsides.'

The man looked uneasy but Collier shook his head.

'He's not the one. That's not Charalambos,' he said.

Chief Inspector Mitsides went wearily through the motions. 'There is another barman?' he enquired.

The man behind the counter nodded. 'Yes. Alexis. My assistant. But he is not here. He is ill.' He scowled, resentful at the perfidy of assistants who allowed themselves to be afflicted with illness. 'For too many days now I have had to manage on my own.'

Collier was not interested in his administrative problems. 'Where's Charalambos?'

The man looked at him blankly. 'Who, sir?'

'Charalambos. The man who was on duty last night. And the night before.'

'I am sorry, sir, but you are mistaken. There is no one of that name who works in this bar. Now and then one of the waiters from the restaurant takes over for a time.' The barman shrugged and made a helpless gesture. 'After all, I must eat. Is that not so? But all the week, during the nights, I have been here alone.'

Collier was flabbergasted. 'But that's not true!' He turned

desperately to Mitsides. 'He's lying. The only man I have ever seen behind this bar is Charalambos.'

The barman's indignation pushed his voice up another twenty decibels. 'I do not lie. Another bar. Some other hotel perhaps.'

Collier was adamant. 'Here. And twice. Last night and the night before.'

The Chief Inspector intervened. 'Do you know this gentleman?'

The man looked almost rudely at Collier. 'I do not think so.'

'You have never served him? Or spoken to him?' insisted the Chief Inspector.

'Maybe. But with so many customers I cannot be certain. It is possible. But, if so, I do not remember him.'

Exasperated by the irrelevance of the exchange, Collier cut in again, his temper getting the better of him. 'Why should he? I've never seen him before. But he's lying. He wasn't here last night.' He turned on the barman. 'Tell the truth. Where is Charalambos?'

Mitsides laid a firm, restraining hand on the Englishman's arm and spoke with sharp authority. 'That's enough, Mr Collier.'

For a moment Collier looked as though he were about to ignore the policeman's injunction but then he thought better of it. With a scathing glance at the barman he turned from the counter and stalked back out into the foyer.

Seconds later the Chief Inspector joined him. He regarded Collier icily.

'I know it must be difficult for you but . . .'

But Mitsides did not let him go on. 'Mr Collier,' he growled. 'At your insistence I was called from my bed before dawn and drove a long way. Together with other police officers I have wasted a great deal of time. I would not advise you to push my patience any further. I suggest that after you have rested you leave for Paphos as you intended and settle your brother's affairs as quickly as possible.'

Collier's bitterness spilled over. 'So that's it then. Case closed, eh? I didn't make it up. That's been ruled out. I imagined it. Everything. All imagination. It was all in my mind.'

'I said that was one possibility,' snapped Mitsides. 'There's another.'

'Which is?' asked Collier sarcastically, opening himself up for the verbal counter punch.

'That you had too much to drink.'

Collier no longer had the energy to be angry. There seemed no way he could convince Mitsides of the truth of what he said. Even as he indicated the bruise on his neck he knew his cause was hopeless. 'And this?' he asked.

The policeman shrugged. 'Unsteady on your feet. You fell down. It is not unknown.'

With nothing now to lose Collier let his scorn have full rein. 'Fine! Marvellous! Drunk and incapable.' He paused for effect. 'Only one thing, Chief Inspector. I don't drink.'

Mitsides held his gaze and then his expression softened a little and he shook his head sadly.

'Well then, Mr Collier,' he said quietly, 'I am sorry. Because there goes the benefit of the doubt.'

And with that he turned and walked briskly across the foyer.

CHAPTER SEVEN

Collier was depressed and tired and as he paused in his packing and glanced in the bedroom mirror he knew it showed. Since his fruitless encounter with Mitsides he had snatched a few hours sleep, shaved, showered and changed into slacks and short sleeved shirt but the improvement in his well-being was still only marginal.

He returned to the wardrobe. There would be no need of a coat on a bright day like this, he thought, gazing at the sports jacket hanging inside it. Anyway, English tweed for autumn hacking would look a little out of place here. He slid the coat off its hangar and folded it over his arm. With the first step he took Barry's wallet slid from its hiding place and thudded on to the floor at his feet.

Collier paused and stared at the wallet fixedly. How the hell had that got there? He picked it up. Mentally he rehearsed his movements of the previous evening. No doubt about it, he had put the wallet with the rest of his brother's things in the chest-of-drawers.

He strode over to the chest and opened the top drawer. Yes, there they all were. He looked again in bewilderment at the wallet in his hand and then, with a shrug, slipped it into the hip pocket of his slacks and, crossing back to the bed, picked up the telephone.

'This is Mr Collier. Room three-o-four. I'm leaving today. Will you make up my bill and order me a taxi in thirty minutes.'

The drive to Paphos had been interesting and relaxing and the taxi deposited Collier outside his brother's house at a few minutes after eleven in a far better frame of mind. With a smile the driver opened the door for him with a flourish and then carried his luggage to the top of the steps leading to the front door. Collier waited for him to return, waved aside the profusion of thanks for the generous tip and turned back to study the house.

Somehow he'd expected Paphos to reflect the rural hinterland of which it was focus and to show at every turn signs of its long and turbulent history. But there was certainly no age old charm here. The street in which he stood was as brashly modern as Barry had been. Perhaps he was being unfair. Many of the streets and buildings which he had glimpsed on the way through the town had been more in keeping with his preconceptions. And the road in which Barry's house stood was, in fact, not far from the bustle and colour of the harbour with all the atmosphere he had expected of Cyprus. But here, on the upper slope, the modern, just detached buildings looked slightly aseptic.

The two storeys of the house which Barry had rented were split between a garage and store space on the ground floor and living quarters on the upper, approached by balustraded stone steps.

As Collier stood staring at this uninformative façade he became aware of the blatantly curious but friendly stares of the Cypriots in the neighbouring buildings. Prompted by a friendly wave of welcome from a stout, middle-aged woman on the balcony opposite, he climbed the steps, picked up his luggage, unlocked the front door and walked into Barry's world.

The apartment as a whole was bright, airy and comfortably furnished although a lick of paint would not have come amiss. A good two coats would have been needed to restore the kitchen, with its battered electric toaster, ancient refrigerator and scarred Formica topped table, to its pristine state.

The same general air of neglect hung over the courtyard beyond the back door. The balcony at the rear of the house hung above a rubble strewn wasteland and overlooked a narrow, ill paved road. Only the harbour in the distance redeemed the otherwise dreary prospect.

Collier turned from the balcony rail and moved back into the kitchen. Idly he opened the refrigerator. It was badly in need of defrosting and was almost empty. Clearly Barry had done most of his eating out.

Closing the refrigerator door again, Collier walked back into the sitting room and inspected it thoroughly and, as he did so, a feeling of pain and depression began to engulf him once more. Everywhere he turned, every record or book he looked at reminded him of his brother. So full of fun and vigour, so cheerfully amoral as he pursued a way of life which Collier had often envied.

Most of the framed photographs liberally adorning walls and shelves were indicative of the principal mode in which that amorality found expression: Barry with one girl or another – or several. But one picture, tucked away in a corner, was different. It showed two grinning schoolboys kneeling on either side of a bright eyed Labrador and watched over by a thin, once-pretty woman of forty plus and a tall, good-natured looking man with one arm around her shoulders.

Collier held the photograph in his hand and studied it, remembering those happy family days when the two brothers had shared the overly-possessive affection of one parent and the well meaning and corrective discipline of the other. Now three of them were dead. And so was the dog.

For a moment Collier felt dead himself. Angrily he shook his head. The past must be packed up and put away. That was what he had come here to do.

He crossed the room, picked up his luggage and walked briskly into the bedroom.

CHAPTER EIGHT

The Kitson Neve construction site was like any other, an apparent chaos of men, materials and machinery from which, gradually, order and form would emerge.

The police car swung through the gate and on to the site. Chief Inspector Mitsides eased himself out of his seat, glanced around interestedly and then headed off in the direction of the hut which served as the Resident Engineer's office. As he neared it the door of the hut swung open and Martin Preece welcomed him with a smile.

'Hello, Chief Inspector.'

'Mr Preece.'

'Something I can do for you?'

'Give me a little of your time, if you will.'

'Of course,' said Preece and led him inside.

Politely ignoring Preece's offer of a chair, Mitsides crossed the office and stood with his back to the open window.

'Would you like a coffee?'

The policeman shook his head. 'Thank you, no.'

His host, reaching for the bottom drawer of his desk, was not to be deterred. 'A scotch?'

'You are very kind, Mr Preece,' demurred Mitsides. 'But some other time perhaps.'

Preece frowned slightly. 'Is this an official visit, Chief Inspector?'

'Routine,' replied the detective dismissively. 'It's more a question of entirely satisfying myself on a matter about which I already have very little doubt.' He paused and then went on. 'How well did you know the late Barry Collier?'

Preece reacted to the question with a look of surprise. 'As one of our Section Managers he was responsible to me,' he said.

'So yours was a strictly working relationship?' Mitsides suggested.

Preece hedged a little. 'Well no, not exactly. A little more than that. There's not many of us from the U.K. working on this project. We tend to stick together.' He smiled. 'You know how it is. "She stood in tears amid the alien corn . . ." '

Mitsides did not like being patronised. He picked up the rhythm of the verse immediately.

' "The same that oft times hath
Charmed magic casements opening on the foam
Of perilous seas in faery lands forlorn." '

Preece's astonishment was rudely plastered across his face. 'I'm impressed.'

The Chief Inspector turned the screw its last inch. 'By Keats? So am I, Mr Preece.' He smiled pleasantly. He had made his point. 'Would you say then that you and Collier were friends?'

Preece paused before answering, trying to recover his poise. 'Well yes, I suppose so. Not close friends. But sure, we were friends. We used to buy each other drinks and occasionally we'd spend some of our time off together.'

The Chief Inspector nodded. 'And how long had you known him?'

'About a year and a half. Barry and I were on the first survey. Right at the start of the project.'

Mitsides suddenly changed tack. 'A project which has taken its toll, wouldn't you say? Including Collier there have been three fatal accidents among your employees in the last twelve months.'

Preece shrugged and let out a quiet sigh of resignation. 'Yes,' he admitted. 'Unfortunately. But all of them due to carelessness. And on a contract of this size and working on the kind of terrain we are you must expect accidents. Some fatal. We've had our share. And that's regrettable. But no more than par for the course I'd say.'

Mitsides turned and stared thoughtfully out of the open window. 'And Alexis Eliades?'

Preece looked bewildered now. 'Suicide. According to the coroner anyway. He was under stress. A sickness of our time, Chief Inspector.'

And nine people in ten, its victims, reflected Mitsides sadly, distracted for a moment by a vision of a golden age when the gods walked the earth and men had not lost sight of heaven. He nodded his acknowledgement abstractedly to Preece who ploughed on, floundering a little.

'I'm sorry but I don't quite see what Eliades' suicide and the other accidents have got to do with Barry Collier. Or my relationship with him.'

Mitsides let him off the hook. 'Nothing, Mr Preece. It was merely an observation. A commentary. On the price of progress. Forgive me.' He turned back to him and smiled once more.

'Tell me,' he went on, reverting to the object of his visit, 'as someone who knew him well, do you have any reason whatever to believe that Barry Collier was involved in anything illegal here on Cyprus?'

'Barry!' exclaimed Preece, stunned. 'Are you serious? Such as what, for instance?'

Since Mitsides had no idea he could offer no concrete proposition. He shrugged. 'Society and the law offer many temptations. Some of them extremely profitable. Trafficking in drugs for example.'

'Oh come now, Chief Inspector!' scoffed Preece. 'Barry was as straight as a die! He wouldn't have got mixed up in anything like that. Or anything else for that matter. He just wasn't the type.'

The Chief Inspector persisted. 'Criminals are not a special breed you know, Mr Preece. They are human beings just like you and me. And often the only difference between them and us is that they get caught.'

'Maybe so. And, okay, perhaps once in a while Barry loaded his expenses a little. But that's all.'

Mitsides studied him closely. 'You are convinced of that?'

'I'd stake my life on it,' answered Preece firmly. 'Anyway what on earth gave you the idea that Barry was crooked?'

The detective was quick to reject the implication . 'I didn't say that. I merely questioned the possibility with you.'

'Even so something must have prompted the thought.'

Mitsides nodded. 'His brother.'

'His brother!' exclaimed Preece. 'I don't believe it.'

'Nevertheless,' insisted Mitsides. 'You've met him. What is your opinion of him?'

'I like him.'

'A stable personality would you say?'

'Certainly. Very stable.'

'Unduly disturbed emotionally by his brother's death perhaps?'

Preece considered a moment before replying. 'I don't think so. Seemed to me he was coping with the situation very well. Shocked by it of course. And deeply grieved naturally. But totally in control.'

'Yes,' said Mitsides thoughtfully. 'I would agree with that. Which really only leaves me with two possible answers. One is that he is not as stable a character as he would appear to be . . .' He sighed and then went on. 'The other is paramythia.'

Preece frowned. 'I'm sorry?'

'That he is a fantasist.'

'A fantasist!' exclaimed Preece. He shook his head in bewilderment. 'I don't understand. What's he been saying, for God's sake?'

Mitsides sighed again, deeply. 'According to Mr Collier, last night he was taken to a deserted village and shown a briefcase which, it is claimed, belonged to his brother. The briefcase contained a small fortune in Swiss francs. Something over fifty thousand pounds in English money.'

'Fifty thousand pounds!' echoed Preece incredulously. He held the policeman's gaze for a few seconds and then, shaking his head in disbelief, reached down, opened the bottom drawer of his desk and took out a bottle of whiskey and two glasses. The slight move of the bottle towards Mitsides was no more than a polite ritual. 'Are you sure?'

Mitsides shook his head. 'Not for me thank you.'

Preece poured a liberal shot for himself and then sipped it.

'But Barry never had that kind of money!' he said. 'And in Swiss francs! It's incredible.'

'Quite so,' agreed the Chief Inspector. 'But no less

incredible than the rest of Mr Collier's story. He claims that he met a woman . . .'

And as Preece listened to what Mitsides had to say so, too, did Eric Morrison, crouching outside the hut beneath the open window.

He had heard everything up to that point and he had to hear the rest. A lot depended on it for him.

CHAPTER NINE

Collier had left the desk till last. The taboo on reading other people's letters and prying into their private life was a hard one to overcome. Even when the person concerned was family and no longer around. Harder perhaps. But bills must be settled, friends notified, debts collected. It had to be done.

And then there was Helene. He could hear her voice now as she spoke about his brother. 'You could say there was a very special relationship between us.' Perhaps there was a picture of her in Barry's 'trophy' album which would bring her back to reality for him. But a thorough search through the photographic records of Barry's many conquests had revealed a lot of small game but no creature nearly so magnificent as Helene. Nowhere in the house had he been able to find a single clue to the association with his brother to which she had laid claim; not among the photographs, not among bits and pieces and hastily scrawled notes which he had found in various drawers in the sitting room. There was no picture of her in Barry's wallet and not one single reference to her in his diary. And the traces of perfume which clung to the pillows in the bedroom didn't fit her either.

And it was the same among the things in the desk, not a letter, not a telephone number or an address, nothing. It was clear that this was one 'special' relationship which Barry had either been determined to keep very much to himself or had been uncharacteristically discreet about.

My God, thought Collier, perhaps she's married, and he found himself strangely disturbed by the prospect. He was still struggling with the possibility when the doorbell rang. It was Martin Preece.

'Hello there,' he said, standing on the doorstep and smiling.

'Hello, Mr Preece.'

Despite the warmth in Collier's voice his visitor pulled a face. 'Martin, please,' he corrected good naturedly.

Collier grinned at him. 'Right then. So, hello Martin.'

'That's better. On my way through to Limassol. Thought I'd just look in. Have you had lunch?'

Collier realised that he had not and suddenly breakfast seemed long ago. With more relish than he had felt since he came to Cyprus he accepted Preece's implied invitation.

An hour later, a good meal inside them and with cups of freshly made, aromatic coffee in front of them on their table overlooking the sea, he was glad he had done so. He might as well enjoy his few days here and simply relegate the Helene episode to a recess in his memory. But then the smoke from Preece's cigarette seemed for a moment to be a puff of gunsmoke from the walls of the ancient Turkish fort overlooking the yacht filled harbour – yachts which, in his mind's eye, turned into a flotilla of ancient ships on their way to rescue another Helen – she who, in the name of love, had set Greek against Trojan and in doing so condemned so many men to die. Preece's voice brought him back to the present.

'You've been through Barry's papers you say? No problems I hope,' he enquired solicitously.

Collier shook his head. 'I don't think so. It all looks pretty straightforward. A few bills to be paid. One or two letters to be answered. That kind of thing,' he said dismissively.

'Well if you do need any help give me a shout,' volunteered Preece. 'I'm sure our legal department would be only too happy to advise you. And if you get snarled up in any way with Cypriot legal formalities, well, the company's got a lawyer in Nicosia who could put you straight on them. Don't hesitate to say, will you? Kitson Neve'll foot the bill.'

Collier was genuinely grateful. 'Thanks. I'll remember if the need arises.'

'There was a Will, was there?'

'Yes,' replied Collier. 'Apparently everything comes to me.'

‘Ah well, that makes things simpler. Presumably you’ll stick around until probate’s granted? Or whatever.’

Collier had not really considered the matter. ‘Depends how long it takes. But I’ll be here for a while I expect.’

Preece picked up the bill from the table and signalled to the waiter. ‘Good. See some more of you then.’

Collier went through the customary protest. ‘Oh no, please! Let me.’

But Preece wouldn’t hear of it. ‘Certainly not. I asked you out to lunch. Anyway, it’s my turn.’

Collier capitulated gracefully. ‘Well thanks very much. I enjoyed the meal.’

Preece dropped a handful of notes on the plate and, without waiting for change, began to shepherd Collier off along the quay.

‘And how are you feeling in yourself?’ he asked as, side by side, they strolled away from the *taverna*. ‘To be honest, you don’t look too good. You okay?’

‘Fine. A bit tired that’s all,’ Collier replied.

Preece smiled. ‘Yes, I heard that you’d had a rather eventful night.’ Collier looked at him enquiringly and he explained. ‘Chief Inspector Mitsides. He came to see me this morning.’

Collier felt peeved. ‘No doubt to get your opinion as to my sanity,’ he said sulkily.

Preece dismissed the suggestion. ‘Just for a general chat really.’

‘In the course of which,’ insisted Collier, ‘he told you about my wild story.’

Preece looked embarrassed. ‘Well, yes, he mentioned it,’ he said and then seemed anxious to drop the subject.

Collier’s initial warm response towards his host had cooled a little by the time they were re-seated in Barry’s sitting room for Preece had been more than a little sceptical at the tale and was still pouring scorn on it.

‘But it really doesn’t make any kind of sense, does it,’ he argued, lighting another cigarette. ‘I mean, if this strange woman had kept the hiding place of the briefcase a secret as it would appear she had, well then, why were you attacked and robbed? And who by?'

Collier shrugged. 'I don't know,' he admitted. 'To tell the truth I'm not even sure it happened myself now.' He studied Preece closely. 'You think I imagined it all, don't you?'

Preece smiled thinly and then tried reassurance. 'I think that once you get everything settled here you ought to have a holiday,' he said. 'Take things easy for a while.'

Collier's protest was cut short by the shrill note of the telephone. He crossed quickly to it, wondering who besides Preece and Mitsides knew where to find him. The voice at the other end was unknown to him.

'David Collier?'

'Yes.'

'My name's Morrison.'

The name rang a bell. Hadn't Barry's friend been called Morrison? Collier checked. 'Eric Morrison?' he asked.

'That's right. Barry told you about me?'

'In his letters, yes. I was hoping to meet you.'

'I was at the funeral.'

'Oh, I wish I'd known.' Collier wondered which of the half dozen unrecognised figures round the grave had owned this voice. Morrison's tone became urgent.

'Look I've got to talk to you. Now. Today.'

Collier welcomed the idea. 'Of course. I'd like that. Come on round,' he urged. 'Any time.'

Much to his surprise his invitation was brusquely rejected.

'No, not there,' Morrison snapped impatiently. 'Not at the apartment. I can't go there. It's too difficult. Look, I'll explain when I see you. Right?'

Mystified, Collier frowned. 'Well if you say so. Where then?'

'A little place called Trimiklini. I'll wait for you there. Around four. Okay?'

'Yes, all right,' agreed Collier rather reluctantly. 'But I just don't understand why you can't . . .'

Morrison interrupted him. 'Look, I told you. I'll explain

when we meet. And don't let me down, will you? I mean, you will come, won't you?'

'Of course,' Collier assured him. 'If it's that important to you.'

'It is. It's important to both of us,' insisted Morrison. 'Believe me.' And then he hung up.

When Collier turned back to Preece it was obvious from his guest's expression that he was more than casually curious.

'Something wrong?' he asked.

Collier shook his head. 'Well no, not wrong exactly. Odd perhaps but nothing more. That was a friend of Barry's. Eric Morrison.' And it was at that moment that he realised. 'But then you know him of course.'

'My senior works supervisor,' confirmed Preece.

'Well he wants to see me. At a place called Trimiklini.'

Preece frowned. 'Trimiklini?'

'Yes. Do you know it?'

'It's a local beauty spot,' replied Preece with a nod. 'But it's a fair distance from here.'

'He said at four o'clock.'

Preece glanced at his watch. 'Oh well you should make it easily by then,' he confirmed. Then, for a second, he looked more than a little annoyed. 'But Morrison's supposed to be working on the site this afternoon.' He sighed irritably. 'And why drag you all the way up there into the mountains, for God's sake? Why doesn't he come here?'

Collier had been wondering the same thing. 'I don't know. Said it was difficult for him. They were close, weren't they? Him and Barry.'

'Almost inseparable,' replied Preece. He stood up.

'Yes, he sounded very upset,' murmured Collier.

Preece nodded. 'Bound to be. But that doesn't excuse him sloping off for the afternoon. Look,' he continued with an apologetic expression, 'I'd run you up there but I've got a meeting with Wyndham at three I'm afraid . . .'

Collier was quick to put him at his ease again. 'I wouldn't hear of it. No need anyway. I can get there all right. In Barry's car.'

'Of course. Well, fine then,' said Preece, clearly relieved, and then, as if to make up for his neglect, he added helpfully. 'If there's a map around I'll show you the best route to take.'

CHAPTER TEN

Collier had thoroughly enjoyed the drive out to Trimiklini. Though the low-slung Triumph Spitfire 1500 sometimes seemed in peril of ripping its exhaust off, it clung beautifully to the bends as he grew in confidence and began to drive it in a style of which Barry would have thoroughly approved. Barry; one of the best drivers he had ever known. Too good to lose even a Spitfire on a simple corner like the one which had killed him, let alone a Landrover. He had meant to ask Mitsides whether the police had checked if the Rover had been on four wheel drive. But then it couldn't have been because if it had been there was no way that Barry could have gone over the edge of that cliff with three good wheels still biting the surface.

Twice as he drove up into the mountains he thought he'd caught a glimpse of a red Alfetta in the wing mirror, way back down the road, but when he straightened up again and looked behind nothing followed him more exciting than his own dust. And when the road finally ran out he had long since stopped looking.

Checking that he was in good time, he got out of the car to keep his mysterious rendezvous. Morrison had not been precise as to the exact spot for their meeting so Collier decided he'd spend the few minutes he had in hand in hard climbing to the top of the ridge that stretched up steeply behind an old and narrow bridge which spanned a dried-up water course just beyond the point where the road petered out.

By the time he had reached the crest of the ridge he was badly out of breath. I'm in bad shape, he thought. Time I took up jogging, played some squash again, even. But that was tomorrow's resolution. Today he was sweating heavily and panting but, looking around from his vantage point, he decided that it had been worth the effort for the view which he now enjoyed.

As he slowly and pleasurably scanned the horizon he became aware of a man sitting in the centre of a small circle of stones in a clearing forty or fifty yards below him on the far side of the slope. That must be Morrison he decided and, as he scrambled down, he called out a greeting so as not to alarm the other man.

'Morrison?'

Morrison looked up as Collier descended the rise towards him and waited.

Collier arrived in a breathless flurry and stretched out his hand. 'Good to meet you. But why here for heaven's sake? It's the middle of nowhere.'

His laugh dwindled as Morrison no more than perfunctorily shook hands.

'Simple. That woman you met last night . . .'

Taken aback at his knowledge, Collier broke in. 'You know about that?'

'I heard.'

'How?' asked Collier.

The other man seemed irritated by the question. 'How doesn't matter. I heard. Okay? She told you Barry was murdered. Right? Well could be she knows what she's talking about. So that's why we're here. See?' Eyes narrowed, he searched Collier's face intently. 'Fifty thousand quid. In Swiss francs,' he challenged. 'That right?'

Collier's excitement grew. 'A little over fifty thousand, she said.'

'That fits,' Morrison muttered, almost to himself.

'Then you believe my story!' cried Collier, his gratitude at finding confirmation of his sanity making his thanks almost hysterical. 'Thank God someone does.'

The other man drew half a step away from him, suspiciously. 'Well I believe the bit about the money anyway. You see, half of it belongs to me.'

'That's incredible!' exclaimed Collier. 'Now I can convince that damned fool, Mitsides, that I'm neither drunk nor mad. Come on. We can drive down to Limassol in less than two hours.'

Morrison scoffed openly. 'Go to the police with you! Are you out of your mind?'

'But you must,' insisted Collier desperately. 'If you confirm the existence of the money then Mitsides will probably accept the rest of my story. He'll have to make a fuller investigation.'

'Too bloody right he will,' snapped Morrison angrily. 'Which is why I'm not going to the police. Clear? That's not why I got you out here.'

'Don't be so damned stupid,' reasoned Collier. 'You have to come to the police with me.'

'Stupid!' snarled Morrison. 'It's not me that's being stupid. It's you that's off your head.' And then he added menacingly. 'And I don't *have* to do anything. See?'

Collier's anger mounted to match Morrison's. 'Then I'll go to them,' he retorted, and he could see from the other man's expression that he believed him. 'I'll tell Mitsides what you've said. Have him pick you up.'

'Don't be a bloody fool!' Morrison's anger degenerated into panic and he grabbed at Collier's sleeve. Collier pulled his arm away angrily and then, like two children fighting over a disputed toy, the pair of them stumbled sideways. And, at that moment, a bullet slammed against one of the rocks only inches from Morrison's head and then sang away in a ricochet which merged with the crack of a rifle that echoed round the hills dominating the clearing.

With a terrified shriek Morrison dived for protection behind one of the other, and even larger, rocks. It took only a moment for an uncomprehending Collier to abandon reason and follow instinct by hurling himself in the same direction.

The second bullet drilled into an adjacent tree in line with the point where Collier had been standing. The silence which followed the dying echoes was total and paralysing, as if all nature had stilled its hubbub to watch the outcome of this hunt with bated breath. Then a single bird, as if recovering from the shock, shrilled its protest and the spell was broken.

Morrison scowled venomously at his fellow refugee cowering alongside him behind the rock. 'You bastard!' he screamed and then he launched himself out across the open ground, weaving from side to side and using every piece of cover on his route to full advantage.

Fascinated, Collier watched his progress, certain, as two more shots rang out, that he must be killed. But, fully alerted, Morrison presented too hard a target for even a highly skilled marksman and the fact that Collier was still alive told him that while he might be dealing with a killer at least he was not at the mercy of a professional sharpshooter. Or so he hoped.

It was only when Morrison reached the safety of the trees that Collier realised that the 'you bastard' had been hurled at him and not toward their unknown assailant. He also realised that he still had to run the gauntlet himself. What's more, this time the killer would be expecting him and would certainly get him the instant he broke cover. There was only one hope. Forget the false security of the car and bolt in the opposite direction, up the hill and away from the road. That at least would be unexpected.

Spurred on by terror and summoning up every ounce of strength in him, he broke from behind the rock and ran as he'd never run before.

He was more than two thirds of the way up the slope when he realised that he had made a terrible mistake. The cover was too scant and the gunman had had ample time to recover and re-align his sights. No. He was dead. Why didn't the swine get it over and done with instead of sadistically savouring every agonising stride until the very last moment.

And then he was at the top of the slope and the killer fired again.

Collier's body spun over the crest of the ridge and crashed down the far side to the last echo of the fourth shot from the rifle and to the frantic funereal chorus of a host of wheeling, frightened birds.

CHAPTER ELEVEN

Collier knew he could only have lost consciousness for a second or two for the small stones which had beaded the fringe of the landslide were still rattling to a halt further down the slope. He ached and stung in a hundred places but, as far as he could tell, no bones had been broken when the root or whatever it was that he had tripped over on the crest of the ridge had sent him somersaulting and cascading down the other side and out of sight of the telescopic eye focussed on the middle of his back.

But for all he knew the rifle was seeking him out again, maybe even zeroed in on him at that moment. He had been lucky, very lucky but he was still a long way off being home and dry. He had to get away.

With difficulty he stood up only to collapse again immediately with a barely stifled shriek. His right ankle would not bear his weight and, after one more painful confirmation of the fact that it must be badly sprained, Collier began to drag himself in a vulnerable crawl towards the shelter of the nearby woods. He knew that it was possible that he could be headed straight toward the would-be assassin but the inborn instinct of a wounded animal to seek cover, any cover, was compelling.

Not long after he had reached the shelter of the trees Collier heard, distantly, a car drive off at speed and assumed that Morrison had made good his escape. And, with a sigh of relief, he judged that by now he, too, must be in the clear. In his crippled condition any determined pursuer would surely have caught up with him within minutes of his fall.

With that thought to console him, he now concentrated his mind on the other problem which faced him; the not inconsiderable task of getting back to Paphos and contacting the police.

It took Collier almost two hours of crawling and scrabbling

around in the undergrowth before he found a branch suitable as a crutch. And then, though painfully mobile, he was still faced with the problem of navigation.

He knew no more than that Paphos lay generally to the south west but with the sun already down over the hills he had little idea of where that might be. Various jumbled bits of scout law about lichens and prevailing winds came uselessly back to him since he had no idea from which way the light breeze was blowing and the trees were uniformly bare of helpful fungi.

Nor was there much prospect in this remote place of finding any kind of assistance. The only living thing that he had seen during the past two hours were an incongruously partnered goat and a ram staring at him from the top of a slab of rock. And he hadn't dared call out to attract the attention of any nearby shepherd for fear that whoever it was who had tried to kill him might just still be in the neighbourhood.

Struggling to his feet and leaning heavily on the improvised crutch he hobbled painfully into the woods.

Darkness was closing in fast when, at last, he limped into a broad clearing in the centre of which stood the workings of a long abandoned copper mine and, more usefully, the tumbledown ruin of a winding shed.

Wincing with pain, he laboriously made for what little shelter it provided, stumbled inside and settled himself down on the ground in one corner and under what remained of the roof.

In what was, by then, the last glimmerings of a momentary Mediterranean twilight he eased off his shoe and sock and surveyed his swollen and discoloured ankle in despair.

It was clearly an even worse sprain than he had first thought and any attempt to make his way any further through the trees in darkness would, he decided, not only be almost impossible but also insane. The only option open to him was to pass the night where he was and as best he could.

Not surprisingly that proved to be not very well, and he

dozed only fitfully until dawn when pain and exhaustion plunged him for a while into a deep, dreamless sleep.

Once again it was his sense of smell which first hinted at the return of consciousness. The acrid tang of woodsmoke brought images of boyhood camps to his waking brain and he lay still, his eyes closed, ankle throbbing, piecing together a mosaic of reality which came together into an unpleasing picture of reality of his present predicament.

Gradually he opened his eyes and reacted, first with astonishment and then with a twinge of fear.

In the centre of the ruins and not more than three feet off from him a camp fire glowed redly in a circle of flat stones. Set firmly amid the wood ash and brilliant embers was a bubbling billy can and a small copper pot with a long handle.

Shifting his gaze a little, Collier saw a loaf of bread lying on a pile of rubble close to the fire and suddenly he was very much aware of just how hungry he was.

However the sound of soft footsteps approaching him instantly dispelled any thought of food and he looked up and across at the remnants of the wall of the winding shed to his right, alarmed and concerned. And what he saw did little to reassure him.

The stranger who appeared around the end of the wall and stood looking at him was certainly not young; fifty or sixty Collier guessed. His unkempt beard, moustache and hair were all streaked with grey. The pirate style headband tied round his forehead divided his hair into two downward curling horns on either side of his face and for an instant Collier was reminded of the ram that had surveyed him so curiously the evening before. The man's solid, slightly paunchy build was lent muscularity by the tattered British army battledress blouse and the baggy, black trousers which he was wearing. He had a canvas haversack slung over one shoulder.

And he was armed; a huge hunting knife protruded from the top of one of his rough leather knee boots and bandoliers of ammunition crisscrossed his chest. But what attracted and held Collier's attention was the bolt action rifle fitted with a telescopic sight which the stranger was cradling in the crook of his left arm.

Instinctively and fearfully Collier, his eyes fixed on the gun, dragged himself further back against the wall. For several seconds the man stood watching him with sharp, bright eyes. Then he swung the rifle out of his arm and propped it against the ruins of the wall, lovingly drew out from inside his battledress blouse a bottle of wine, three quarters full.

The stranger gazed at the bottle reverently then uncorked it and, throwing back his head, drank liberally from it without pausing for breath. Smacking his lips in relish, he re-corked the bottle and slipped it back into his blouse.

Collier watched, mesmerised. But then to his further bewilderment the man, after his initial interest, proceeded to ignore him totally.

He crossed to the fire, squatted down beside it, unslung his haversack and opened it.

From it he took a crumpled packet of coffee, a plastic spoon and a small, none-to-clean mug.

Two heaped spoonsful of the coffee were dumped into the boiling water in the copper pot and stirred until the rising froth threatened to fountain over the top. Then the stranger removed the pot from the embers. This process was repeated twice more before the brew passed muster and was decanted into the battered mug. After hacking a chunk of bread from the loaf with his lethal hunting knife, and with the mug in one hand and the bread in the other, the man stood up, crossed to Collier and held out the food and drink to him. Collier eyed him warily.

'Who are you?' he asked in as level a voice as he could manage. 'What are you doing here?'

The man did not reply but merely pressed the bread and coffee on him with an insistent gesture.

Collier's hunger stabbed at him again and he reached out and took the offerings and alternated urgent bites into the bread with sips of the scalding and quite delicious coffee.

His good samaritan said nothing, simply settled on his

haunches beside him and waited until he had finished eating. Then he gently raised Collier's injured ankle for inspection.

He didn't need the Englishman's gasp of pain to tell him just how badly sprained it was. One look was more than enough to confirm that.

Tenderly lowering the leg again, the man stood up and returned to the fire to examine the bubbling contents of the billycan.

It was clear to Collier now that, despite his initial fears, the stranger meant him no harm. Quite the reverse apparently. He decided to try to establish some kind of contact.

'You just found me here,' he enquired with a smile. 'Is that it?'

The man did not even turn his head. He cut three lengths of cloth from a strip of linen which he dug out of the haversack. The two narrower ones he rolled up neatly into bandages. Then he folded the larger one into a solid pad and, dipping the blade of his hunting knife into the billycan, began to spread it with a gooey, malodorous, greeny-brown paste.

Collier spoke again.

'Look, I must get to a telephone. But I can't walk. Is there any way you can help me?'

It was as if the stranger had not heard the question. He stood up and approached Collier holding the steaming poultice.

The Englishman was distracted from the moment of actual impact by the revolting smell of the medicament but flinched at the heat of it a moment later. Surprisingly the pain from the freshly boiled unction vanished in seconds and was followed by a pleasantly numbing sensation which spread through the whole lower part of Collier's leg. But he knew that this didn't make it any the less imperative for him to somehow make the man understand his other and almost equally pressing needs. He tried again and loudly this time as the thought struck him that his benefactor might well be deaf which would account for his lack of response so far.

'It's very urgent,' he said, enunciating carefully. 'You see

I've got to get in touch with the police. I know this sounds crazy, but someone tried to kill me yesterday.'

But once again the man ignored his entreaty. He gathered up the various implements and utensils and scoured them out with dirt and grass before returning them to the haversack. The fire had been partly extinguished by the dregs from the coffee pot and now the stranger raked soil over it with his foot, covering it completely.

'Don't you understand?' Collier shouted. 'Someone tried to kill me. I must tell the police.'

His packing completed, the man reached into his battle-dress, took out the wine bottle and drank from it once more.

Collier suddenly realised his stupidity. He had been speaking English to a Cypriot peasant. He gestured wildly in an elaborate mime.

'You don't speak English, is that it?'

Still there was no reply. No reaction of any kind. Collier tried again in that strange pidgin language with which foreigners are usually addressed, to their complete confusion, by the English, either abroad or in Piccadilly Circus.

'You not speak English, yes?'

The man slung his haversack over his shoulder, crossed to Collier, bent over him and, with great gentleness, began to work the injured foot back into its sock and unlaced shoe.

Collier was becoming frantic now.

'Police! Police!' he bellowed. 'You understand that? Police?'

His companion made no sign of having heard a word and despairingly Collier decided that he had to be more than just a little hard of hearing. He might even be dumb too for all he knew.

Oh great! he thought to himself. Alone in a wood with a deaf mute. That's going to get me nowhere fast.

He made one last, fatuous attempt. 'You not hear, yes?' He flapped his fingers. 'You not speak?'

He didn't really expect an answer and he didn't get one.

The man gathered up his rifle and disappeared from view for a while around the end of the wall. When he returned he was leading a very docile looking mule. The sight of the beast gave the Englishman renewed hope. Perhaps his message had got through after all. He smiled and nodded enthusiastically.

'Yes! Yes!' he exclaimed. 'Telephone. You take me to a telephone. Right?'

He tried to get to his feet but even with the support of the skilfully applied bandage, his ankle would still not take his weight and let him know it in very painful terms.

With almost nonchalant ease the shepherd, for this was what Collier now decided he must be, scooped him off the ground and swung him up onto the back of the mule. Then, as he led the burdened animal out of the ruins and across the clearing, his taciturn features broke into a smile and a deep, rich bass made the woods ring with song; a song which, although he didn't understand any of the words, Collier just knew from its inflections had to be bibulous or bawdy. Or both.

They had been travelling a good hour, climbing higher and higher into the mountains, before Collier recognised a sense of unease creeping up on him. Surely they were going further into the wilds, not back towards civilisation, telephones and policemen.

Just as he was about to voice his anxiety his guide stopped and stared down into a valley to their left. There at the end of a narrow track on the open mountainside stood a typical Greek Orthodox monastery.

From his seat astride the mule Collier could see no sign of life, but that did not worry him. This must be why his rescuer had brought him here. He could rest while the monks sent someone to the nearest village for help.

But if the deserted air of the building caused Collier no concern it seemed a positive source of delight to his companion.

Eugene Hellman kept his eyes on the display panel as the computer signalled its next move, then he looked up and across at the two men standing just inside the doorway to the stateroom.

'He didn't come back to the apartment last night,' mumbled Travis.

Olsen nodded in confirmation. 'We've asked around.'

Outside, gulls lazily circled the yacht and in the open expanse of sea between it and the shore, water-skiers rode the wake of powerful motorboats.

Hellman, sitting at an ornate chess table, sighed. 'Discreetly, I hope.'

'Naturally,' Olsen assured him defensively. 'No one's seen him since early afternoon yesterday.'

Hellman looked away from them and studied the chess board. He made a move in answer to that of his electronic opponent.

'And you found nothing when you searched Barry Collier's place in Paphos, you say?'

'Not a thing.'

'But suddenly his brother's not around any more,' mused Hellman, his eyes still on the chess pieces. 'Interesting.'

'You think he's gone under cover?' ventured Travis, more as a hesitant suggestion than a question.

Hellman nodded thoughtfully. 'That. Or perhaps he's just visiting. Taking stock. Making an inventory perhaps.' He looked up at the two men again. 'Either way, find him,' he snapped brusquely. 'I am most anxious to talk to Mr David Collier.'

'And if he doesn't go for the idea?' asked Olsen.

Hellman frowned. 'Then persuade him,' he replied, fixing the pair of them with a hard, piercing look. Then he paused and the merest trace of a smile came on to his lips. 'Persuade him that it would be to his advantage.'

CHAPTER TWELVE

Collier was grateful when his 'shepherd' swung him off the mule and carried him across the threshold of the monastery. His ankle still hurt, if not quite so badly, but he felt exhausted and he longed to rest. But first he must get in touch with the outside world.

'There is a telephone here?' he asked. It was difficult to mime when being carried bridal fashion but he tried. 'A telephone? Here a telephone?'

Again there was no response and Collier decided to let the matter drop until he had been safely deposited wherever they were going. He was not kept waiting long. They halted halfway down a long, stone-pillared colonnade with rough wooden doorways leading off on either side.

The stranger pivoted through ninety degrees and prodded one of these doors open with his foot. Stooping slightly he stepped inside and gently laid his burden down on a simple wooden bed draped with a colourfully embroidered Cypriot coverlet.

While he plumped up two cushions to slip behind the Englishman's back, Collier gazed around.

The room was small and barrel-vaulted like a wine cellar. The walls were whitewashed but otherwise unadorned except by the leafspun pattern of light thrown by the sun through a single, narrow arched window high in the wall opposite the door. In one corner stood a low pine cupboard and a stool. On top of the cupboard a brass tray bore two plain pottery beakers and an earthenware jug.

But spartan convalescence was not what Collier needed. Not now anyway.

'No, look!' he protested. 'This is very kind of you, but you don't understand. A telephone. That's what I want. I must get in touch with the police.'

He might as well have addressed the whitewashed walls for all the difference it made to the other man who had now unslung his rifle and pack and dumped them on the floor by the cupboard. With a sigh Collier realised that if he was to get any immediate action then he must clearly make his own way to the monks who were presumably to be found in some other part of the monastery and explain to them. He swung his legs to the floor and again tried to stand but, once more, the pain was too much for him and he fell back onto the bed.

The stranger turned to him. 'Rest,' he said quietly.

Collier was exasperated by the absurdity of the advice. 'Rest! How can I while . . .' He broke off suddenly appreciating that the sphinx had spoken. 'You're not deaf then! Nor dumb. And you do speak English!'

The man looked at him and smiled. 'No, my hearing is excellent,' he assured him. 'And yes, I speak English. Also French, German, Latin, Spanish, Hebrew. Many languages. Including, of course, Greek.'

Collier felt irritated that he was being teased now after having been ignored for so long. 'Then you've understood everything I've said to you?'

'Perfectly,' came the unrepentant reply.

'So why bring me here?' asked Collier. 'You know I've got to get to a telephone. Someone tried to kill me yesterday.'

Again the other man seemed unperturbed. 'Yes. So you said.'

'It's the truth,' insisted Collier.

The man nodded. 'I believe you.'

Collier pressed on. 'So I have to get in touch with the police.'

'And you will,' came the reassuring reply, but Collier felt he was being fobbed off and his impatience burst out.

'Now! Right away!'

Patiently he was put down again. 'That is not possible. The nearest telephone is some distance from here. And you are injured. Travelling is not easy for you. Later. When you are rested. You will see.'

'It can't wait,' said Collier despairingly.

'You cannot walk. And my mule is tired. As I am tired. As you are. So for now, rest. Sleep.'

The calm logic of this argument convinced Collier that the significance of his plea had not been understood.

'But I wasn't alone. There was someone with me. He was shot at too. He ran but I don't know for sure that he's okay. And even if he did get away he could still be in danger. He has to be protected.'

Again the response was entirely logical. 'If he is alive, this man you were with, do you not think that by now he will himself have gone to the authorities?'

Collier had to concede the point. 'I imagine so.'

'Then your concern for his safety is unnecessary,' stated his companion simply. 'And if he is dead, well . . .' he shrugged. 'Then there is no need for haste, is there? Better you should look to your own well being, friend.'

Collier was shocked by the man's apparent callousness and when the stranger merely smiled at his indignation it spilled over into words.

'Screw you, Jack, I'm all right. That's a charming attitude.'

The other was not to be put out. 'It is a practical one. And pragmatism is not without its merits as an ethic.'

Collier had to admit that his own ethics in the past forty-eight hours had not been untinged with pragmatism. But just who the hell was this inhumanly philosophical and incongruously well-educated shepherd?

'What's your name?' he asked.

'Basileos.'

Collier moved his right leg in an attempt to ease the dull ache beneath the poultice.

'It hurts?' enquired Basileos solicitously.

Grimacing, Collier nodded. 'Yes, it hurts.'

'The poultice will heal it,' he was assured.

Collier looked doubtful. 'Maybe.'

'Put your trust in nature, Englishman,' affirmed Basileos. 'For in it is all that is divine.'

'The common cold?' retorted Collier bitterly. 'Piles? Cancer?'

Basileos nodded solemnly. 'Yes. In those things too.'

'Thank you,' laughed Collier scornfully. 'We could do without them.'

'But also in the rose,' continued Basileos. 'And in your first breath. Rest. And have faith. The salve will mend your ankle. It is an old and proven recipe.' He turned to the cupboard and, picking up the jug, poured wine into the two beakers. 'And as for the pain you feel now, well this will ease that.'

He crossed over to the bed, a beaker of wine in either hand, and offered one to Collier who eyed it suspiciously.

'What is it?' he asked.

The pride in Basileos' voice was evident as he replied, 'Wine. The best in all Cyprus.'

Collier shook his head. 'No thank you. I don't drink.'

Basileos was clearly shocked. 'Not even wine?' he exclaimed.

'No.'

'Why?' asked Basileos.

'It goes to my head.'

Basileos laughed. 'As it should. To your head and to your heart.' He chuckled. 'Wine is to the spirit what food is to the body. Comfort, fuel and substance.'

Collier glanced pointedly at the neck of the bottle protruding from his battledress blouse. 'Well your spirit should be in pretty good shape.'

Basileos looked down at the bottle and nodded. 'Succour and pleasure for the needy. And for myself, a vindication. But a travelling companion. Nothing more.'

Then, like a man in love, he raised his beaker and gazed fondly into the red liquor it contained, savoured the bouquet and sighed with pleasure. 'This, though, is something special.'

He sat on the edge of the bed and once more proffered the other beaker but Collier again declined. 'I'm sure it's everything you say it is, but no thanks.'

Basileos tried persuasion. 'It has medicinal qualities too. It will take away your pain.'

'I'm sure. If I drank enough of it I don't imagine I'd feel

anything.' Collier tried to turn him away with a laugh but the other man took the proposition quite seriously.

'That is so. But taken in the right amount you feel everything. Except pain. Wine can open doors within you which you did not even know were there. Let alone that they were closed.'

'*In vino veritas*,' quipped Collier.

Basileos shook his head and then fixed him with a gaze. 'No. The truth is not in wine. The truth is within everyone. Wine is merely a mirror in which to see it. To know oneself as one really is. And that perhaps is the reason why you do not drink it, eh? You are afraid.' He paused and then added, challengingly, 'Of you.'

He held the beaker out to the Englishman once more; tempting, taunting him with it.

Collier scowled and hesitated. But the challenge was too blatant for him to ignore it. Defiantly he reached out and took the beaker and drank from it.

As Basileos had promised, it was an excellent wine, mellow and full bodied. Collier relished the taste and then drank from the beaker again, deeper this time.

Basileos was studying his reaction closely. 'It is good?' he enquired with a quiet smile.

Collier nodded. 'Very good.'

Basileos was obviously pleased. 'Did you not have my word on it? And the key to so many locks. So, Englishman.' He raised his beaker in a gesture of toast. '*Yassu, sante, prosit, salud, na Zdrarovie, lechaim.*' He grinned. 'Cheers.'

Collier lifted his beaker in acknowledgement and drank from it once more. Already he felt better. Sleepy still, sleepier, even, but a lot better. Far more relaxed. He focussed on Basileos and smiled. 'Where are we? What is this place?'

'It is a monastery.'

'You live here?' Collier was surprised to find that he slurred the question a little. He took another drink from the beaker. It really is rather special, this wine, he thought.

'Here and elsewhere. I travel a great deal,' replied Basileos in an offhand tone.

Collier made a vain and half-hearted attempt to bring the conversation round again to the topic uppermost in his mind – getting back to Paphos. 'Well I certainly shouldn't be here.' And he had some difficulty making that unequivocal statement too.

'Oh, but you should,' Basileos assured him. 'For now anyway.'

'Why?'

Basileos shrugged. 'To rest. If for no other reason. And there are those who say that nothing is chance. That each man has his destiny. Who knows, in being here, perhaps you are fulfilling part of yours. Who can say? But is it not an interesting thought? That you should be a small part, however insignificant, of some vast plan for the cosmos. That you have a positive role to play. That you are needed.'

'Well, I'm wanted, that's for sure,' retorted Collier. 'By someone. But dead it would seem.' As he drained his beaker an unpleasant thought occurred to him. 'And you were in the mountains yesterday, weren't you? With a rifle.'

Basileos ignored the implication and refilled the beakers. 'Hunting. And Englishmen are out of season. This person who tried to kill you. You have no idea who it was?'

'None. Or why. But then a lot of things have happened to me since I arrived in Cyprus and I don't understand any of them. There was this woman . . .'

He broke off, trying to decide whether to tell his story and disguising his hesitation by a long pull at his beaker. But what was the point? Basileos would only think that he was crazy. Everyone else had. Perhaps he was. But then Morrison had confirmed that Barry had been murdered. Well almost anyway. Still the rest of the story was pretty way out.

'What woman?' enquired Basileos, waiting for him to continue.

Collier lowered his beaker. 'Forget it,' he said.

Basileos tactfully changed the subject. 'You like women?'

Collier shot him a look of surprise. 'I've never considered any alternative,' he blurted. And then he giggled.

'You have a woman?'

'Not currently. But I've known a few.'

'And enjoyed them?' enquired Basileos with the obvious relish of a man to whom the point was important.

Collier was amused. This mysterious man had already demonstrated his love of wine and song so what more naturally earthy than to complete the trio.

'You make them sound like a meal,' he said and then raised his beaker again. 'Or a cup of wine!'

Basileos took the analogy literally. 'What is the difference? Hunger, thirst, desire. They are all needs to be satisfied. And in that satisfaction there should be enjoyment. For without it, satisfaction is as arid as the desert. If you have truly enjoyed the women you have known and if they have truly enjoyed you then be grateful. For you have lit some small flames in the darkness of loneliness. And in giving and taking with joy there is obligation, each to the other. And for eternity. However brief the relationship. And obligation is love.'

'That's quite a philosophy,' commented Collier, a little surprised at the earnestness with which the proposition had been put.

'One which I recommend to you for your consideration,' said Basileos.

'And which you've adopted?'

Basileos nodded. 'From my earliest days. And in my time I have contracted many obligations, believe me. And for each of them I am grateful.'

Collier found himself losing track of the conversation. He felt so tired; contented, very contented, but tired. And, as Basileos had prophesied, the wine had eased the pain in his ankle considerably. He felt more than ready for sleep.

As his eyelids drooped he knew that Basileos was smiling and he felt the beaker gently lifted from his hand. And the last thing he was conscious of was the comforting clack of the wooden latch on the door as his rescuer quietly left the room.

CHAPTER THIRTEEN

When Collier awoke he felt fully rested and very much at peace with the world. He was, therefore, doubly surprised when he looked at his watch and saw that he had slept for less than three hours.

He stretched contentedly and lazily drew his legs up towards his chest.

It was then that he realised. And the realisation came as something of a shock which quickly turned to bewilderment. The movement of his legs had caused him no pain whatever. He sat bolt upright and looked disbelievingly at his right ankle.

The bandage once pressed tightly against the swelling now hung loosely around a limb of normal size. Cautiously he reached down and unwound the strips of linen. The poultice was quite dry and came away easily in his hands in crackling flakes like dried bay leaves.

Collier blinked in astonishment. There was no swelling and no sign whatever of a bruise. Tentatively he prodded his ankle. No pain. It was as Basileos had so confidently assured him. The poultice had worked; the sprain was healed. Collier shook his head in disbelief at what appeared to be nothing less than a minor miracle. He decided then and there that he must get his new-found friend to give him the recipe for such an incredibly effective salve. Properly marketed he could make a fortune with it back in England.

He saw it all; the scepticism and then the confusion of the General Medical Council, the publicity, the acclaim of a grateful public and all the money which would pour into him as sole proprietor and manufacturer of Collier's Instant Cure, the eighth wonder of the world.

Still smiling at his flight of fancy, he swung his legs over the side of the bed and stood up. No question about it. It was as if he had never suffered a sprain of any kind, let alone a bad one.

Shaking his head in astonishment again, he rewound the bandages into a neat roll and put them, together with the pad on which Basileos had spread the poultice, on top of the pine cupboard alongside the wine jug and the two beakers.

Then he set out in search of human contact and a telephone.

Retracing the route along which Basileos had carried him, he passed through the stone colonnade and then, realising that the way he had chosen would only lead him back to the front door of the monastery, he changed direction and crossed an open courtyard to a flight of steps which led to the floor above.

The stairway opened on to another long corridor and it was then that Collier first caught the sound of distant laughter coming, it seemed, from behind the partly opened door at the far end. He headed towards it and as he did so he heard the laughter again.

Not wanting to intrude in any way on the monks inside, nor to alarm them by his sudden appearance, Collier cautiously pulled the door open a little wider and peered round it.

He found himself gazing out across a narrow gallery above what looked at first glance to be a refectory. And what he saw below first astonished and then filled him with anger.

Seated at the head of a long oak table laden with food was Helene, sensuously and delicately eating a peach. On her right sat Charalambos neatly cutting himself a slice of cheese and, on her left, Basileos, his face buried in a wine goblet.

Collier was utterly bewildered.

There was an air of quiet and confident familiarity about the trio and it was obvious from the relaxed atmosphere surrounding them that this was not their first meeting. They knew one another. And very well indeed if he was any judge.

Had Helene and Charalambos been here all the time, he wondered, or had they just arrived? Not that that was important. They were here. With Basileos. That was enough. Why they were here and what they were up to was just one more mystery within a confusing maze from which there seemed no way out. But whatever their game was

Collier was in no doubt now that, in some way, he was part of it and that they were using him. Although how and for what purpose he had no idea.

Charalambos said something which Collier did not catch but which clearly amused his two companions and set them laughing again.

And their laughter only made Collier more angry. All right, let them enjoy their little joke, no doubt at his expense. If he could contact Chief Inspector Mitsides and get him out here then the last laugh would be on them.

Slowly he began to back away from the door and, as he did so, for just a moment he had the faint but uncomfortable impression that Helene had flicked a momentary glance up towards him as if she knew and enjoyed the fact that he was there and had seen them. But when he looked hastily down into the refectory to check he felt certain that he had been mistaken. Helene was concentrating on her peach and licking the juice from her slender fingers.

Collier moved quickly and silently back along the corridor and down the steps to the courtyard again. Seconds later he slipped through the outer door by which he had first entered the monastery and gratefully put himself outside its walls.

He started to head for the trees on the far side of the forecourt of the building but then he saw Helene's red Alfetta parked not far off from the entrance. Right, he thought. Let them do a little walking for a change. He altered course and was pleased to find that the driver's door was unlocked, though, of course, the key was not in the ignition. Still, that should present no problem. The facia panel was not fully sealed and the ignition wires were easily accessible.

But then, as he eased himself into the driving seat, he hesitated. As far as Basileos and his two companions were concerned he was still asleep in the cell. If they heard the car start, as they must, then they would be alerted. Charalambos might even have another car parked at the rear of the building in which to give chase. And pursuit from Basileos' rifle would be even swifter and could be deadly.

He shot a look across at the mule. The animal was

regarding him solemnly, as if reading his mind, and there was something about its expression, particularly the evil glint in its eyes, which warned him that what he was contemplating would be a mistake.

Better on foot, he decided. There had to be a village not too far away.

Carefully he got out of the Alfetta and pressed the door to before setting off at a jog through the woods in what he calculated, from the position of the sun, must be roughly a southerly direction.

It was an hour of hard going, which involved crossing two sizable stream-threaded valleys, before he reached a narrow, tarmacadamed road and more than thirty minutes after that before a passing lorry shuddered to a halt. The driver threw open the nearside door of the cab for him.

So it was close to two hours after his hasty departure from the monastery that he, at last, reached a telephone.

CHAPTER FOURTEEN

'Morrison knows about the money. He claims that half of it belongs to him.' The police car was speeding in the direction of the monastery.

After he had at last managed to persuade a very sceptical and weary voiced Mitsides that he could now lead him to the mysterious Helene and not just Charalambos but yet another equally odd associate of her, Collier had left the telephone box in the centre of the village square and taken shelter from the sun under the thatched awning of the local *taverna* and waited.

And the wait had been a long one. He had drunk two brandies and four cups of coffee before the car had arrived but now they were making up for lost time.

'And did he explain how he and your brother came by such a large sum?' asked Mitsides.

'No. But he as good as said that Helene was right about Barry having been murdered.'

The Chief Inspector sighed quietly. 'And then you were shot at, eh?' He glanced across at Collier. 'Three times?'

The bloody man's humouring me, Collier thought, and he scowled angrily. 'I don't know,' he snapped. 'I can't remember. Three. Four. Does it matter?'

Mitsides shook his head. 'No. Not really.' He gazed absently out of the window. 'Since fortunately neither of you were hurt.'

Sergeant Karaolis, sitting beside the uniformed driver, glanced up into the rearview mirror and Collier saw the scornful look in his eyes.

'We were both very lucky,' he countered defensively.

'Indeed you were,' replied Mitsides quietly.

Karaolis sniggered silently and grinned, as the driver swung the car on to a dirt road and accelerated up it in a cloud of dust.

Within half a mile the road deteriorated into a deeply

rutted track and the going was slow until, finally, they bumped and rolled on to slightly more even ground once again and then pulled up in the forecourt of the monastery.

And as he stepped out of the car Collier's heart sank; the red Alfetta was nowhere in sight and neither was the ill-disposed mule.

Mitsides, Karaolis and the driver came to the front of the car and surveyed the forecourt.

'The car!' exclaimed Collier. 'It's gone!'

'Again!' Now the sarcasm in Mitsides voice rang out loud and clear.

'It was here,' Collier insisted angrily.

'And the mule?'

Collier pointed. 'It was tethered to that tree.'

Mitsides and Karaolis exchanged looks. The Detective Sergeant raised his eyes despairingly.

Collier ran across the forecourt and darted in through the open door. With a gesture Mitsides indicated to Karaolis and the constable that they should check the rear of the building and then he strolled leisurely in pursuit of the Englishman.

Collier was standing in the doorway of the room where he had slept when Mitsides came up alongside him.

The policeman gazed around the small whitewashed room and hissed impatiently through his teeth.

There was a bed, but no coverlet on it such as had been described to him. Not even a mattress. And where were the bandages and the poultice which his informant had claimed he had left neatly rolled beside a wine jug and the beakers? Come to that, where were they? Certainly nowhere the Englishman had said they would be, for the top of the pine cupboard was bare and, at first glance anyway, appeared to be lightly filmed with dust.

Scarlet with frustrated anger and embarrassment, Collier swung round and raced back down the colonnade, across the courtyard and up the flight of steps.

When Mitsides ambled slowly on to the gallery the Englishman was staring down dejectedly into the refectory, fiercely gripping the wooden railing and breathing heavily, but not through exertion.

In the room below the furniture was all neatly stacked in a corner and if anyone had enjoyed a meal there recently then they had left behind no evidence to confirm the fact.

'They were sitting at that table,' moaned Collier despairingly. 'Eating. I saw them.'

Against his better judgment Mitsides found himself feeling sorry for the wide and wild-eyed man standing at the railings.

'This monastery has not been occupied for more than a year now,' he said gently.

Collier swung round to face him. 'All right. So they didn't ask permission. But they were here,' he reiterated defiantly. 'Helene, Charalambos. The man with the gun. They were here this morning. And so was I. They must have gone up to the room and found I'd left. So they cleared out and took everything with them.'

'Why?'

'They guessed I'd make for the nearest telephone. I told you. When I first met her Helene said she didn't want to get involved with the police. And this Basileos character wasn't very enthusiastic about my contacting you either.'

'Why?'

Collier shook his head and sighed deeply. 'I don't know.'

'And these three strange people. What is their interest in you anyway?' asked Mitsides.

Again Collier had no answer. 'I don't know that either,' he admitted. 'But it happened. Everything happened. Just as I said it did. My meeting with Helene. The attempt on my life. And my ending up here. It all happened.'

Mitsides studied him closely for a few seconds and then turned on his heel and led the way back to the forecourt. Karaolis and the constable were waiting for them.

'Did you find anything?' queried Mitsides perfunctorily, and then reacted with a look of surprise when the Detective Sergeant nodded and then guided them around to the back of the building.

Barry Collier's Triumph Spitfire was parked under a tree.

Karaolis handed something to his superior. 'This was in the glove compartment,' he muttered grimly.

Mitsides glanced at the piece of pasteboard in his hand and then wagged it in Collier's direction.

'A membership card,' he said. 'Of the Limassol Nautical Club. Made out in the name of Barry Collier.' He indicated the Triumph. 'This is your brother's car?'

Collier nodded lamely.

'Which, according to you,' Mitsides continued, 'you left in Trimiklini.'

Again Collier nodded.

'Where someone tried to kill you.'

'Yes,' mumbled Collier.

His eyes fixed on him, the detective drew in a deep breath. 'Tell me, Mr Collier,' he demanded in a low and steely edged voice. 'Just what kind of game are you playing with us? And why?'

And then Collier remembered. Morrison! Eric Morrison.

He smiled arrogantly. 'Oh no, Chief Inspector,' he said, gloating over the trump card which he had suddenly realised he had been holding and which he now played. 'Not again. Not this time. Not about the attempt on my life anyway. Because, you see, this time I have a witness.'

Martin Preece gave a slight, apologetic shrug. 'Well, I'm sorry, Chief Inspector,' he sympathised. 'But I'm afraid you've made a wasted journey. He's not here.'

Collier had followed the police car in the Triumph throughout the journey down from the mountains to the construction site and Preece had looked up from his desk surprised and puzzled when, accompanied by Mitsides, he had entered his office and the policeman had said that he wished to speak to Morrison.

The Chief Inspector saw the surly expression on Collier's face but disregarded it. He smiled understandingly.

'I see. Then perhaps you would be good enough to tell me where I might find him.'

Preece shrugged again. 'I've really no idea,' he replied. 'He lives in Paphos. But I don't think he spends much time there. A girlfriend. You understand. He's probably with her.'

'When did you last see him?' asked Mitsides, frowning slightly.

'Yesterday afternoon.'

'He came back here yesterday afternoon!' exclaimed Collier.

Preece shot him a look. 'Yes. Why?'

'Well didn't he say . . .' Collier began eagerly only to be curtly interrupted by Mitsides.

'Thank you, Mr Collier. But I will ask the questions.'

Preece was clearly even more puzzled now. 'What's this all about?' he asked.

The Chief Inspector ignored his question and pressed on. 'At what time yesterday did Morrison return to the site?'

'I'm not sure,' said Preece. 'But it was lateish when I saw him. Around five, five-thirty.'

'And did he appear to you to be upset in any way?'

'Upset?'

Mitsides elaborated. 'Worried, concerned, agitated. Afraid even.'

'Afraid!' Preece laughed. 'No. He seemed perfectly normal to me.' But then his smile faded and suddenly he was concerned. 'Why? Has something happened to him?'

'There is some doubt as to that,' the Chief Inspector murmured with a sigh. 'But personally I do not think that you need worry.'

'But he's not here, is he?' insisted Collier.

Mitsides snapped him a warning look. Then he turned his attention back to Preece and smiled again. 'It is perhaps his free day,' he suggested.

Preece shook his head. 'No. Matter of fact he's on leave. As of now.'

Mitsides looked vaguely troubled by this news. 'For how long?' he asked.

'Two weeks.'

'Leave which was arranged some time ago?' ventured the Chief Inspector tentatively.

'Of course.' Preece sounded pained. 'We can't have people just taking off at a moment's notice. The company wouldn't like that one little bit.'

Mitsides smiled again. 'I see. And when you last saw him you say that you noticed nothing strange about him.'

'No. He was the same as always.'

'He did not, for instance, give you the impression of being a man who thought he was in danger? Or of someone who had recently survived an attempt on his life?' Mitsides probed casually.

Preece exploded into laughter. 'Are you joking!' he burst out. But then when he saw from the detective's expression that the question had been put to him in earnest he checked himself and shook his head.

'He was out there on the site. Getting on with the job cool as a cucumber.'

'He was covering up,' Collier interjected vehemently.

'Be quiet, Mr Collier,' ordered Mitsides, and there was no mistaking the finality of the warning. The detective paused to make sure that it had been heeded and then when he was satisfied that it had been, he smiled at Preece again and made a gesture as though begging for tolerance.

'If you would just bear with me a little longer. Now yesterday I understand that you had lunch with Mr Collier.'

'Yes,' Preece replied, nonplussed.

'And tell me, during the time you were with him did he receive a telephone call?'

The Resident Engineer seemed embarrassed by the question and shot a look at Collier before replying. 'Yes,' he said cautiously.

'And do you know who it was from?'

Preece nodded. 'Well, yes. David told me. It was from Morrison.'

'Arranging a meeting.'

'So I understand.'

'And later when you saw Morrison, did you mention this telephone call to him?'

Preece was visibly discomforted by Mitsides' gaze and his persistence with this line of questioning.

'Look here, Chief Inspector,' he exclaimed with a mild note of protest in his voice. 'I really don't see . . .'

Mitsides was not interested in Preece's views, only in his answers. 'Did you, Mr Preece?' he demanded.

'Well yes, as a matter of fact I did,' admitted Preece grudgingly.

'And what did he say?'

Preece's discomfiture was mounting with every second. 'Look, I only brought it up in passing.' He looked at Collier. 'I just wanted to make sure you'd found your way to the place okay,' he explained.

Mitsides repeated his question. 'So what did he say?'

'He said . . .' Preece broke off and turned to Collier, embarrassed and confused. 'I'm sorry, David. What the hell's this all about?'

Collier had no chance to reply.

'Please answer my question, Mr Preece.' Mitsides' tone was polite but there was a cutting edge to his voice now.

Preece hesitated. Then, after giving Collier a helpless, trapped look, he shrugged.

'Well he was surprised,' he said quietly and lowering his eyes. 'According to him he didn't make any telephone call. He said he'd never spoken to David. Let alone met him.'

Mitsides let out a long, deep sigh of resignation. Then, his eyes fixed on Preece, he nodded. 'Thank you,' he said quietly. 'And please forgive me for troubling you.'

Collier caught up with him as he was getting into the police car.

'But don't you see?' he pleaded, 'Morrison was lying to Preece. Question him yourself.'

Mitsides rounded on him, the effort to control his temper crushing his lips to a thin line.

'Mr Collier,' he said, and the note in his voice was chilling. 'I am being charitable in not charging you with laying false information with the police. But my charity ends here. Understand that. I suggest that you wind up your brother's affairs as quickly as possible and then leave

Cyprus. I would also suggest that you consult a doctor. But I warn you. One more incident like this and . . .' He broke off as if not trusting himself to say more, got into the police car and gestured impatiently to the driver.

CHAPTER FIFTEEN

David Collier was still smarting angrily from Mitsides' reprimand as he opened the front door of his brother's house in Paphos. For a moment he did not see the man standing in the middle of the room with his back to him. Then he pulled up sharply.

'Morrison!' he exclaimed. 'What are you doing here?'

Morrison whirled round and looked at him venomously. 'Just taking a look see. Fair enough?'

'How did you get in?' demanded Collier angrily.

Morrison pulled a key from his pocket and waved it at him. 'Barry and me were mates. Remember?'

'And just what were you looking for?' asked Collier, as he moved further into the room leaving the door open behind him.

'Lost property. And I found it,' retorted Morrison. Then he stepped aside a little so that Collier could see the briefcase lying open on the table. 'Look familiar does it?'

Collier reacted with a look of consternation. It was the briefcase which Helene had given to him in the deserted village. And the money was still in it.

Morrison picked up one of the bundles of notes and waved it contemptuously at Collier.

'You lying bastard. Had it all the time, didn't you? Barry would've played straight with me. But not you. Oh no. You wanted it all, eh?'

'I don't know what you're talking about,' protested Collier.

'Then how come I find this in the wardrobe?'

Collier shook his head. 'I don't know. I don't understand. Look, this is crazy. I promise you that briefcase wasn't in this apartment when I left to meet you yesterday.'

It was plain enough that Morrison did not believe him. 'No? All right then. So maybe you lost a tooth, eh? And the fairies were feeling generous. Lucky you.'

Collier's frustration and anger bubbled over. 'Oh, for God's sake, don't be so bloody stupid.' He stepped in closer to the table and Morrison moved in quickly between him and the briefcase.

'Now don't come it with me, friend. All surprise and innocence. Caught you with your knickers off, didn't I? You know what you're about. You were lying. Right down the line. It was all lies, your story, wasn't it? Well most of it anyway. And I nearly swallowed it too. But it smelt wrong. Fishy. Know what I mean? I thought I'd just take a look around for myself. Just as well for yours truly, eh?'

'I tell you that briefcase wasn't here yesterday,' repeated Collier.

'Well it's not going to be here tonight and that's for sure.' Morrison sounded pleased with himself but Collier chose to mistake his meaning.

'No. We must hand it over to the police.'

'Police!' Morrison snorted. 'Well, you are a trier. I'll give you that.'

Collier realised that the other man genuinely believed that he had been doublecrossed.

'Look, do you really believe I've been lying? That I had the money all the time? That I'm mixed up in all this? Whatever it is that's going on?'

'What do you think?' snarled Morrison.

Collier's anger grew. 'Then you're dead stupid. Because if that were true then why did I go to the police and tell them about the briefcase in the first place?'

'To throw them off the scent,' replied Morrison. 'Could be you thought they were on to something. So you came up with a story that has them running round in ever decreasing circles. And one that makes you look like you're wide eyed and virginal. All outrage and screaming "Someone put his hand up my skirt".'

Collier tried once more to be reasonable. 'Then if that's what I had in mind all I had to do was to stick to my story and I was home and dry. I certainly didn't need to play charades with you. So who the hell took those pot shots at us then?'

'Maybe you know the answer to that better than I do,' countered Morrison. 'Maybe some of your story was true. The bit about the beautiful bird perhaps. Barry had more than his fair share of them. Could just be that he told his current one what was going on and got her to stash the money somewhere for him. He ends up dead, she's scared and comes running to you. And you get alongside her.' He sniggered insultingly. 'And on top of her for all I know. Yes, I'd buy that.'

'So it was her shooting at us. Is that what you're saying?' demanded Collier.

Morrison latched on to the suggestion. 'Her. Or her barman friend. Just another grain of truth perhaps.'

'All right then. So answer this one. Why?'

'Because you knew all along that half of this money's down to me. And three into fifty works out better than three into twenty-five.'

Morrison put the bundle of notes he was holding back in the briefcase and closed it. Keeping his eyes fixed warily on Collier, he fumbled with the catches but succeeded in clicking only one of them home.

'Well you made a big mistake, friend. If you'd treated me right you could've had what was due to Barry. No hassle. I wouldn't have argued about that. But you're greedy. You've got naturally sticky fingers. You tried to cheat me. So now I take the lot and you're out in the cold with nothing. Have fun.'

He snatched up the briefcase in his left hand and headed for the still open door. Collier intercepted him and grabbed at his sleeve.

'Nobody's got anything. I'm taking that briefcase to Chief Inspector Mitsides and you're coming with me.'

'Piss off.' Morrison jerked his arm free and pushed Collier violently in the chest, sending him staggering back.

For Collier this was the last straw. So far he had managed, by and large, to keep his temper in check. But this was too much and now he lost control.

With a roar of animal rage he launched himself after the retreating Morrison in a rugby tackle and they both crashed to the ground. The briefcase flew from Morrison's hand, bounced against the wall – springing the one closed catch and spilling half a dozen bundles of notes across the floor.

Punching and kicking, the two men threshed about on the floor in unscientific and ineffectual fury for half a minute before Morrison, using his superior strength, managed to struggle to his feet and make a grab for the briefcase, ignoring the bundles of francs which had already bled from it in his eagerness to get clear. But then, when he made for the door again he found his way blocked by Collier. Lowering his head and bellowing, he charged. There was no way Collier could avoid the onrush of his opponent and the impact of it drove the wind out of him, but he managed to cling onto Morrison and again force the briefcase from his hand before they crashed through the doorway together and then rolled down the steps and into the street.

The object of their battle was now quite forgotten as the two men fought for supremacy with primitive concentration to the delight of the crowd which quickly gathered as neighbours appeared from their houses, attracted by the noise. Some began chanting encouragement to the contestants while others, no less noisy, shouted for them to stop.

Collier was gradually getting the worst of the exchange and he tried to gain a respite by grappling Morrison to him as the two men stood swaying face to face. He was ready for the obvious knee in the groin and blocked it with his thigh but the savage, woodpecker blow from Morrison's forehead across the bridge of his nose was something he did not anticipate and it sent him reeling back, tears streaming blindingly from his eyes and blood pouring from his nose. He could not now even see his opponent except as a dim blur. He could see very little, in fact, so he was unaware of the sudden appearance of the two policemen running down the street towards them. But Morrison, at the foot of the steps and on his way back up into the house, saw them and knew that explanations would be demanded by them. And there was one thing he knew that he could never explain to their satisfaction. 'Shit!' he cursed and then made a run for it, dodging through the crowd and out of sight around the corner of the road.

As the pain receded a little and his vision cleared, Collier focussed on the two constables now standing in front of him. One of them spoke to him in Greek and Collier shook his head.

'English. I don't understand you.'

The policeman's English was reasonable but not fluent.

'This is bad. Fighting is not allowed. Why did this happen?'

Collier brushed this aside. 'Later. Later.' He beckoned the policeman to follow him back into the house. 'Come with me. There's something I want to show you.'

The man hesitated, then gesturing to his colleague to disperse the crowd, followed Collier as he climbed the steps a little unsteadily.

'And when you've seen this I want you to telephone Chief Inspector Mitsides in Limassol. Understand?'

Despite his bruises Collier was exultant. Now he had some evidence. He led the constable into the living room and then consternation swept over him once more. The case was gone. And so was the money. All of it. Collier gazed about him in bewilderment. It was impossible.

The policeman looked at him suspiciously. 'Well what is it that you have to show me?'

Without answering Collier darted into the other rooms but not really expecting to find anything. His glance out of the back door was no more than perfunctory. He was beaten and he knew it. Slowly and dejectedly he returned to the living room.

The policeman tried again. 'What is it? Where is it?'

Collier sighed. He dare not approach Mitsides again. Without evidence he'd either have him locked up or certified. 'It doesn't matter. Forget it.'

The policeman produced his notebook. 'You are English?'

Collier nodded.

'Your passport.'

Resignedly Collier crossed to the desk, took out his passport and handed it over. The policeman examined it and then wrote Collier's name and other details from it into his notebook.

'You live here?' he asked.

'It's my brother's apartment,' replied Collier. 'He's dead. An accident. A few days ago.'

The policeman returned the passport. 'You said I should telephone Chief Inspector Mitsides in Limassol.'

'Yes. But it doesn't matter now,' said Collier.

The policeman was obviously not quite sure whether it mattered or not. 'You know the Chief Inspector?'

'Yes. I know him.'

The questioner proceeded warily. 'You are friends?'

'No,' said Collier wryly. 'Not even cards at Christmas. But we've met. Once or twice.'

The policeman, satisfied that he was not stepping on highly placed toes, became more formal.

'Why were you fighting?'

Collier had no intention of telling him the real reason.

'It was a personal matter. A disagreement. An argument. We lost our tempers.'

This was carefully noted down. 'And the other man. What is his name?'

'Morrison. Eric Morrison.'

'And where does he live?'

'I don't know,' replied Collier casually, then catching the policeman's disbelieving look added, 'I really don't.'

And he didn't care either. Other questions were uppermost in his mind at that moment, questions such as who had put the briefcase in the wardrobe? And why? And who the hell had it now?

CHAPTER SIXTEEN

If the man in the car had not been a sadist as well as a killer Morrison would never have made it. A good sprint, though, can beat most cars from a standing start for up to about eighty yards and Morrison had been granted a fifty yard handicap as well.

On the other hand, he didn't realise at first that he was in a race – for his life.

He had stopped at a public tap half way down a long, narrow side street to wash the blood off his face and then, refreshed by the clear, cool water, had breathed out in satisfaction and, wiping his face with his handkerchief, straightened up.

The midnight blue Mercedes, rolling silently down the slight incline advanced on him with all the deadly intent of a mamba, and Morrison was suddenly very afraid. He turned and ran.

The car filled the narrow street within six inches of either wall and as soon as Morrison had looked around and had seen it the driver, hidden behind the heavily tinted windscreen, fired the ignition and engaged gear.

The narrowness of the street prevented the driver accelerating flat out but the Mercedes gathered speed far more slowly than was necessary if it were in the hands of a competent driver. It was as if the person behind the wheel knew that however hard the now panic stricken Morrison ran he would be caught long before he reached the safety of the square at the far end.

With only an occasional glance back over his shoulder, Morrison hurtled down the street and he was in no doubt that he was running for his life.

Inexorably the Mercedes closed the gap between them as it gathered momentum. In vain Morrison looked for an open door, a back yard or some other sanctuary but there seemed to be nothing which offered any kind of safety. He had no choice but to keep running while the black cat at his heels played with him cruelly.

When the Mercedes, picking up more speed now, was no more than five yards off from him, Morrison saw, on the opposite side of the street, a garbage strewn runnel no more than a donkey width wide which had previously been hidden from him. In a gamble which he had no option but to take, he darted across the path of the speeding car and just made it, the bonnet of the Mercedes missing him by not more than six inches and he felt the wind of death on his heels as the limousine swept past the opening of the alleyway.

When Morrison found that his escape route led only to a stout wooden gate which was locked and impossible to scale, he spat out an obscenity. He was trapped. But then he realised that even if the Mercedes had been braked hard it still couldn't have stopped less than twenty yards down from the opening into which he had dodged. The narrowness of the street would prevent the driver from getting out and the car could not reverse after him nearly as fast as he could run.

He swung round and doubled back, and as he emerged cautiously from the alleyway he saw the Mercedes turn into the square and vanish from sight.

Morrison ran back up the slope the way he had come, the sweat running from his body more the product of terror than of exertion and the smell of his own fear made him all the more frightened.

At the top of the incline the fear multiplied a hundred fold and nearly stopped his heart for good. For there, parked predatorily on the opposite side of the major road into which he re-emerged, and only sixty yards away, was the Mercedes.

The traffic here was still sparse and might well leave the road empty for minutes at a time. And then he would once again present a perfect target. To redouble back down the street again would only invite the driver of the car to come after him in pursuit once more. He had to find another way to put distance between him and his would-be killer.

And then he saw it.

Just down the road, on the same side on which he stood,

was an excited group of Cypriots. He had passed them earlier in his retreat from Collier's house deep in animated conversation and gesturing wildly. Now they were boarding an ancient, single decker bus shaped more like a Victorian bath tub than a motor vehicle.

The roof rack of the bus was stacked with bales and packages of all shapes and sizes and crowned by two crates containing loudly protesting chickens. The women and children, all dressed in their Sunday best as were the whole group, had already scrambled aboard and now their menfolk were following them.

Panting, Morrison was the last in. The driver levered the door shut and noisily engaged gear.

As the bus chugged and spluttered its way up the road the Mercedes slid smoothly away from the kerb and followed.

There was a carnival spirit aboard the bus and a lot of chatter and exchange of news and views but Morrison couldn't understand a word of what was being said. That everyone knew everyone else was clear enough though but, despite this, none of the passengers as much as queried with a glance the presence of the stranger among them. Indeed the passengers did all that they could to make him welcome. The bus was crowded with a score of men and boys packed into the centre aisle but after a great deal of shouting, gesticulating and squeezing up a seat was found for the Englishman in the back row just below the rear window.

Morrison accepted the arrangement gratefully as he did the wine, raisins and oranges which were thrust on him and knowing anyway that to refuse would cause deep hurt among his fellow travellers, for in Cyprus hospitality is not an obligation but an instinct. To a Cypriot to have and not to offer to others would be as impossible as to be born with lungs and not to breathe.

And for the people of Cyprus to be unkind to children would be as unnatural as to have a heart and not feel it beat. Therefore, Morrison did not protest when the woman sitting alongside him beamed at him and then sat her wide-eyed son of four or five on his lap.

Morrison, who loathed children, smiled weakly at the boy

and patted him on the head. He had reason enough to be grateful for this overloaded refuge and he could afford to be generous with his affection, however feigned. But then he looked back through the rear window and once more felt terror gripping at his throat.

The midnight blue Mercedes was cruising easily along not more than thirty yards behind the bus, the afternoon sun glinting on its tinted windscreen.

A few miles outside Paphos the bus turned off the main road and started to climb laboriously into the foothills of the central mountain range. It twisted and turned, gaining altitude with each bend. And the Mercedes, keeping a safe distance back from it, clung to it as though magnetised.

At last the motorised bath tub, clanking and steaming, came to an indecisive halt in the square of a small village whose shabby bilingual nameplate had proclaimed it to be Omodhos.

The square was empty and silent and there were neither vehicles nor people in sight. Shops and *tavernas* were shuttered. It was as if the entire village had business elsewhere – as indeed it had.

Into this vacuum there poured, in a sudden gush which emptied the bus in less than two minutes, the stream of cheerful humanity which had been Morrison's protective accompaniment for the past two hours.

Even the driver, a carefully wrapped parcel in his left hand and a half full bottle of wine in his right, scrambled out to join the passengers and moments later the driver and passengers alike had vanished up a side street and Morrison was left sitting alone in the old bus as it settled down, the engine creaking as it cooled.

But not quite alone.

Lurking in the shadows of the opposite corner of the square was the sleek shape of a large, dark blue saloon, the three armed star on the bonnet winking in the sunlight like a malevolent eye.

Vainly Morrison hurried to the door of the bus and gazed out in the direction taken by the noisy throng with whom he had shared the ride.

There was no sign of them. The square was again empty of people. And to follow the group would mean that Morrison would have to pass within a few feet of the waiting Mercedes.

He withdrew nervously to the back of the bus once more and peered through the window. As he watched, greatly to his relief, the limousine began to move slowly further into the square and the movement triggered Morrison out of his paralysis of fright. If he stayed where he was he would be shot down without a chance. If he ran for it he might just have a slender one.

The car's movement round one side of the square meant that the path to the street down which the others had gone was now unguarded. He ran down the aisle, jumped down from the step and began a zigzag run across the centre of the square, not daring to look back at the Mercedes which had now stopped. He heard a car door open and slam and then a second later, as he rounded the corner of the street for which he had headed, chips of plaster flew off a wall not more than three feet away from his head as a bullet slammed into the brickwork.

There was no report, only the ominous thunk of a silencer and, as far as he could tell, no second shot either. But then, as he ran down the street, he heard a car door slam again and this was followed immediately by the fierce revving of an engine and then the squeal of tyres.

This time, however, the streets were criss-crossed with alleys and lanes at every angle and Morrison was confident, after dodging down three or four of these, that he had lost his pursuer. For the time being at least.

He turned one more corner for luck – and got it, to the accompaniment of *lutas*, fiddles and accordion.

Heading towards him was a procession led by the musicians with a priest in ornate robes only a few paces behind them. And trailing behind the priest was what appeared to be the entire population of the village plus his erstwhile travelling companions and several excited, yapping dogs.

Morrison waited for the column to draw abreast of him

and then, when it was almost past, plunged into the tail of the throng.

The procession halted outside one of the houses in the street to sort itself out and then to give pride of place to the traditionally escorted bride and groom before setting off in full flood once more; the musicians striking up a lively tune and setting the pace.

Eric Morrison was going to a wedding; not, after all, to a funeral.

CHAPTER SEVENTEEN

The Honda motorcycle on which Morrison roared up to the vineyard did not belong to him. No doubt even at that moment some wedding guest, eager to make an impression at the feast, was vainly searching for his two hundred and fifty cubic centimetres of noisy pride and joy, but Morrison had put a good sixty kilometres between himself and the scene of the festivities.

Now he swung the bike back onto its stand and eagerly scanned the rows of women who were picking grapes with a ruthless, mechanical monotony in the last warmth of the sun.

Amongst them one woman stood out spectacularly. Not for beauty, though in a blowsy way she was not lacking that, but for her sheer voluptuous sensuality. Thrusting breasts, broad hips, full lipped mouth and lazy eyes all promised more than a passing acquaintance with the pleasures of the flesh. The man who enjoyed her was destined for a good time and Morrison had never been one to shirk the more pleasant demands made on him.

He called out to her urgently, 'Maria!'

Maria looked as pleased as she did surprised, and, with an uninhibited shout of 'Eric', she dropped the grapes she was holding and ran through the vines towards him. He was almost bowled over as she flung her arms about him and planted an open-mouthed, tongue-searching kiss on his lips.

The women working the rows nearby cheered and whistled and made ribald comments but Morrison must have disappointed them. Embarrassed and pre-occupied, he swiftly disentangled himself. Scornfully Maria made a crude gesture at her fellow workers and then, smiling, looked at Morrison.

'What are you doing here?' She did not even wait for an answer to her first question as she noticed the bruises on his face and became, in an instant, all solicitude. 'What happened to you?'

Morrison drew her aside. 'I need your help,' he said urgently. 'I'm in a bit of bother.'

Alarmed, Maria jumped at once to what, for her, was the obvious conclusion. 'The police!' she exclaimed.

'No, nothing like that,' Morrison reassured her hastily. 'Look, I'll explain later. But it's not the law, right? Only I have to keep out of sight for a while.'

Maria had the solution to his problem in an instant. She smiled seductively at him. 'Stay with me,' she tempted. 'I would like that. And so would you, I promise. Much better than just every now and then.'

'No, not your place,' Morrison snapped dismissively. 'Somewhere else. Somewhere more private. Like in a village. And with someone who won't ask any questions.'

Maria responded with a spate of questions, giving him no time to reply to any of them. 'What's wrong? What is this trouble you are in? Someone is after you? You have been fighting, haven't you? What is it, Eric?'

He tried to calm her. 'It's nothing for you to worry about. Nothing I can't handle. Believe me. I just need to be somewhere out of Paphos for a week or so. You know anywhere?'

Maria thought for a moment and then nodded. 'My cousin, Antonis. He has a garage. He lives alone. We could go there.'

'We?' questioned Morrison, slightly taken aback.

Maria smiled and, her eyes on his, slowly ran the tip of her tongue around her lips. She moved in close to him and Morrison could feel her nipples erect and hard against his chest.

'You will not need someone to keep you warm at night?' she murmured. Then, suddenly, she frowned, stepped back from him again and demanded, challengingly, 'Or perhaps you think you will find someone else, eh?'

Realising that he had made a mistake and knowing how much he needed her, Morrison gave her a pained look, took her into his arms and drew her close to him once more.

'Now don't be bloody silly,' he wheedled. 'You and me. That's how it is. That's how it'll always be.' He kissed her passionately but briefly to emphasise the point. 'The two of us. Right? You know that.'

Mollified, Maria smiled again and Morrison gave her a wink. 'This cousin of yours,' he went on. 'Where does he live?'

'I will take you there,' said Maria. 'As soon as I have finished work.'

She winced slightly as his grip on her tightened.

'No. Now, Maria,' he urged. 'It has to be now.'

Maria hesitated, studying him closely. Then she shrugged.

'Okay,' she said. 'If that is what you want.'

Morrison led her over to the Honda and, flouncing out her skirt, she settled herself astride the pillion.

'I like motorcycles,' she murmured, her head against his back and wriggling on the seat. 'They excite me so.'

What doesn't, thought Morrison as he kicked the starter. 'Well, don't get too attached to this one,' he shouted above the harsh roar of the engine. 'I stole it.'

The garage was certainly isolated enough in that it stood back from the main road some quarter of a mile outside a village high in the foothills of the Troodos. There was a forecourt with three pumps, a workshop, a lubrication bay and a vehicle yard filled mainly with tractors and trucks. It was evident that nearly all its trade came from local farmers rather than passing traffic and Morrison had wondered how Maria's cousin managed to make a living.

He gazed out of a window overlooking the forecourt while Maria fussed around the room, tidying it and flicking at the dust on the furniture with a grimy, oil-stained shirt which had been lying across one of the two chairs. A gangling, sloe eyed youth was sitting on top of a tilted oil drum, picking his nose and reading a comic. The man who Maria had introduced on their arrival as her cousin, Antonis, came out of the workshop and idly kicked the drum out from underneath the youth who crashed uncomplainingly to the ground. Antonis laughed but sounded bored rather than spiteful.

At that moment Maria crept up behind Morrison and slipped her arms around his waist. He turned to her.

'The room. It is all right?' she asked.

'It'll do,' said Morrison grudgingly.

She kissed him and again her tongue plunged deep into his mouth. 'You will see. You will be okay here. Comfortable. I will see to that,' she said as she at last drew back from the kiss. Taking his hand, she guided him over to the bed and tested the springs with her fingers. She smiled archly. 'It is a good bed, eh?'

Morrison pulled back the corner of the brightly coloured bedspread and grimaced at the rough blankets beneath.

'If Antonis has no linen I will bring some from my house,' Maria assured him, seeing the look on his face.

'You're going back home?' exclaimed Morrison, clearly very disturbed by the idea.

Maria nodded. 'I have to. There are things I will need.' She smiled coyly. 'Things to make me pretty for you. Things you like. And if we are to be here for some time then you will need fresh clothes. Give me your key and I'll bring them up for you.'

Morrison reacted sharply to the suggestion. He grabbed her by the arm again. 'No! Stay away from my place. Understand?'

Alarmed by his suddenly raised voice, Maria frowned. Then she sighed resignedly. 'Yes, all right.' She shook herself free from his grasp. 'If you say so.'

'And if anyone asks you any questions about me. Anyone. You know nothing. Right?'

'Of course,' Maria pouted. 'I am not stupid.'

Morrison relaxed a little and gave her a smile. 'No, you're very clever. And beautiful with it.' He added a kiss for good measure which Maria took as an invitation.

Smiling, she wound her arms round him and pulled him down onto the bed but Morrison shook his head and disentangled himself from her embrace.

'Later. Later,' he protested and then, to console her in

her obvious and petulant disappointment, he quickly added, 'These blankets look pretty rough to me. You'd feel you were being screwed on the back of a goat.'

Maria giggled and sat up.

Taking out his wallet, Morrison gave her twenty pounds.

'Buy me a couple of shirts, a razor, some shaving cream. Stuff like that.' Then, conscious that he had been ordering her about a little unromantically, he gave her bottom an encouraging pat and added. 'Hurry back, eh?'

And, despite all that he'd been through and the fear which still nagged at him, suddenly the thought of her naked in his arms, her back arched against his thrusting eagerness, her fingernails scoring his back and crying out as she was engulfed by the first spasms of a climax, was very attractive.

She looked down at the swelling bulge in his slacks and smiled triumphantly. 'That's the way I like to see you,' she whispered. 'Hungry.'

She slipped off the bed and crossed the room. Then, as if to further tantalise him with thoughts of the delights to come she paused in the doorway and flipped up her skirt and he caught a glimpse of thigh and of brief, moist-crotched panties.

Antonis must have sensed her excitement as she came out through the side door and crossed to him. He grinned. 'Your man. He is happy with the room?' he asked.

Maria looked at her cousin – sharp eyed, good looking, roguish, no more than thirty – and decided that though she fancied him she didn't like him. Nor did she trust him. It would be better to put him in his place from the outset, she thought. She shrugged. 'He says it will do.'

'Oh, his Lordship is used to better, eh?' countered Antonis, pulling a face.

'It is not very clean,' said Maria primly.

'Those in need cannot complain,' smirked Antonis. 'It is going to cost him, you know. Being here.'

Maria had had his measure years ago and did not bother to hide her contempt. 'Of course, my dear cousin. Since when did you do anything for nothing?'

Antonis leered, quite uncrushed. 'And a double room too.'

'He will pay. I have to go back to my house to collect some things and then into Limassol. I will need to be driven.' She was as haughty now as any aristocrat and Antonis reacted like the tradesman he was.

'That is a long way. And petrol is expensive.'

'Put it on the bill.' Maria might have been buying caviar at Fortnums.

Antonis gave her a mock salutation of respect. He'd do just that. And then some. 'Dimitrios!' he shouted. 'Get the pick-up. Take my lady cousin where she wants to go.'

Maria pointed at the Honda motorcycle standing just inside the workshop. 'Can you get rid of that?'

Antonis laughed. 'Of course. Don't worry.' He winked. 'It's as good as sold.'

CHAPTER EIGHTEEN

Travis and Olsen had come close to grabbing David Collier that morning. They had parked their car and were approaching the house in Paphos when their quarry had exploded through the front door grappling with a man who was a stranger to them. And, as the fight had developed in the street, they had stood in the background of the small crowd which had gathered around the combatants.

And when, somewhat to their surprise, Eric Morrison, having floored Collier, had run off instead of enjoying his moment of triumph, it seemed a good moment to step in as solicitous friends of the loser and whisk him away. But, even as they had edged their way through the spectators, they had also seen the two policemen bearing down fast on the scene and they had withdrawn discreetly and returned to the yacht to report the incident.

Eugene Hellman was interested in what they had to tell him but he clearly attached no great significance to it. He double checked. 'A brawl you say?'

'One hell of a fight,' Olsen confirmed.

'And you've no idea who his opponent was?'

'No. But from the way he was swearing I'd say he was another Limey.'

Hellman's face took on a pained expression. 'So vulgar! And in public too.' He sighed disdainfully and then shouted, 'Pull!'

Hellman was standing at the rail of the yacht, trap shooting. From further along the deck a clay sailed out high over the water. Expertly Hellman snapped the Winchester pump action shotgun to his shoulder and fired. The clay shattered.

The marksman watched the fragments fall into the sea. 'David Collier is very important to me,' he had informed them. 'Pull!'

Another clay, another shot, another hit.

'He is the key,' Hellman continued. 'His brother either cut him in on the deal before he came out here. Or somehow or other he picked up the threads on arrival. Pull!' This time the barrel of the Winchester swung down with the clay as it fell and the target was less than six feet above the gentle swell when Hellman fired and the clay disintegrated.

'Anyway now he's in the driving seat,' he continued. 'And I need him.'

'And he needs you,' Travis assured him.

'Not necessarily. He could shop around.'

'He'd be better off dealing with you.'

Hellman nodded and worked the pump of the shotgun. 'Undoubtedly. But he must be convinced of the fact. That's why I need to talk to him. Pull!'

Travis waited for the shot and watched the soaring clay fragment before replying. 'We'll call on him again tonight.'

Then, for the first time, Hellman turned from the rail to glance at them. 'Stress the mutual advantage of our getting together.' He smiled thinly and enquired sarcastically, 'Think you can handle that?'

Resentfully and smarting from the jibe, Travis held his employer's mocking gaze for a few seconds and then, angrily, he strode over to the rail, unbuttoning his jacket as he did so. 'Pull!' he shouted.

Another clay leapt from the trap and arced in the clear, blue sky.

Almost lazily, Travis reached in under his jacket, smoothly and swiftly drawing his Walther automatic from its holster and, holding the pistol in a rock-like, double handed, straight-aim grip, fired.

Falling, the clay exploded spectacularly under the impact of the bullet.

Re-holstering the Walther, Travis turned from the rail smiling smugly. At that range, with that gun and with such a target it had not been simply a good shot, it had been a brilliant one. And he knew it.

'Impressive,' Hellman acknowledged with a thin smile and a nod. But then suddenly he was no longer smiling. 'But you know how I abhor violence,' he hissed quietly.

'Except in self defence. And when there is no other alternative. David Collier is useless to me dead.' Then, with a warning look at both men, he added, 'Remember that.'

And Travis and Olsen both had his warning echoing in their minds as that night they crossed the waste ground behind the house in Paphos and crept up the steps to the back door.

It took Olsen fifteen seconds to pick the lock, an improvement of two seconds on their first visit, when they had searched the place. The two men stepped quickly into the kitchen and Travis closed the door behind them.

There was a faint click and the beam of a high powered torch held them dazzled and transfixed. The voice of the man who greeted them from the darkness behind the torch was unmistakably English, and the barrel of the rifle which had them covered was unwavering.

'Good evening.'

Travis went for his gun but then froze as the rifle barrel flicked in an instant on to his chest and the man spoke again.

'That would be a mistake, Mr Travis.'

Travis saw the truth in this and slowly raised his hands. Unbidden, Olsen followed suit.

'Really,' the man behind the gun continued, and now with a gentle note of reproval in his voice, 'you should know better. Breaking and entering is illegal. Your weapons please.' The two men hesitated. 'Your weapons,' demanded the man shrouded in the darkness, and the slight movement of the barrel of the rifle added weight to his command.

As, together, Travis and Olsen reached for their guns the man tutted gently. 'No. With the other hand,' he instructed. 'And carefully.'

Travis and Olsen did as they were told.

'On the floor. Gently. And now kick them over here.'

The brace of automatics slid over the linoleum and into the darkness.

'Excellent. Well I think that's all. Except to say that you are not welcome here. Now or at any time in the future. Goodnight.'

Disarmed and looking down the barrel of that rifle,

Travis, like his companion, knew he was beaten. But if force was no longer open to them, reasoned argument might still succeed.

'We have a message for you,' he said with a smile and blinking into the glare of the torch. 'From Mr Hellman.' He spread his hands in a bewildered gesture and put on an innocent, hurt expression. 'That's why we're here. He wants to talk to you about . . .'

He got no further. 'Goodnight,' said the man, interrupting and insistent.

The two Americans hesitated but then as the rifle barrel swung up a little higher, indicating beyond all doubt that any further argument was useless, Olsen reached behind him and opened the door. Then, with their eyes still fixed on the gun, he and Travis stepped quickly back into the night and the torch was extinguished.

For a few moments there was no movement in the kitchen, but then a figure moved across the faint shaft of light coming through the window and closed the back door again.

In the distance, from across the waste land at the rear of the building a car started up and was driven away at speed.

Charalambos, standing by the window, struck a match and lit a cigar. Slinging his rifle onto his shoulder, Basileos stepped in beside him and for a moment his face was illuminated in the flame of the match.

'I think I did that rather well,' he said, reverting to his own voice.

Charalambos considered him critically. 'I could have done it better,' he said confidently and then blew out the match.

At that moment, in the bedroom, David Collier, waking from a nightmare which was instantly forgotten, sat up in bed and gazed in sleepy shock and bewilderment across the room.

Sitting in the armchair, toying with a handkerchief, smiling gently and studying him closely, was Helene.

CHAPTER NINETEEN

'You were dreaming,' Helene said quietly.

Collier stared at her in disbelief. 'And I'm not now?'

She stood up, crossed to the bed and sat on the edge of it; close to him. 'No. Not now.'

Collier found himself more than a little discomforted by the nearness of her. 'I'm glad,' he said, gazing into her eyes. 'I was beginning to believe that you never existed.'

Helene smiled again. 'Oh, I exist.' And to prove it she took his hand and laid it against the warm, velvet softness of her cheek. 'See, flesh and blood.' She held his gaze and Collier made no attempt to remove his hand from hers.

It was she who broke the momentary spell. Laying his hand back down on the bed, she stood up. 'We have to talk,' she said.

And with that she turned and crossed to the bedroom door.

Instantly Collier snapped out of what had been another and very different dream. 'Yes, you're right,' he muttered angrily. 'We do. And you have a hell of a lot of explaining to do.' Scowling, he swung his legs over the side of the bed and, grabbing up his dressing gown and struggling into it, followed her into the sitting room.

Helene had switched on the lights and was standing by the fireplace studying a photograph of one of Barry's conquests with a faintly amused expression on her face.

Tolerant too, thought Collier. Or maybe she doesn't reckon that one to have been any kind of competition. And she was right, of course. The strident blonde featured in the photograph had nothing to match the beauty of the woman now holding the picture.

'How did you . . . ?' Collier began but then realised, glanced across at the front door and nodded. 'Of course. You told me. You and Barry had a special relationship. I wonder just how many keys to this place there are floating around Cyprus.'

Helene replaced the photograph on the mantelshelf and turned to him. 'I also told you that your brother's death was not an accident. I showed you the briefcase with the money in it. I gave it to you.'

'And then ran off.'

'Because you said you were going to take it to the police. I wanted you to do that but I could not become involved.'

'Why?'

Helene moved slowly across the room and settled herself on the settee. 'I have my reasons.'

'Because you are also mixed up in whatever it is that Barry got himself into. Is that it?' Collier demanded.

She shook her head. 'No. At least not in the way you mean, anyway. But you didn't take the briefcase to the police, did you?'

'No. Because when I left the village I was jumped on by a bunch of thugs who knocked me out and snatched it.'

Helene frowned. 'Yes. I was afraid that something like that might have happened when Bambos told me that he had seen my car in a ditch on the side of the road to Aghios Georgios.'

'Bambos?' This was a new name to Collier.

'It is short for Charalambos,' explained his visitor. 'The man who served you in the bar of the Curium Palace. He is my friend. He was concerned when I did not return and came looking for me. We used his car to pull mine back onto the road.'

Well that answers that question, thought Collier. We're making progress.

'I see,' he said. 'So that's how come it wasn't there when I went back with the police.'

Helene shrugged. 'I did not know then what had happened. An accident I thought. You were not around to say and I did not wish to leave it there.' She looked at him enquiringly. 'Do you have any idea who these men were who robbed you?'

Collier shook his head. 'None.'

Helene frowned. 'Strange,' she mused. 'How could they have known that I was planning on taking you to the money?'

'Good question. You didn't say anything to anyone?'

'No.'

'So how did Charalambos know where to come looking for you then?' Collier challenged suspiciously.

'Ah yes!' She smiled and nodded. 'Bambos. He knew. But, as I told you, he is my friend.'

'So what was he doing playing at being the barman at the Curium Palace? The real barman's called Nikos and he claimed he'd never heard of your friend Bambos.'

Helene shook her head sadly. 'Poor Nikos. Of course he would have had to say that. You see Nikos is in love.'

Collier regarded her blankly. 'So?'

'So the woman he is in love with is married,' Helene continued with a smile. 'He can only visit her while her husband is at work which happens to be at the same time when Nikos should be behind the bar. So from time to time Bambos covers for him.'

Somewhat grudgingly Collier accepted her explanation. It made sense. Then he frowned again. 'Well, Nikos lying like that really dropped me in it with the police. And then you and Charalambos and that way-out character, Basileos, running from that monastery the way you did finally put the lid on it for me. Now Mitsides thinks I'm out of my mind. Why did you do that?' he asked plaintively. 'Pull out I mean?'

'Bambos took some food up to you and discovered that you'd gone. It was obvious that you intended to contact the police.'

'And the three of you didn't want to be around when they turned up.'

'No. It is the same for all of us. We cannot become involved. Not directly anyway. And not with the authorities.' She sighed with a hint of impatience. 'I have told you that.'

'Yes. But not why. You haven't explained that.'

Collier sat down in the armchair alongside the settee and,

close to her again, was immediately lost in her gaze once more.

'You will just have to trust me,' she said softly. 'Trust the three of us.'

'Why?'

'Because I ask you to. And because you really have no other choice.'

Collier sank further into the warmth of her brilliant pale blue eyes. 'I want to. But it's not easy,' he replied, almost in a whisper. And he meant it.

Helene leaned in towards him and laid her hand on his arm. 'We wish you no harm. Believe that.'

At that magic moment Collier would have believed anything she told him. Her face was only inches from his, her lips, slightly parted, were in reach and her perfume was intoxicating. 'I do,' he murmured. I'm going to kiss her, he promised himself. And she's not going to stop me, I'm sure of that.

But then, even as he slowly moved his face closer to hers, she drew back a little and smiled again. Once more the spell was broken.

'May I have a drink?' she asked.

'Yes, of course,' stammered Collier, cursing himself for having misread the message in her eyes and feeling foolish as well as disappointed.

He stood up and walked quickly over to the sideboard. 'What would you like?'

'A whisky please.'

Collier nodded. At that moment a stiff scotch seemed like a good idea. 'I'll join you,' he said.

As he poured the drinks Helene rose from the settee and moved in on the sideboard. She frowned questioningly. 'Bambos said you didn't drink. Just tomato juice.'

'I only recently acquired the taste. Basileos waxed lyrical about alcohol. Wine in particular. I tried it. He's made a convert. He's another friend of yours, eh?'

Helene nodded. 'Another good friend.'

The two liberal Cutty Sarks in his hands, Collier turned

to her. 'Odd him finding me in the middle of that forest, wouldn't you say? Something of a coincidence.'

'A lucky one,' she agreed. 'For you.'

'And nothing more than a coincidence?' Collier pressed, his eyes again on hers.

Helene made no attempt to avoid his searching look. 'I had told him about you,' she replied patiently. 'That I wanted to find you. That I was worried. He was out hunting.'

'With a rifle,' Collier said grimly.

Helene nodded. 'After moufflon. Wild sheep. It is illegal. But not everyone observes the law.'

'No, I imagine not. Interesting though, isn't it? Just a little earlier and not too far away from where he found me someone else had been loosing off with a rifle. Only they weren't after moufflon. They were after me. And a man named Morrison.'

Helene looked concerned. 'Yes, Basileos told me that you had said someone had tried to kill you. But he didn't mention anything about another man. Who is this Morrison?'

'He worked with my brother. He claims that half the money in the briefcase belongs to him.' He held up the glasses and looked at her enquiringly. 'Ice?'

She smiled. 'Please.'

Collier carried the two whiskies into the kitchen, put them down on the table and opened the door of the refrigerator.

The frost-encrusted ice trays would not budge. He was still struggling with them when Helene followed him into the room and stood regarding him in the doorway.

'Don't bother,' she said. 'Just some water will do.'

Gratefully Collier gave up the struggle and, closing the refrigerator, crossed to the sink and added water to their drinks.

He handed one of the glasses to her. 'Thank you,' she said. Then she sipped the drink and assured him, 'That's fine.' She raised her glass to him in salute. 'Yassus.' She could see from his expression that Collier did not understand the Greek toast. 'Roughly translated, "Your health and happiness",' she elucidated.

'I see.' Collier sipped his drink and then added, wryly, 'Well right now it's my health I'm more concerned about.'

Helene nodded. 'Yes. You must be careful,' she said gravely. 'But why should anyone wish to kill you? That I don't understand at all.'

'Neither do I. But then there's a hell of a lot I don't understand. Your part in all this for instance.'

Helene studied him over the rim of her glass. 'A vested interest.'

'In Barry.' Collier nodded. 'Oh yes, of course,' he sighed irritably. 'That "special relationship" again. Only Morrison thinks it might have been you or one of your two friends who shot at us.'

She searched his face with her eyes. 'And what do you think?'

Gazing at her, Collier was again captivated by her beauty and her proximity. 'You said that I should trust you,' he reminded her quietly.

'Thank you.'

'For what? I'm trying, that's all. Reserving judgment.'

Helene accepted the reservation with a graceful inclination of her head. Then she turned from him and led the way back into the sitting room.

'If only we could find out who stole the money from you and where it is now,' she said.

'Well I can tell you where it was yesterday afternoon. Here in this apartment.'

Helene swung round and gave him a look of total bewilderment.

Collier shrugged. 'Yes, I know. It's crazy. But it's the truth. I walked in and found Morrison standing at that table with the briefcase open in front of him. He'd searched the place and said he'd found it in the wardrobe in the bedroom.'

'But you said . . .'

'I know. I know,' he admitted wearily. 'But there was the briefcase large as life on the table.'

'But this is ridiculous.' Helene frowned. 'First the money is taken from you and then . . . Who? Why?'

'God knows. Morrison claimed my whole story was a pack of lies and that I was trying to cheat him out of his share.'

'And he took the money?'

'No.' Gently Collier touched the right side of his jaw with his fingers. It was still very tender. 'He tried to but we had a slight disagreement about that. The money was here when the punch-up started. Lying all over the floor. But when I came back into the room, just a little while later, it had gone. And Morrison didn't take it. I know that for certain.'

'Then who did?' persisted Helene. 'And who put it in the wardrobe in the first place? It doesn't make any sense.' And then a thought occurred to her. 'Unless . . .' She took another drink from her glass.

'Unless?' prompted Collier.

'Someone is using you.'

Collier let out an exasperated sigh. For a moment he thought she might have come up with something which hadn't already occurred to him.

'Someone has to be. The question is who and why?'

Helene sat down on the settee again. 'You didn't report this to the police?' she asked.

'Hardly. Not with Mitsides already thinking I'm a nut case. If I'd gone to him with one more crazy story he'd have had me certified.'

'And you've absolutely no idea who could be behind all this?'

Collier held her look. 'Apart from you, no,' he replied levelly.

Helene smiled up at him. 'And you don't really believe that, do you?'

'I told you,' he said shortly. 'I'm reserving judgment.' And then he went on, floundering. 'Look, I don't even know how Barry got hold of that kind of money. It's clear enough now, though, that he didn't come by it honestly. There's no way he could've done. But I have no idea what he was mixed up in with Morrison. And according to you, neither have you.'

'No. But you do at least now believe that your brother was murdered.'

Collier nodded. 'Morrison as good as confirmed that.'

'So what do you intend to do about it?'

'What can I do about it?'

'See that whoever killed him gets what is due to them,' Helene countered.

Collier raised his eyes in desperation. 'How? The police won't listen to me.'

'You could make some enquiries on your own,' she insisted.

'Oh, for God's sake!' exploded Collier. 'I'm not a detective. I've already been hit on the head, robbed, shot at, got into a fight and had a senior officer of the local constabulary suggest that I leave the country soonest. I'm out of my depth.' He drained his glass.

'But you can't just walk away from it,' Helene protested. 'Someone killed your brother. At least you have to try to find out who was responsible for his death. You owe Barry that.'

Collier spread his hands in a hopeless, pleading gesture. 'And where would I begin?'

'You ask questions. And you go on asking them until you get the answers. Talk to Morrison. Force the truth about the money out of him. There has to be a lead in that. Bambos. Basileos. Me. We will help you. You won't be entirely on your own.'

Collier was not impressed. 'No? Well, maybe not. So that adds up to four amateurs instead of one. Just what kind of chance do you think we've got?'

'Perhaps more than you think,' she replied quietly and there was something about the way she said it which prompted Collier to shoot a puzzled look at her.

She smiled at him and shrugged. 'Who knows?'

Collier turned the idea over in his mind. 'All right,' he said. 'So I start asking questions. Start looking for Morrison. So we all work together on this. We'll have to compare notes. Cross check what we find out. If anything. I don't even know where you live. Where I can reach you. Any of you.'

'We'll keep in touch,' she assured him.

'Why not out in the open?' demanded Collier. 'Side by side.'

Helene was about to reply but he sighed wearily and raised a hand to silence her.

'I know. There are reasons.'

'That bothers you?'

Collier nodded. 'Somewhat. You're surprised?' He shook his head, dismissing her proposition from his mind. 'No, it's a crazy idea anyway.'

'Then not with us,' she suggested. 'There must be someone here on Cyprus you trust. Someone you could turn to. Someone who'll believe you. Someone who knew Barry, perhaps, and liked him enough to want to see his murderer punished.'

Again Collier shook his head. 'Who is there? I can't think of anyone.'

He glanced at the glass in her hand and saw that, like his, it was now empty. He reached out and took it from her and she did not protest when he crossed to the sideboard and poured another drink for them both.

'Certainly not Martin Preece,' he continued. 'He's as convinced as Mitsides is that I'm about ready for the funny farm. And there isn't anyone else.'

Shaking his head sadly he went into the kitchen and crossed to the sink and added a dash of water from the tap to the two glasses. 'No, look. Face it,' he argued, raising his voice so that it would carry into the next room. 'It would just be a waste of time.'

He strode back into the sitting room. 'And anyway I don't think . . .' He pulled up sharply and broke off in mid sentence.

Helene was no longer sitting on the settee and the front door stood slightly ajar. Then, as he stood there gazing round in amazement, Collier heard a car pulling away from the house.

'Oh no!' he burst out, his astonishment now brimming

into anger. 'Not again. I don't believe it. Helene!' He crossed quickly to the front door and out onto the top step.

The red Alfetta was making a right hand turn at the head of the street and the chuckle of its exhaust and a winking indicator were his visitor's only farewell.

Fuming, Collier stormed back into the sitting room, kicking the front door shut as he did so. 'What the hell?' he cursed savagely. 'The stupid . . .' He checked himself. No, she's not a bitch, he thought, not that one. But his charity ended there and the disqualification did nothing to assuage his anger.

He slammed the two glasses down on the table and, flicking off the lights, strode into the bedroom.

It was as he was taking off his dressing gown that he saw Helene's handkerchief lying on the arm of the chair in which she had been sitting.

It was very feminine, made from the best linen and embroidered and edged with lace.

His expression softened a little as he picked it up and then held it to his nose, savouring the hint of the expensive and exciting perfume which clung to it. With a deep sigh he crossed to the drsssing table, pulled open one of the top drawers and laid the handkerchief in it.

And there was the piece of paper, the page which Eugene Hellman had torn from his memo pad and given to him when they had talked in the Curium Palace Hotel.

Collier picked it up, unfolded it and gazed thoughtfully at the telephone number which the American had written on it in case of need.

CHAPTER TWENTY

'A cave!' Maria exclaimed excitedly.

Morrison, watching her reflection in the mirror of the wardrobe, pulled on his trousers. She was sitting naked on the bed, her knees drawn up to her chin, amidst a jumble of sheets.

He nodded. 'Yes. A damned great hole. Full of antiquities.' He caught the look of incomprehension that came on to her face and grinned. 'Old things,' he explained. 'Statues, pots, wine jars, plates. Thousands of years old. The kind of stuff collectors pay a fortune for.' He zipped his fly and turned to her. 'And that's not all. There's treasure there too.'

Maria's eyes gleamed. Just the thought of treasure was even more stimulating to her than the anticipation and preliminaries of being screwed. And she could feel herself responding to the stimulus and she enjoyed it.

'What kind of treasure?' she demanded.

'You name it,' he said casually.

'Bracelets? Necklaces?'

'And then some.'

Maria gasped. 'How did you find it?' she asked, scrambling to the end of the bed.

'We got lucky. We sort of, well stumbled on it. A while back.'

'And that's how you got the fifty thousand pounds?'

'That's how Barry got it. For just two stones. Sapphires.' Morrison sat down beside her. 'Imagine. Fifty thousand quid. Just for them. And that's nothing. There's more. Much more.'

Maria put her arms around him and hugged him. She smelt of sweat and the dried residue of feverish copulation.

'So, what does it matter then if Barry's brother has stolen the money from you?' she argued. 'If there is all that you say there is in the cave then you are right. Fifty thousand is nothing.'

Morrison scowled. 'Maybe. But it's the principle of the thing. I don't like anyone ripping me off. I'll break his bloody neck if I get the chance.'

'Forget him,' Maria coaxed, slipping her hands beneath his still unbuttoned shirt and caressing his nipples. 'Just think how much you stand to make when you sell the rest of the things. Hundreds of thousands.'

'Closer to a million sterling I'd say.' Morrison tried hard, but not quite successfully, to sound nonchalant. Maria was staggered by the prospect of such a sum.

'A million! Really? A million! Oh, my darling! Such things we can buy. Such things we can do. We could even get married.' She mauled Morrison against her in an even tighter hug.

Marriage was the last thing Morrison had on his mind, then or at any other time, and momentarily his expression betrayed the fact.

'You *do* want to marry me, don't you?' Maria sulked.

Morrison was quick to make amends. He needed her. 'Sure. Of course I do,' he soothed. 'You know I do. Haven't I always said?' Carefully, so as not to offend her further, he removed himself from her embrace, stood up and crossed to the window. 'But before you start sending out the invitations there's a problem. And it's a big one.'

Maria frowned. 'What is it?'

'I've got to find a buyer for the stuff,' Morrison said. 'Someone who knows what it's all about. Someone who deals in that kind of merchandise. And someone who's got that kind of money.'

'But whoever bought the sapphires from Barry. Surely they would . . .'

Morrison interrupted her. 'Yes, they probably would. Only trouble is I don't know who the buyer was.'

'But if you and Barry were in this together you *must* know.'

Morrison rounded on her. 'Only I don't. Right?' he snapped. 'Barry made the contact. He fixed it all up. He comes to me one day and says that he's on to a likely prospect. Someone big. But he wouldn't say who. The next morning he gives me the thumbs up sign and tells me everything's fixed. And that was our last conversation. Twelve hours later he's lying on a slab in the hospital mortuary.'

He shuddered at the thought of how nearly he had found himself stretched out in the same place. 'I didn't know then that he'd already been paid for the stones,' he went on. 'It wasn't until his brother turned up to bury him that I found that out.'

'I see,' said Maria. 'And you've absolutely no idea who Barry dealt with?'

'No. And nothing to go on. No way of following it up.'

Maria shrugged dismissively. 'So we find someone for ourselves,' she declared. 'Another buyer.'

Morrison restrained himself with difficulty. 'It's not quite as simple as that,' he muttered, trying to keep a cutting edge out of his voice and with only partial success. 'We're not trying to unload a secondhand car. Or some unwanted Christmas present. We're talking about a fortune in antiquities that legally belong to the Cyprus Government. So we can't exactly put an advertisement in the papers, can we?' Then he put the brake hard on the sarcasm and switched to practicalities. 'We've got to find someone who buys and sells in that kind of market,' he explained. 'And someone who can come up with cash on the table. And not petty cash either. And we've got to act fast.'

'Why?' queried Maria suspiciously, and with a hint of alarm in her voice. 'Does anyone else know about this cave?'

Morrison wondered just how much he should tell her and decided just enough but not everything. 'All I'm saying is that Barry Collier dying in the way he did was no accident,' he said meaningfully. 'And someone's already had two goes at knocking me off.'

Now Maria was visibly alarmed. 'Who? The brother?'

Morrison shook his head. 'No. He's not fully in the picture. I'm sure of that now. He just found the briefcase and went for broke on that.' His face contorted into an ugly mask. David Collier's obvious betrayal still rankled. 'Greedy bastard!' he spat out as an aside and then, his features relaxing again, he continued. 'Besides he was with me the first time. He came close to getting killed himself.'

'Then who?' asked Maria.

'I think I know,' Morrison said cagily. 'In fact I'm pretty sure. But I couldn't prove it. And anyway I'm not about to go to the police, am I? And it's better for you to know nothing about that. Believe me. Right? But you see how it is. We can't hang about.'

Fear acted as a spur to Maria's thought processes and, coupled with her greed, it brought on a sudden inspiration. 'Antonis!' she exclaimed.

Morrison regarded her scornfully. 'Your cousin!' he scoffed. 'Him that runs this place? Oh come on, you've got to be joking.'

'No. Not to buy,' said Maria. 'But he could perhaps find a buyer. He knows many people. And few of them are honest.'

'Small time stuff,' sneered Morrison.

'Yes. But maybe through his contacts he could lead us to the right door and open it for us,' Maria suggested.

Morrison considered the possibility. It was certainly better than anything he had been able to come up with. 'Do you trust him?' he asked.

'No.' Maria was unequivocal. 'He is a thief, among other things.'

'Well, that's the kind of pedigree we're looking for.' Morrison thought the idea out for a little longer and then nodded. After all, what alternative did he have? 'All right,' he said. 'Have a word with him.'

Maria got up from the bed and began to dress.

'If he is interested say nothing to him about what really happened to your friend Barry,' she warned, fastening her brassiere. 'Or about someone trying to kill you. If you do he will be afraid. All right?' Maria knew her Antonis.

Morrison nodded. 'All right.' Then he frowned and added bitterly. 'Although I don't see why he shouldn't join the club.'

*

Antonis was intrigued. 'There are many artefacts you say?'

'More than you've ever seen in your life. In or out of a museum,' Morrison assured him.

The two men stood facing one another in the junk filled workshop.

'And treasure, Maria tells me.'

'Jewels. Gold. The lot. A fortune.'

'And you wish to find a buyer.'

Morrison gave him a look of disdain. 'No. I'm going to give it away.' But his sarcasm was wasted on the other man.

'Tell me,' said Antonis, 'this cave, where is it?'

The Englishman had been waiting for this. He regarded Antonis coldly. He has to be off his head if he really thinks I'm going to tell him that, he thought. No way. 'Get off,' he growled.

Antonis grinned philosophically. It had been worth trying.

Morrison grew impatient. 'Well, can you handle it?' he demanded.

'Yes, I think so. I will ask around.' Antonis tried to adopt a condescending air of importance but was no match for Morrison.

'Great. So who's keeping you?'

'Oh no.' Antonis was not about to be pushed into doing anything. 'Softly. Softly. I must be careful. And very discreet. Such things are not arranged in a hurry.'

'Perhaps not,' conceded Morrison. 'Normally. But I'm in a hurry.'

Antonis was quick to react, sensing an advantage. 'Oh, why?'

Morrison tried to be casual, to make a joke of it. 'I want the cash. So I can settle up with you for the luxury accommodation. I don't like being in debt.'

The other man was clearly not convinced but he didn't pursue the matter any further. 'I'll do my best,' he said.

'I'm sure you will. You're in for ten percent,' Morrison announced.

Smiling, Antonis quickly corrected him. 'Twenty five.'

Morrison knew he was being taken but he also knew that

in his position he could do nothing about it. He scowled. 'Okay. Twenty five.'

'You have a sample of what is on offer?' The question threw Morrison off balance, but Antonis' next remark showed it to be a reasonable one. 'If I find someone who is interested, without something to show them, they will not even begin to negotiate. No one will buy blind. And first they must be teased. You have something?'

'No,' Morrison said curtly.

'But you could draw from stock, eh?' Antonis persisted.

'Not easily.'

Antonis shrugged. 'Then my hands are tied. Without bait, even if I drive the fish inshore, they will not bite.'

'It would mean travelling. And I'm not too keen on being seen about just now,' admitted Morrison.

'I understand.' Antonis was just a little too sympathetic. 'Then let me collect some trifle for you,' he suggested helpfully. 'I would be only too willing.'

Morrison snorted. 'Yes, I'm sure you would.' But if no one else could be trusted then he had no alternative but to risk being spotted and go himself. 'All right,' he said unenthusiastically. 'I'll get something.'

'Today?' Antonis pressed him.

'If you can provide some transport.'

'A pleasure,' said Antonis, beaming. 'And for nothing.'

'That's big of you,' retorted Morrison remembering the rhyme about the smile on the face of the tiger. But you just try anything friend, he thought. You just try. He nodded. 'Today then.'

'Good. Then I will start making enquiries without delay.' Antonis swelled with self-importance. 'And if I am successful then soon we shall all be rich, eh?'

'Very,' Morrison encouraged him, thinking, only some of us will be richer than others.

And Antonis wondered why the Englishman laughed.

CHAPTER TWENTY-ONE

'I cannot tell you how pleased I am that you decided to accept my invitation after all,' purred Eugene Hellman as he waved Collier into one of the two leather armchairs, separated by a coffee table, which dominated the centre of the stateroom.

'It's good of you to see me,' stammered Collier. 'But I'm afraid this is not exactly a social call.'

Hellman frowned. 'Well no but then I didn't imagine . . .'

'The fact is, Mr Hellman,' continued Collier, interrupting him, 'I need your help. Apparently Barry was mixed up in something illegal. And everything now seems to point to the fact that he was murdered. And a lot's happened to me since we last met. And all of it very odd indeed. I doubt if you'll believe a word of it. But I promise you it's all true. I just don't know what to do about it. Frankly, I'm drowning. And, well, seeing that you were a friend of my brother's, that's why I called you. I'm hoping you'll listen to me, accept my word that it's not some kind of fairy story and that together we might just be able to make some sense of it all. And maybe even come up with a few answers.'

It had been a day of surprises for both of them.

For Hellman the first surprise had been the telephone call from the man for whom he had been searching and who, only the night before, had disarmed and held off Travis and Olsen with a rifle while they were breaking into his house. And the American's second and even greater surprise had been his quarry's urgent request for a meeting.

But even that in no way matched his bewilderment at Collier's blurted and embarrassed outburst now.

For Collier his surprise had come only moments after he had climbed the boarding ladder from the motor launch which had ferried him out to the yacht and he had stepped on to the deck. Travis and Olsen had been waiting for him, standing on either side of their employer and, as he had moved forward to greet Hellman, they had intercepted him and expertly run their hands over his clothing. And when they had found nothing they had looked not only disbelieving but positively disappointed.

'What was that all about?' Collier had enquired, mystified, as Hellman led him to the stateroom.

The American had smiled quietly.

'I imagine they were hoping you had brought their toys back,' he had answered enigmatically.

And Collier had not understood.

Now Hellman was regarding him with a mixture of stunned amazement and curiosity. And he didn't understand that either.

Hellman sat down in the armchair beside him and reached for the coffee pot on the table between them and when he looked up he smiled pleasantly.

'Coffee, David?' he enquired.

Collier nodded and then, as he sipped and savoured the Markus gourmet roast, he told the American everything.

Helene rode the horse at a canter through the low water which ran over the stones and gravel in the centre of the otherwise dried up river bed. Her hair was flying in the wind and the horse's hooves kicked up a fine spray.

She had not ridden far when she spotted Charalambos sitting on a rock on the crest of the ridge overlooking the river and she turned the horse and trotted it up the slope towards him. As she got closer she heard the strains of the wistful, somewhat plaintive melody which he was playing on a harmonica.

Helene reined in alongside the rock. Charalambos took the harmonica from his lips, tapped the spittle from it into the palm of his hand and then looked up at her.

'He has found a friend,' he said. And he knew that was true for he had been watching through binoculars as Collier had boarded Hellman's yacht.

Helene turned her head and looked out towards the not too distant coastline. And then, as she smiled, Charalambos again raised the harmonica to his mouth and began to play once more.

Collier waited nervously for Hellman's reaction to his story with all its wild improbabilities. The American stood at the glass doors which opened on to the sun deck, gazing thoughtfully out over the sea. Then he asked, 'And you haven't even got a suspicion as to what Barry might have been into?'

'Not a clue,' replied Collier. 'But with that kind of pay-off it has to have been something big. I don't even like to think about it.'

Hellman shook his head in wonderment. 'Well it sure is one hell of a scenario. Pity I'm not in the movie business.'

Disappointment welled up in Collier. 'I see,' he said mournfully. 'You don't believe me either.'

Hellman rounded on him, frowning. 'On the contrary. I believe everything you've told me.'

'You do!' exclaimed Collier.

'Sure. Shouldn't I?'

'Well, yes but . . .' His relief left him almost speechless.

Hellman returned to the table and put his coffee cup down on it. 'Why would you come here and lie to me? What's in it for you? And you're not crazy. I'd lay odds on that.'

'Thank you. That's reassuring. It's been suggested.'

Hellman studied him. 'So you said. By the police.'

'And others,' Collier added honestly.

'Forget it.' Hellman dismissed both the police and others with a flick of his well manicured fingers. 'So, right, it's a pretty wild story. But you're as sane as I am. So these things happened. Just the way you've spelt them out. I accept that.'

'At last!' Collier breathed a deep sigh of relief. 'I can't tell you what it means to me just having you say that, Mr Hellman.'

'Eugene,' smiled Hellman. 'Okay?'

'Right. Thank you.'

Hellman crossed to his desk. 'We've got a lot to do if

we're going to solve these riddles and tie up all the loose ends,' he said briskly and with an air of authority. 'Then dump the whole shebang in Mitsides' lap and watch him squirm.'

Suddenly Collier realised just what kind of an imposition he was placing on his host; a man who was practically a stranger.

'Look, I know I said I needed your help. And I do. But thinking about it, well, this is my problem. I can't really drag you into a mess like this. I don't have the right.'

'Right?' echoed Hellman. 'Sure you do. Friendship. Isn't that right enough? Your brother and I were friends. And now you've inherited that friendship. At least that's the way I see it. Besides I care. Okay, so maybe Barry got fouled up somewhere along the line and dirtied his hands in some crooked deal or other. And remember we don't even know that for sure. Not yet. Anyway, as far as I'm concerned he was a great guy. I liked him. I liked him a lot. And if someone killed him, well I want them to get what's coming to them. So as for dragging me into it, forget it. You just try keeping me out.'

Collier gave him one last chance. 'Well I'm grateful of course. And I could certainly do with you on my side but . . .'

Hellman crossed back to him. 'Now you listen here, David,' he said, with a trace of impatience in his voice. 'Friendship and all that apart. You come to me with an intriguing story like this, a story that raises many questions. If you think I'm just going to stand aside and not do everything I damn well can to find the answers to those questions. Well, correction. You *are* crazy.' He smiled. 'I'm in. You're stuck with me. And you sure as hell do need me. I've got the time, financial resources and the manpower for just this kind of operation. So no arguments.'

Collier shook his head and returned the American's smile. 'No arguments.'

'Good.'

'So where do we go from here?'

Hellman was now in charge. 'We dig. Dip deep. Now

this woman, Helene. And her friends. What are their names again?'

'Charalambos and Basileos.'

'The bandit character?'

'Well he looks like one.' Collier recalled the wild yet sympathetic character who had helped him. 'A poacher anyway, and that's for certain.'

'And you're totally in the dark as to what their interest is in all this?'

'Totally. Except it's pretty obvious that Helene and Barry had something going for each other. It could be that she's just out to nail his murderer. And the other two are helping her.'

'You really believe that?' Hellman clearly didn't.

'It's a possibility. An explanation.'

'Sure.' Hellman was derisive. 'But I don't buy it. If all that lady wants is to see justice done then why doesn't she talk to Chief Inspector Mitsides? And why is she playing hide and seek?'

Collier repeated Helene's defence. 'She says that she can't get involved with the police. That none of them can.'

'That has to be because she's scared. They're all three of them scared.'

'Of what?' asked Collier.

'Who knows? Maybe of ending up in gaol themselves.' Hellman caught Collier's look of doubt. 'Oh come on! They haven't exactly been acting like law abiding citizens, have they?'

'But it was Helene who gave me the briefcase with the fifty thousand pounds in it,' countered Collier.

'And just how long did you keep it? Ten minutes? Fifteen? Half-an-hour at the most. Right? And she told you herself. No one else knew where the money was hidden or that she was planning on giving it to you.'

'Except Charalambos.'

'Exactly.'

Collier shook his head. 'But that's ridiculous. Why give me the money and then rob me of it?'

'A smokescreen maybe,' suggested Hellman.

'To cover what?'

'Their own implication perhaps.' Hellman worked Collier gently round to his view.

'Are you saying that whatever Barry and Morrison were into Helene and the others were in it with them?'

'No,' said Hellman. 'Not with them. But how about in opposition? Now that's a possibility too, isn't it? And that's what we're dealing in right now. Possibilities.' He wandered back over to his desk again and sat down at it. 'Like it's also just possible that it was Helene or one of her friends who killed your brother.'

Collier was truly horrified at the prospect. It had been bad enough to suspect that Helene had been using him, but that she might have killed Barry was too awful to contemplate. She couldn't have done. Not Helene. Nor could she have ordered such a thing. Or could she? Perhaps *that* was the special relationship she claimed to have had with Barry, the bond between killer and victim.

'My God!' gasped Collier as the full implication of what Hellman had suggested sank in. He got up from the suddenly uncomfortable depths of the armchair and, going to the window, stared out at the enigmatic sea.

'That thought hadn't occurred to you?' Hellman enquired.

'Not that they might have murdered Barry. No.'

'Then hold on to it. It might save your neck some time.' Hellman was remorseless. 'Where do they hang out, these three?'

'I have no idea. But last night Helene said she'd keep in touch.'

'I bet,' said Hellman bitingly. 'Well, we might just flush them out first, eh? As I see it for starters we have to get alongside Morrison. He's the one who can answer the sixty-four thousand dollar question. What kind of racket he and Barry were working. If it was a racket. And, if not, then how did they lay their hands on a small fortune in Swiss francs? The rest we can take from there. Have you got any thoughts as to Morrison's whereabouts?'

Collier shook his head. 'Not on the construction site that's for sure. He's officially on leave. He's got a girlfriend

I understand. He could be with her I suppose. But then he could be anywhere. It's a pretty big island.'

'So it's hunt the 'possum time. And for that we need to bring in the dogs.' Collier clearly didn't understand what he meant, so Hellman enlightened him. 'Travis and Olsen. They can handle it. They've got the right kind of background.' He picked up a soft leather notebook and miniature gold pen. 'Can you give me a description of Morrison?'

'Better than that,' said Collier, pleased to have something to contribute at last. 'I've got a photograph of him.' Pulling Barry's wallet from his hip pocket, he crossed to the desk and handed it to Hellman, opened at the photo of his brother with Morrison and the two Cypriot girls.

The American nodded. 'May I keep this?'

'Of course.'

Hellman extracted the snapshot from the plastic envelope. Then, idly, he flicked through the other photographs in the wallet. The one of the naked girl caused him to exhale appreciatively. 'Not bad, eh?'

'Part of Barry's collection.'

'Yes, he did okay for himself in that department, didn't he?' said Hellman, leafing on. He reached the last picture and frowned. Collier saw that his attention was riveted on the shot of the hieroglyphics. 'What's this?'

Collier shrugged. 'Search me. Some kind of inscription. I imagine it's from one of the archaeological sites here.'

'Could be,' agreed Hellman.

'Any idea what it says?'

The American laughed and shook his head. 'Not my line of country. Wall carvers will be prosecuted, maybe.' He handed the wallet back to Collier and held up the photograph of Morrison with Barry and the two girls. 'This'll be a great help. I'll get Travis and Olsen started on tracing him right away.'

'And what do I do?'

Hellman grinned at him. 'Relax.' He held up a hand to check any protest. 'Listen, let my legs do the running around, eh? They get paid enough. When they come up with something solid, well okay, you and I'll move in front and centre. Meanwhile unwind a little.'

He pressed a bell push on his desk then stood up, moved around from behind his desk and put his arm around Collier's shoulders. 'Look, David,' he said avuncularly, 'you've had a pretty rough time these last few days. The first sign we're getting anywhere near close to Morrison and I'll be in touch immediately. Count on it. But for now just let it ride. Take things easy.'

Slowly he began to steer Collier towards the door of the stateroom. 'Rest and recreation. Know what I mean?' Then, half way across the room, he had an inspiration; snapped his fingers and paused. 'Say, I've got a wonderful idea. I'm giving a party on board tomorrow night. Quite a number of interesting people are coming. Some of the local brass. A few ex-pats.' He grinned. 'And I wouldn't be a bit surprised if there weren't one or two unattached and very attractive women on board too. Something for you to add to *your* collection. How about it?'

Collier hesitated.

'Oh come on,' urged Hellman. 'Give yourself a break. You've earned it. Around eight. What do you say?'

It would be ungracious to turn him down, thought Collier, when the American was being so helpful. He smiled. 'You've just made me an offer I can't refuse.'

Hellman laughed. 'Great.'

The door opened and Travis, summoned by the bell, stepped into the stateroom. He glowered at Collier.

'Have the tender take Mr Collier ashore,' Hellman ordered brusquely. Then he held out his hand to the Englishman. 'Till tomorrow night then.'

Collier had not felt so easy in his mind since he had arrived in Cyprus and his gratitude was sincere. 'What can I say?' he enquired with a helpless shrug, shaking hands. 'Except thank you. For everything.'

'Forget it,' said Hellman. 'Now watch how you go.'

As Collier stepped into the tender Hellman waved to him from the deck, then he turned on his heel and strode back into his stateroom. From a drawer in his desk he took a sheaf of enlarged colour photographs and began to go through them, examining each one carefully.

There was a light tap on the door and Travis and Olsen entered and crossed to the desk.

'Was he co-operative, sir?' asked Travis.

Hellman put his photographs away and drummed his fingers thoughtfully on the desk. Then, as if hearing Travis' question for the first time, he replied. 'Extremely. But without realising it. David Collier is a very confused man. And right now so am I.'

'What's his play? Where does he figure in this?' queried Olsen.

'He doesn't. It's out in the open now. He's clean. A child wandering in the wilderness. He knows nothing. But he came up with the lead we've been looking for.' Hellman picked up the snapshot Collier had given him and tapped the figure on the right. 'Eric Morrison.'

Travis looked at the picture. 'Hey! That's the guy Collier was fighting in Paphos.'

Hellman nodded. 'Find him,' he ordered. 'He's the one we want. The real key to the whole operation. And while you're looking for him there are three other people you need to run a check on.'

Olsen was still perplexed by this unexpected development. He double checked. 'Collier's clean you say, Mr Hellman?'

'As an antiseptic.'

'Then why didn't he call the police when he found me searching his hotel room?' asked Travis, almost as bewildered as his companion. 'Why did he chop me and then just dump me back in the car out cold?'

'He didn't,' Hellman replied. 'Not that I asked him. But I'm pretty sure he didn't. There has to have been someone else in that room.'

Travis frowned. 'But who?'

'That's one of the things we're going to find out.'

Olsen made one more attempt to get this new situation straight in his mind. 'And if Collier is in the clear then who was on the other end of that rifle at his place last night?'

Hellman studied the two men, enjoying their confusion.

'Would you believe a poacher, maybe?' he said, with a quiet smile.

CHAPTER TWENTY-TWO

Eric Morrison came out of the side door and looked around cautiously.

Maria was standing alongside the Datsun pick-up which the boy, Dimitrios, had left parked on the forecourt for him. There was no sign of Antonis.

Still peering about him, Morrison crossed to the truck.

'Where's Antonis?' he grunted.

'He has gone. To Nicosia.' Maria put her arms around his neck. 'How long will you be away?'

'A while,' replied Morrison flatly, as he freed himself from her embrace.

Maria tried again. 'This cave. It is far from here?'

Morrison grinned inwardly. Oh yes, wouldn't you like to know, he thought. You and that cousin of yours. What do you both take me for, an idiot? Why do you think I waited until he was well clear of the garage before I even thought about leaving? He nodded. 'A fair distance,' he said.

'Be careful,' Maria pleaded and she looked genuinely concerned.

'I am. Always,' Morrison assured her grimly. And with that he climbed into the cab of the Datsun, slammed the door and drove the pick-up on to the road where he turned left and accelerated.

From his vantage point among some trees bordering the narrow track on rising ground above and behind the garage, Antonis watched the pick-up pull away and grinned. He waited for a few seconds to give Morrison a good head start. And then he started the engine of his much prized and lovingly maintained Ford Cortina, engaged first gear and glided away down the slope in pursuit.

For the first four or five minutes of his journey Morrison flicked a glance up into the rearview mirror every few seconds. But then, satisfied that he was not being followed, he relaxed. Prising a packet of Marlborough from his breast pocket, he shook out a cigarette and lit it. Feeling pleased with himself, he inhaled deeply and settled down for the long drive to the cave.

Antonis, half a mile back, was feeling no less pleased with himself. The pattern of the road as it wound its way down the mountainside meant that he could hang well behind and, always on higher ground than the pick-up, easily keep it in sight while remaining hidden himself. For the next ten or eleven miles there were only three turns off the road Morrison was taking and Antonis, knowing the road well, was able to position himself in good time and in such a way as to observe whether or not the Englishman turned on to any of them. He didn't.

The only slight problem Antonis could foresee would come when this minor road joined the coastal highway. There he would have to close up a little in order to check which way his quarry went, but even there he reckoned that there was little chance of his being spotted by a driver intent on seeking out a safe gap in the main stream of traffic on the busy link between Limassol and Paphos.

The last series of bends before the highway was made up of tight hairpins with short, straight stretches between them. The slope on either side of the road was not more than twelve or fifteen degrees, but was so boulder strewn as to be unnegotiable to any vehicle, however rugged.

Antonis closed the gap a little between the Cortina and the Datsun and watched Morrison negotiate the first leg of the bend immediately below the Ford. And then, momentarily, he lost sight of the pick-up as it swung into the second turn of the hairpin. Accelerating, losing height but gaining ground, he steered the Cortina into the left hand bend in Morrison's wake, came out of it and immediately spun the wheel over to twist through the opposite turn and then gun the car into the next straight.

It was then and only just in time that he saw the obstruction.

Cursing viciously, he stamped on the brake and, as the clutch followed it home, the rear of the car wagged sharply two or three times before Antonis brought the Ford under control and it stopped with a squeal of protesting rubber just two yards from a flock of goats.

The first few animals had only just crossed the road, meandering downhill, but the remainder were jostling their way in a solid phalanx across his path. And they were in no hurry. Nor was the cloaked and hooded goatherd squatting impassively in the shade of a rock half way up the hillside.

Antonis honked his horn furiously but neither the goats nor their guardian took the slightest notice of him.

It was a full three minutes before the last of the herd had skittered far enough across the road for Antonis to squeeze past them with a final blast on his horn. He took the remaining double bends at Grand Prix speed and roared into the last straight and up to the junction.

But he was too late; he had been delayed too long. The pick-up was no longer in sight in either direction.

Furious, Antonis jerked on the handbrake, got out of the car and scrambled on to the roof to give himself a better view. But to no effect. There was traffic enough on the highway, travelling both east and west, but in neither flow could he spot the Datsun he had been following.

Livid with frustration, Antonis turned to face uphill and shout an obscenity back at the distant goatherd. Then he jumped down on to the road again, climbed angrily back behind the wheel of the Cortina and, with no other alternative now open to him, turned the car left on to the highway in the direction of Limassol where he would pick up the road for Nicosia.

And far up on the hillside Basileos threw back the hood of the shepherd's cloak and laughed.

'No, I'm sorry, but I have absolutely no idea where Mr Morrison is,' said Preece.

The two men looked affable and their enquiry had been polite enough but there was something about them which he found slightly disturbing. And although they hadn't introduced themselves he had seen them somewhere before. 'Have you tried the place where he lives?' he asked.

'Yes. No luck though,' replied Travis.

'No one at home,' chimed in Olsen.

Preece shrugged. 'Well, he's on leave so he could be anywhere. He might even have gone to Athens. He's done that before.'

'He didn't say what his plans were?' Travis probed gently.

'No.'

'And you didn't ask?'

Preece looked surprised. 'None of my business.'

'His girlfriend . . .' Olsen made a show of racking his memory. 'You know. What's her name . . .'

'Yes,' Preece agreed. 'He might be with her of course.' Again he shrugged. 'I'm sorry I can't be more helpful.'

'Well thanks anyway, Mr Preece.' The two men swung round from him and started to move away across the site.

'Is it important that you find him?' Preece called after them.

Travis and Olsen stopped and turned slowly back to him. 'Not that important,' said Travis with a smile.

It was Olsen who explained. 'It's just that, well the three of us invested in a lottery ticket and, what do you know, the number came up.'

'So we want to settle with him,' added Travis.

'Lucky man,' exclaimed Preece enviously.

Travis nodded. 'Yes. No complaints from us either. It's not a fortune but a third of something's better than being a loser, eh?'

'It certainly is,' agreed Preece. 'And what a pleasant surprise for him to come back to. He'll probably be broke. If I see him first I'll tell him you called. You're . . . ?'

Travis fielded the question. 'The bringers of good news, wouldn't you say? We'll leave a note for him at his place. Thanks again.' Then he turned once more and, with Olsen at his side, strolled over towards their car which was parked by the gate.

Preece watched them go, his expression questioning and more than a little troubled. So many people seemed to be taking an interest in the whereabouts of Eric Morrison.

CHAPTER TWENTY-THREE

When Morrison returned to the garage and showed Maria what he had brought with him it was she who, once she had caught her breath again and somewhat reluctantly returned the artefact, suggested that they celebrate. And for her celebration meant one thing only.

They were lying on top of the bedcovers and still celebrating when Antonis pounded up the stairs and into the room. He pulled up sharply a foot or so away from the bed and grinned broadly, enjoying the spectacle.

Morrison found the intruder's presence somewhat off-putting and he could feel his enthusiasm fading fast. And so could Maria. And even if normally she would have objected to presenting her cousin with such erotic entertainment for free she was at that moment too close to an orgasm to be cheated out of it by anyone.

'Don't stop! Jesus and all the saints! Don't stop! Don't come out! Don't come out!' she moaned frantically, undulating wildly under Morrison and wrapping her legs around him.

And then, with precious little further help from her partner, she made it and, throwing her arms out sideways and spreading and stretching her fingers, she screamed out in her ecstasy.

Distracted, Morrison hadn't been so lucky. Not that he cared really. He'd made it twice before that afternoon already. As he rolled off Maria she turned on her side, eyes closed and sobbing with pleasure.

Morrison swung his legs over the side of the bed, sat up and glared at Antonis. He considered hurling himself at the man and beating him to a pulp but then, sitting there naked, he suddenly felt very vulnerable and somewhat ridiculous. No, this isn't the time for a brawl, he decided. He scowled and reached for his underpants which were lying on top of a heap of clothes on a nearby chair.

'Don't bloody well bother to knock, will you,' he snarled angrily.

'Pimp! Poncing queer!' shouted Maria without moving and without opening her eyes.

Antonis went on grinning. He spread his hands in an apologetic gesture. 'I'm sorry,' he said. 'I did not think. So early.' He shrugged. 'But then why not? What better way to pass the time, eh?' He glanced at Maria. 'And you have such an appetite for it, haven't you cousin?'

Morrison was scrabbling into his trousers. 'For what I'm paying I expect privacy. Right?' he snapped.

Lazily and with a contented expression on her face, Maria sat up in the bed and reached for a cigarette from a packet on the bedside table. 'Deduct ten pounds from what was agreed,' she suggested. 'It's worth that for the show we just gave him. And you enjoyed it, didn't you, dear Antonis?'

'It was all right,' acknowledged Antonis grudgingly. 'But ten pounds.' He shook his head. 'That is too much. For ten pounds I could watch an even better whore than you on the job.'

Maria made an obscene gesture in his direction and Morrison's scowl deepened. 'Watch your mouth,' he warned.

'Okay! Okay!' appeased Antonis. 'I have said I'm sorry, haven't I? I didn't mean to interrupt.' He turned and moved back towards the door. 'It's just that I thought you'd want to know that it looks like I've found a buyer,' he threw in casually over his shoulder.

'You have!' Excitement replaced anger on Maria's face. She threw her cigarette down into the ashtray, leapt from the bed and, running across to Antonis, grabbed at his sleeve. 'No, don't go. Tell us.'

Antonis ran his eyes over her body, relishing it. 'Oh, but if I am interrupting,' he teased.

'Shut up,' snapped Morrison.

'Later perhaps. When you are not so busy,' Antonis suggested to Maria with a wink, pushing his luck.

Morrison lunged at him, seized the lapels of his jacket and twisted them savagely. 'Now,' he hissed dangerously.

Antonis knew that he had gone too far and he was afraid.

Wide-eyed, he stared into Morrison's face and nodded. Resentfully Morrison released him.

'This buyer,' Maria asked eagerly. 'How did you find him?'

Recovering his composure and conceit, Antonis strutted back into the room. 'It was so easy,' he said. 'I spoke to a few people I know and gave them just a hint of what was on offer. Just a hint. No more. And then, in less than one hour, someone made contact. In the *taverna* where I waited.'

'Who?' demanded Maria.

'An agent. For a big spender. A man who is in the market for exactly such things as we wish to dispose of.'

Morrison wanted more details. 'What's his name? Who does he work for?'

Antonis pulled a face. 'Such confidences we did not exchange.'

'It could be a trap,' Morrison suggested. 'The police, maybe.'

'No. The man I spoke to comes recommended,' Antonis assured him.

'Who by?'

'My friends of course. Otherwise they would not have sent him to me. And they are careful those ones. They have to be.'

Maria frowned uncertainly. 'You are sure?'

'Of course. I tell you. He is all right.'

Morrison got down to details. 'Cash?'

Antonis nodded. 'In the hand. On delivery. But first he wants to see the quality of the merchandise. Did you get something to show?'

Maria smiled knowingly and shot a conspiratorial look at her lover.

Morrison, his eyes on Antonis, hesitated for a few seconds. Then he pointed to the chair. 'Give me my jacket,' he ordered.

Antonis picked it up and gave it to him.

From out of one of the side pockets Morrison drew a folded handkerchief and handed it to the other man.

Holding the handkerchief in the palm of his hand, Antonis

unfolded it and in an instant his studied nonchalance was replaced with wonder.

The necklace was solid gold and made up of a chain with a tier of finely engraved and beautifully proportioned and interrelated panels. It was clearly a genuine antiquity but it was in mint condition and it radiated a light of its own, almost as if it were a living thing.

As Antonis stared at it, stunned, Maria smirked and Morrison, trying to sound as offhand as he could, asked, 'That do?'

Slowly Antonis pulled himself out of the spell cast on him by the necklace. 'Oh my friend!' he whispered. 'My friend.' He held the necklace up to the light and stroked it with the fingers of his other hand.

Morrison reached for the artefact. 'So when do I get to see this feller?'

His eyes still fixed on it, Antonis surrendered the necklace to him. 'Tonight,' he said. 'He will meet us tonight.'

'Us?' Morrison frowned.

Antonis nodded. 'Of course.' He smiled wilily. 'The meeting place. It is a bit out of the way,' he explained. 'And I would not want you to get lost.'

It was only later as they parked outside the chosen rendezvous and close to a red Peugeot 304 that Morrison's suspicions that Antonis was more concerned about protecting his investment than he was about him losing his way, were confirmed.

Directions on how to find an open air cinema would have been easy enough to follow, especially to this one which, although somewhat isolated, just outside a village, was only a little way off the road from Limassol and not more than twelve miles from the town itself. But Morrison said nothing, just got out of the car and moved round the front of it to join his companion.

The soundtrack of the film was clearly audible but it was in Greek and Morrison could not understand a word of it. But to judge from the laughter the audience seemed to be enjoying it.

Beckoning to him, Antonis led the way round the side of the building and to a small doorway.

The door opened into a broad space between the rear wall and the large screen on to which the film was being projected.

As Antonis closed the door behind them, Morrison looked around warily.

The only light was that which filtered flickeringly through the screen itself and the whole area was dominated by the reverse images of the giants who were entertaining the audience that night. The amplified boom of their dialogue resonated around the building.

Three-quarters of the way down the width of the screen stood a man. He had his back to them and he was shrouded in a haze of tobacco smoke. Morrison shot a questioning look at Antonis who nodded and guided him towards the stranger.

The man was dressed in a well cut if somewhat loud pinstripe suit and he was smoking a cigar. When lazily he turned to face them while they were still some yards off from him, Morrison decided that he must have sensed their approach, because he certainly could not have heard anything above the din of the soundtrack.

Charalambos nodded a greeting to Antonis and then stood studying the Englishman through eyes half closed against the veil of tobacco smoke which surrounded him.

Morrison took in the dapper shirt and the broad, jazzily-patterned silk tie which the stranger was also wearing.

His inspection of the Englishman completed, Charalambos glanced at Antonis. 'Let us not waste time,' he said. 'You have brought something to show me?'

Antonis nodded but Morrison, who had taken an instant dislike to the man, hesitated.

Charalambos looked from one to the other of them and his face took on an expression of faint irritation. 'Well?' he sighed.

Antonis nudged his companion and, unenthusiastically, Morrison took the handkerchief from his pocket and unfolded it to reveal the necklace.

Charalambos regarded it disinterestedly for a while and

then, moving in closer, he picked it up and examined it carefully and with the eye of an expert.

Anxiously Morrison and Antonis awaited his verdict.

His examination concluded, Charalambos looked at the two men again, his face still betraying no emotion. He nodded. 'Good. And there is more like this, you say?'

'Much more,' confirmed Antonis, obviously eager to please. 'Jewels. Statues. Many things. And all very old.'

Charalambos shook his head. 'Relatively modern,' he corrected him flatly. 'Third century B.C.'

Morrison had not taken his eyes from the stranger. 'Are you interested?' he asked.

'Personally? No.'

Morrison frowned and shot a look at Antonis.

'But then I am only an intermediary,' Charalambos went on. 'An agent. I have little doubt, however, that my employer will be most interested.'

Morrison looked relieved. 'In the lot? Everything?'

Charalambos nodded. 'Almost certainly.'

'See! Didn't I tell you,' exclaimed Antonis triumphantly.

Morrison was still not fully convinced. Everything seemed to be going too well. 'And payment would be in cash?' he demanded.

Charalambos gave him a disdainful look. 'Naturally,' he murmured.

'How much?'

Charalambos held up the necklace. 'For this?'

'For all of it.'

Charalambos shrugged. 'An appraisal would be necessary. Of the individual items. Only then could an offer be made.'

Morrison frowned. 'For that I'd have to take you to the cave.'

The stranger nodded. 'Together with my principal.'

'How do I know I can trust you?' challenged Morrison. 'Or your employer?'

'You don't.' Charalambos shrugged and held out the necklace. 'But then perhaps you have another buyer in mind,' he went on. 'Someone you do trust.'

Morrison was trapped in a dilemma and he knew it. There

were only two choices open to him if he was to make any money; one to reveal the whereabouts of the cave and risk being doublecrossed and the other to cut his losses nd settle for the sale of the necklace alone.

'How much for just that?' he asked, pointing at the necklace.

'Are you crazy?' burst out Antonis angrily.

'Shut up,' snarled Morrison.

Charalambos shook his head again. 'My principal does not deal in bits and pieces,' he said. 'It's all or nothing.' Again he held out the necklace to the Englishman. 'You wish perhaps to think about it? To try elsewhere. I will contact you. In, say, two or three weeks from now.'

Morrison reacted with a look of alarm. 'No! I can't wait that long.'

'So?' Charalambos shrugged.

Morrison took less than five seconds to think about it and then he nodded. 'Okay. The lot.'

'Good,' breathed Charalambos. He fed the necklace into the palm of his other hand. 'You do realise, of course, that before taking the matter any further my employer will first need to see this. We will go now, eh?'

'Where?'

'Limassol.'

Panic seized the Englishman. He had already come further from the garage than he thought was safe. There were too many people who knew him in Limassol; he remembered what had happened to Barry, and he heard again the sound of the bullets ricocheting off the rocks when he met David Collier at Trimiklini.

'Can't your boss come to me?' he asked.

Charalambos regarded him coldly. 'It is the salesman who travels,' he reminded him. 'Not the buyer. The mountain never did go to Mohammed. Believe me.'

'You don't understand,' explained Morrison. 'It's not that simple. I've got . . . well, problems. I can't move around too much. I can't risk it.'

The stranger appeared completely disinterested in his

problems and merely shrugged. 'If you say so.' Then he suggested, 'Your associate then.'

'Yes, that's the answer,' volunteered Antonis with even more eagerness than he had shown before. 'I can go.'

This did nothing to relieve Morrison's sense of unease. He trusted Antonis just about as much as he did the stranger. Again he hesitated, turning the problem over in his mind. Charalambos waited patiently and then, apparently bored by the Englishman's indecision, he looked pointedly at his watch.

'I'm sorry,' he said, 'but I am expected elsewhere. On other business.' And there was a note of finality in his voice.

Antonis, alarmed at the prospect of the sale slipping through their fingers, pulled Morrison a little to one side. 'What's the problem?' he whispered urgently. 'I will go with him and bring the answer back to you at the garage. And then how and when, that will be up to you.'

Biting his lip, Morrison stared at him thoughtfully and then he nodded. 'All right.' He turned back to Charalambos. 'You got a car?' he asked.

'Of course.'

Morrison held out his hand to Antonis. 'Give me the keys to yours then.'

Antonis took them from his pocket and handed them over.

Charalambos slipped the necklace into his jacket pocket and strolled slowly away in the direction of the side entrance. Antonis was about to follow him when Morrison grabbed his arm.

'I'll wait for you,' he spat out grimly. 'And if you doublecross me . . .'

'Oh come on now,' protested Antonis and interrupting him. 'As if I would.' And his face was a picture of injured innocence.

Outside in the fresh night air again, Morrison stood alongside the Cortina and watched while Antonis and the stranger crossed to the Peugeot 304.

'Here,' said Charalambos, tossing the keys of the car to his companion. 'You drive. I am tired.'

Antonis shrugged, unlocked the door and slid in behind the steering wheel. The Peugeot swept past Morrison but he did not move and stood gazing after it until its tail lights were no longer visible.

The two men drove in silence, Charalambos, his cigar almost finished, gazing out through the windscreen apparently lost in thought. Then he snapped out of his reverie, looked at his cigar and wound down his side window and tossed the butt out into the darkness. Winding the window up again, he checked his watch. 'I am going to be late,' he muttered. 'I must telephone and explain.' He looked ahead through the windscreen again and pointed. 'Pull in there.'

Ahead of them was a roadside station, a combination restaurant and coffee house. Antonis nodded and, as they drew level with the forecourt, swung the Peugeot on to it.

There was a lighted telephone box just outside the entrance to the building and about thirty feet away from where the car was parked.

Charalambos opened his door. 'I won't be a minute,' he said.

'Okay,' replied Antonis.

Charalambos got out of the car, slammed the door behind him and crossed to the telephone box. Antonis saw him step inside it, pick up the telephone and begin to dial a number. Then he remembered, the stranger was carrying the necklace, and for one panic stricken moment he considered getting out of the car and crossing to the telephone box himself. But then he relaxed again, reasoning that the man was in full sight where he was anyway and, besides, he was hardly likely to make a break for it on foot, was he?

Antonis took out a cigarette and lit it with the lighter from the dashboard. Then he turned on the radio. Humming to the music of a popular song, he glanced once more across at the telephone box. The stranger was speaking urgently into the instrument.

It was to the accompaniment of an old Elvis Presley record currently enjoying a revival that, ten minutes later, Antonis flicked the end of his cigarette out on to the forecourt, sighed deeply and glanced across for the twentieth time at the telephone box. The stranger was apparently still speaking. Antonis began to drum his fingers impatiently on the steering wheel. What's keeping him for God's sake, he thought. I won't be a minute, he had said. Bloody hell, he'd been on that phone ages. He decided that if the man wasn't back in the car in another sixty seconds he would go over to him and demand an explanation.

And it was as he made this decision that the police car eased its way on to the forecourt and pulled up alongside him.

The two constables got out and converged on the Peugeot; one on either side of the car. The man on the nearside tapped on the window and, hopefully concealing the alarm which gripped him whenever he was confronted by the police, Antonis leaned across and wound it down. The policeman stooped and looked into the car. '*Kalispera*,' he said.

Antonis only just managed to smile '*Kalispera*.' He snapped his head round to look at the second policeman who was now peering into the car on his side, and thought it wise to include him in the greeting. '*Kalispera*.' The policeman gave him a curt nod.

'Is this your car?' enquired the policeman on his left.

'Yes, of course,' Antonis assured him but then quickly corrected himself. 'Well, no, not mine. It doesn't actually belong to me.'

'No it doesn't, does it?' said the policeman, gazing into the car over his shoulder. Then he reached in and plucked the keys from the ignition. 'Because the owner reported it missing from outside his house in Larnaca this afternoon, didn't he?' He opened the door. 'Out,' he ordered.

'But you've made a mistake,' protested Antonis volubly and with some confidence. 'This car belongs to a friend of mine. Ask him.'

'Oh yes,' sighed the constable disbelievingly.

'Yes,' countered Antonis defiantly, going into the attack. 'And he will confirm it. Ask him.'

The policeman on the left-hand side of the car straightened up and looked around the forecourt. 'So where is he then?'

Antonis scrambled out of the car. 'Making a telephone call,' he snapped. 'That's him over . . .' He looked across at the telephone box, his jaw dropped in amazement and his expression took on a look of stunned bewilderment.

The telephone box which had been obscured from his view during his exchange with the two policemen was empty.

Antonis scowled as his reaction turned to one of anger and then of concern for himself. He had been had. And now he had to find some way out of the mess he was in. The policeman looked away from the telephone box and shook his head. Then he glanced across at his companion and smiled.

'Maybe this friend of his was the man who rang in and tipped us off about the car, eh?' he suggested as a joke.

His companion laughed. But Antonis didn't find it amusing.

CHAPTER TWENTY-FOUR

Morrison hurled the cup, half filled with coffee, across the kitchen and it exploded against the wall.

'It was bad enough David Collier ripping me off,' he shouted vehemently. 'But that flashy little Cypriot creep.'

He hadn't slept all night and he was exhausted and now, with the sun high over the mountains behind the garage, it was only his temper which kept him on his feet, pacing the room back and forth. 'I'll kill the bastard.'

'If you ever see him again,' said Maria morosely, sitting at the table and peering into her coffee cup to see if the grounds in it promised a future happier than the present.

'What exactly did Antonis say when he called?'

Maria sighed. 'I've told you a hundred times.'

'Well tell me again,' demanded Morrison savagely.

Maria shrugged. 'He just said that he had been arrested for stealing a car. That he was innocent but that the man he'd been with, the one whose car he was driving, had disappeared.'

'Nothing else? You're positive?'

'I'm positive. That's all. What else could he say? He was speaking from a police station.' She peered into her coffee cup again.

Morrison began to pace once more. 'So I lose out again! Great!'

Maria put in a plea for her cousin. 'What about Antonis! He could end up in prison. And for something he did not do.'

'Screw him! He should have been more careful. The moment I saw him I didn't trust the smooth-talking git he came up with.'

Maria sighed again. 'Then you should have gone to Limassol with them.'

'How could I?' snapped Morrison. 'I'd've been sticking my neck right out, wouldn't I?'

'All right. So don't blame Antonis. He was only trying to help.'

'He was in it for his cut,' Morrison scoffed contemptuously.

Maria looked at him angrily. 'And you were doing it for charity!' she jeered. 'At least you're not in gaol.'

A sudden thought struck Morrison. He frowned. 'He won't talk, will he?' he asked anxiously.

Maria regarded him as though he were a child. 'About what he was doing in that car? With that man? And land himself in even worse trouble. Are you crazy?'

'So he'll be all right, won't he?' said Morrison, reassured, in a sullen attempt to ease Maria's unexpected anxiety about Antonis. 'Driving a car away without the owner's consent. That's nothing. The most he'll probably get is a fine. But I've lost the bloody necklace.'

Maria shot a look at him. 'We've lost the necklace,' she said firmly.

Morrison saw the look in her eyes and hastily corrected his mistake. 'Okay, so we've all been robbed. And we're right back where we started from.'

There was a knock on the side door. Maria got up from the table and opened it. It was the boy, Dimitrios. He shot a frightened glance at Morrison and then spoke to Maria in Greek. She reacted with a look of surprise and bewilderment and turned to Morrison.

'Dimitrios says there is a man on the telephone who wants to speak to you.'

'Me?' checked Morrison warily. 'He asked for me by name?'

Maria shook her head. 'No. He just said "the Englishman". He says it is about the things you have for sale. And the sample you gave him last night.'

Morrison reached the telephone in the workshop yards ahead of Maria and Dimitrios and he was already speaking when they ran in through the doorway.

'Look, what the hell's going on? Just what kind of game are you playing? What happened last night . . . ? All right. All right. But I'd still like to know what's . . . Yes, okay.

I'm listening . . .' He frowned deeply. 'Where . . . ? Yes, I've got it . . . Well, I don't have much choice, do I?'

He removed the telephone from his ear and Maria could hear the dialling tone. Looking perplexed and worried, Morrison hung up.

'Who was it?' Maria asked.

Morrison shrugged.

'Well, what did he say?' she persisted.

Morrison gazed thoughtfully into space. 'That I ought to go to church,' he replied.

The bell of the old and lonely mountain chapel was tolling as Morrison drove up in the pick-up truck and parked close to the door.

He got out of the pick-up and looked around. There was no one in sight. Climbing the steps, he entered the chapel and peered into the gloom surrounding him but he could see very little. A dozen thin candles flickered in the sand of an ornate holder before an icon and threw a pool of soft light on the floor. The yellow of the flames reflected off the gold in the elaborate Byzantine frescoes behind the altar and gave an almost black viscosity, like blood, to the reds. The chapel appeared to be deserted. So who's ringing the bell, pondered Morrison.

High in the wall three fingers of sunlight came probing through the windows, each to spotlight a square yard of marble floor.

Suddenly a thick, hairy hand and forearm, severed at the elbow by the sharp edge of the beam, was thrust into one of the shafts of light. A finger beckoned.

'Over here please.' The voice was a resonant bass.

Slowly and warily, Morrison moved in the direction indicated. And he was in no way reassured when a burly figure stepped fully into the light and stood watching him sternly as he advanced. He noticed that the man wore crossed bandoliers of cartridges over an old British army battledress blouse. And he could see the hilt of a hunting knife protruding from the top of one of his boots.

'You are late,' the man reprimanded him as he came up close and Morrison caught the smell of wine on his breath.

'It wasn't easy finding this place. And I don't understand. Where's the man I met last night?'

The bearded man shook his head. 'I know nothing of that,' he said. 'I was merely asked to pass on a message to you.'

'What is it?' asked Morrison.

Basileos did not reply immediately but studied Morrison intently and with a look of concern tinged with compassion for several seconds before speaking. 'Do you ever pray?' he enquired.

'Pray! What's that got to do with . . . ?'

'Do you?' pressed his interrogator.

Better humour him, Morrison thought. I don't like the look of that knife. He shrugged. 'It's been a long time.'

'It's never too late,' pronounced the stranger quietly. 'And who knows when one may be called to account for one's life?'

Morrison nodded irritably. 'I'll bear that in mind,' he assured him. 'Now what's the message?'

Basileos did not answer immediately. Again his eyes searched Morrison's face. The Englishman, discomforted by his scrutiny, scowled. 'Well?'

'I must first ask you another question,' countered Basileos. 'Do you still wish to sell?'

'Of course I bloody well do,' growled Morrison.

'Yes. I felt certain that would be your answer.' Basileos' voice had taken on a tone of great sadness. 'Very well then. Tonight. The buyer will meet you tonight. Now listen . . .'

Still speaking, he drew Morrison deep into the shadows behind them while outside the chapel bell now tolled, as if for a funeral.

CHAPTER TWENTY-FIVE

The yacht looked magnificent, sitting on the water sparkling with lights and opulent awnings while the sound of music wafted across the sea.

Collier sat contentedly in the back of the tender determined to follow Hellman's advice and relax and enjoy himself. He had felt a little embarrassed when he had boarded the motorboat to find that all the other guests on that trip were in evening dress, but the warmth of the American's welcome when his host greeted him as he stepped on to the deck of the yacht immediately put him at ease.

'Hello there, David!' Hellman pumped his hand enthusiastically and with a firm grip. 'Good to see you again.'

Collier smiled self-deprecatingly. 'Thank you.' He indicated his grey lounge suit. 'But a bit underdressed, I'm afraid. I didn't realise it was formal.'

'Forget it! It doesn't matter. Just so long as you are here.'

More guests came up the accommodation ladder behind them and Hellman flicked a glance in their direction. 'We'll talk later, eh?' he suggested, taking a glass of champagne from the tray of a passing waiter and handing it to Collier. 'Mingle. Have fun. Pick yourself out a girl.'

Tactfully Collier moved on, briefly acknowledged Travis and Olsen who, as usual, were standing back at a distance and flanking their employer. The two men gave him a curt nod. Sipping his champagne, he filtered his way through the throng of recent arrivals concentrated around the reception area and strolled on to the forward deck.

The deck was a picture of luxury under a web of coloured lights strung over the rails and among the rigging.

An appetising and tempting *haute cuisine* buffet had been set out, amid gleaming silver, spotless linen and expensive china, on a long table on the port side. By the foremast, there was a bar offering every kind of drink. In the centre of the deck, immediately in front of the quartet of musicians, a small space had been left clear for dancing.

There was an air of opulence and power among most of the people in the groups standing around chatting and laughing. There were a number of good-looking, younger men and among them, as Hellman had promised, several seemingly unattached and very attractive women.

Martin Preece was talking to one of them, a politely attentive, lazy eyed and very desirable brunette. As Collier approached them he caught the tail end of the story Preece was telling.

'. . . and there I was, covered in brick dust with the flowers in one hand and this great brass bell-pull thing in the other.'

The girl laughed and at that moment Preece caught sight of Collier.

'David!' he exclaimed, surprised but pleased.

Collier nodded. 'Hello, Martin. Didn't think I'd see you tonight.'

'No, I must say the invitation came as a bit of a surprise to me too. I've only met our host once before. But then it looks as if just about everyone on the island's here. Well this is pleasant. I'd no idea that you knew Hellman.'

'I don't,' admitted Collier. 'Not really. He was a friend of Barry's.'

Preece frowned slightly. 'Really! Barry never mentioned him.' He shrugged. 'Still, why should he? How are you?'

'Fine.'

'Sure?' Preece pressed him. 'No more, er . . . problems?'

'Do you mean am I still imagining things?' Collier took him up sharply. 'I never was.'

'No, of course not.' Preece hastily changed the subject. 'Oh I'm so sorry. How rude of me. I haven't introduced you. This is Barbara Newcombe. Barbara's in public relations. She works for one of the big hotels.' He turned to his companion. 'David Collier. Just out from England.'

The girl had been studying Collier from the moment he had joined them and she liked what she saw. Turning his head to look at her, David caught the unmistakable interest in her eyes.

'Hello, David,' she said quietly and with a warm smile. And as she spoke, with only the slightest of movements, she clearly detached herself from Preece. 'How do you like Cyprus?'

'Well I've only been here for a few days,' replied Collier, holding her gaze. 'And it hasn't really been a holiday. But from what I've seen . . .'

Barbara cut in on him. 'Do you dance?' she asked. And even before Collier had a chance to reply, she took his hand and, with a sweet dismissive smile at Preece, led her partner on to the dance floor.

Preece watched as Collier took the girl into his arms and they began to samba. Then he shrugged resignedly, turned and made for the bar.

It was four dances later that Hellman came up behind Collier while he was waiting patiently in line at the buffet to fill two plates, one for himself and one for Barbara, who was waiting for him at a table in a relatively quiet corner of the deck.

The American looked across in Barbara's direction and grinned. 'Having a good time?' he asked.

'Great,' said Collier with feeling, relishing the thought which had formed in his mind from the moment when the girl had led him into their first dance and which, with her body warm and tight against his, she had encouraged from then on.

'Good,' said Hellman. 'Spare me a moment though, eh?'

Collier held up the two plates. 'Well I was just . . .' Hellman didn't let him finish. He beckoned to a waiter who was at his side in an instant, took the two plates from Collier and handed them to the man. 'A little of everything,' he ordered. 'And more than a little of the caviar.' He glanced at Collier. 'It's rather special,' he assured him. Then he turned his attention back to the waiter. 'And then take them across to the table in the corner where the young lady in the green dress is sitting.'

The waiter nodded and quickly moved to the buffet.

'What you don't like, well, leave it,' said Hellman with a broad grin, taking Collier by the arm and guiding him forward along the deck. 'And you can always come back for more of what you do.'

It wasn't until they were standing in the bow of the yacht and well clear of the other guests that Hellman spoke again.

'I just wanted to tell you that we may have a lead on Morrison,' he said in a low confidential tone. 'You know that girlfriend of his you mentioned?' Collier nodded. 'Well Travis and Olsen followed up on her. Apparently she works in one of the vineyards. But it seems that she's dropped out of sight too.'

Collier frowned. 'So where does that get us?' he asked blankly.

'Who knows? But it's interesting, isn't it, her not being around just now? And it seems she's got cousins. Lots of them. But there's one in particular. He runs a garage up Troodos way. Pretty isolated by all accounts.'

Collier reacted with a look of excitement. Hellman nodded. 'It just could be,' he confirmed. 'Anyway I'm having the place checked out first thing tomorrow.' He grinned and patted the Englishman on the back. 'Well that's all I've got to say. And I'm keeping you from a very lovely lady.' He winked. 'I'm glad you took my advice. The pick of the bunch I'd say.'

And with that he led Collier back into the party. Neither of them was aware that throughout their conversation Martin Preece had been watching them with considerable interest from the shadows of the starboard wing of the flying bridge.

Preece dropped his cigarette onto the decking and ground it under his foot. Then he turned and started to move over to the bridge companionway. As he did so he almost collided with a woman standing just behind him in the shadows. Nothing more than a vague but shapely outline. He pulled up sharply and frowned. Either she'd been there all the time and he had not noticed her or she had come up silently on to the flying bridge while his attention had been on Hellman and Collier.

The woman spoke. 'I'm sorry. Did I startle you?' Her voice was electric in its effect.

'A little,' smiled Preece.

'It's peaceful up here, isn't it?' she said as she stepped out of the shadows and into the light of the companionway.

Preece gasped; her beauty was breathtaking as was the low cut evening dress which she was wearing. And, set off to perfection against her evenly tanned skin, was the gold necklace which Morrison had reluctantly handed over to Charalambos. Preece's eyes were drawn hypnotically to it. 'Yes,' he replied quietly, his thoughts elsewhere. And then, as if mesmerised by the necklace, he stepped in closer to her.

The woman, obviously pleased by his interest, raised a hand and ran her fingers lightly over the finely engraved gold panels. 'You like it?' she enquired quietly.

'Very much,' breathed Preece. Then looking up quizzically into her face. 'May I ask where you got it?'

Helene smiled.

CHAPTER TWENTY-SIX

In an old, derelict stone warehouse some two hundred yards back from the quayside of the harbour in Paphos, Morrison waited for the buyer. The warehouse was quite empty. A meagre light from the harbour lamps filtered through a single, grimy window high in one wall.

Morrison had arrived early, parking Antonis' pick-up in the shadows and cautiously reconnoitring the area before trying the door to the building. It had opened easily and he had slipped quickly inside and quietly closed the door behind him in one movement.

When he had set out for his appointment he had been in a state of suppressed excitement but now he sweated as he waited in the dark, pacing nervously up and down.

He stiffened suddenly and cocked his head to one side, listening, as he caught the sound of a car approaching and pulling up outside. He moved quickly to the door and put his ear to it.

After a moment or two someone tapped gently on one of the panels. The beads of sweat stood out on his forehead as Morrison licked his lips before speaking.

'Who is it? Who's there?' he whispered hoarsely.

'You are expecting someone I believe,' answered a man in a muffled voice.

Morrison hesitated and then he said in a slightly louder voice, 'It's open.' Cautiously he began to back away from the door and into the false security of the shadows deeper in the warehouse.

Very slowly the door swung open and the caller stood silhouetted in the doorway. Morrison retreated even further down the length of the building as the man stepped inside and shut the door behind him.

For a moment he was almost invisible but then, as he walked forward and came level with a thin shaft of light strained to a glimmer by the encrusted panes of the window, his face could be seen dimly. Morrison gave a low, long drawn out gasp.

The man was Martin Preece.

'Hello, Eric,' he said with a cruel smile. 'Gone into business on your own I hear.'

Shocked and afraid, Morrison pressed back against the wall. 'How did you . . . ?' he stammered. But before he could say more Preece cut in on him.

'A little bird told me. A rather lovely one as a matter of fact.'

Morrison tried to pull himself together. 'I don't know what you're talking about,' he said.

'Oh come on now,' chided Preece. 'I've *seen* the necklace. And what about the two other little trinkets that are missing?'

Morrison opened his mouth and tried to speak but no sound came. Preece shook his head in mock sadness. 'You couldn't wait, could you? You and Barry.'

Fear spurred Morrison to switch to the offensive. 'Wait! Look, there were seven of us when we found that place. Ted Willet, Jack Ransome, Dusty Miller, Alexis Eliades, Barry, me and you. We'll all keep our mouths shut, you said. It'll take time, but stay *stum* and I'll find a buyer and we'll all make a fortune, you said. So we did. And then what do you know? Twelve months later four of 'em are dead. Ted, Jack and Dusty all had "accidents" and Eliades conveniently ups and kills himself. Well, Barry and me, we thought that was just too much of a bloody coincidence.'

Preece smiled and nodded. 'You caught on. Ten little nigger boys and all that.' He sighed. 'Still, it was bound to happen sooner or later I suppose. So you decided to help yourselves. Pity about that. From my point of view. Still, my own fault. I really should have taken care of both of you sooner, shouldn't I?'

Slowly he reached inside his jacket and pulled a Luger automatic fitted with a silencer from the waistband of his trousers.

At the sight of the gun and face to face with death,

Morrison, almost vomiting with fear, stretched out his arms as if to ward off a blow.

'No, don't! Please don't!' he pleaded, feeling his bowels loosening. 'It was Barry's idea. He sold the sapphires.'

'Who to?' Preece asked curtly.

'I don't know,' said Morrison abjectly. 'All he told me was that he was on to the buyer you'd got lined up.'

'Was he? Clever!' Preece said admiringly as he raised the automatic slightly. 'I underestimated him.'

Trembling violently, Morrison tried to appease his executioner.

'He set up the deal. It was him who picked up the cash. I never got more than a smell of it.' He raised a shaking hand as though taking an oath. 'So help me, God! And I didn't get anything for the necklace. You know that's the truth. But look!' he urged. 'There's the fifty thousand Barry pulled in for the jewels. It's yours,' he bargained. 'All yours.'

'Where is it?' demanded Preece.

Morrison was not going to hold anything back now. 'David Collier's got it. He tried to pull a fast one on me. But it didn't work. I found it in Barry's apartment. In a briefcase.'

Preece frowned and Morrison, in a desperate attempt to make him believe his story, gabbled on, the words tumbling from him in a scarcely coherent torrent.

'I had my hands on it. Only Collier came in and we had a bit of a bundle and I couldn't get clear with it. It's probably still there. Or he's hidden it away somewhere. I'll help you find it,' he wheedled. 'And I won't say a word to anyone. About anything. And the money, well you can have it all. Every penny of it.'

Preece nodded thoughtfully. 'Why not?' he said, and then he smiled malevolently. 'Fifty thousand's fifty thousand. And you won't be needing it, will you?'

He took careful aim and squeezed the trigger of the Luger.

The automatic thunked twice and Morrison was slammed back against the wall by the impact of the bullets. With two neat holes punched in his chest and with his back blown out, his mouth open and his eyes already beginning to glaze over, he slowly slid down the wall leaving a thick red smear on the faded whitewash.

For a moment Preece stood listening, his ears straining to catch any sound outside the warehouse. But he heard nothing to disturb him.

Slipping the Luger back into his waistband, he strode over to Morrison, stared down at him thoughtfully for a moment and then, squatting beside him, began to go through his pockets.

Quietly and expertly Charalambos manipulated the lock of Barry Collier's apartment and slipped inside. Softly he closed the door behind him and stood in the darkened sitting room, gazing around.

He looked down at the key in his hand as if to remind himself of its size. It was about two inches long with a plastic tag attached to it on which were printed a number and the words 'Larnaca International Airport'.

Charalambos looked up from the key and around the room once more. Then he made up his mind.

He crossed to the bookshelf, removed three books and carefully slid the key to the back of the shelf. Then he replaced the books neatly and stepped back, smiling contentedly.

After another quick look around the room, he crossed swiftly back to the front door and let himself out as silently as he had entered.

'You giving her a lift?' asked Hellman with a nod towards Barbara Newcombe who had already made her farewells and was half way down the accommodation ladder.

Collier smiled. 'Seemed like a good idea,' he said.

The American gave him a knowing grin. 'You better believe it. She's taken to you for sure.' His grin broadened. 'So make the most of it, why not.' He put out his hand. 'Well, goodnight, David. Thanks for coming.'

'Thanks for inviting me. I've had a wonderful time.'

'I'm happy to hear that,' beamed the American. 'Like I said, you'd earned yourself a break. And I'll call you, right? Let you know the moment they come up with anything.' He indicated Travis and Olsen who were standing to one side.

'Thank you,' said Collier. 'Goodnight.' He nodded to the American's guardians. Unsmiling, the two men nodded in return as Collier started down the ladder.

Looking thoughtful, Hellman watched until the Englishman stepped into the tender and the motorboat began to pull away. He waved, and then, his smile fading, he turned to Travis and Olsen.

'I want Morrison here on this yacht tomorrow,' he commanded. 'Clear?' Then reflectively he looked up at the stars and added in an undertone. 'It's time we got this all wrapped up.'

Sitting in the stern of the tender, Barbara Newcombe snuggled up close to Collier.

'My place or yours?' he asked. The girl gave him a questioning, teasing look. 'For a nightcap,' he added with mock innocence.

Barbara laughed. 'Mine. It's nearer,' she said, squeezing his arm. Then a thought occurred to her and she pouted a little. 'Only thing is it's a small flat. And I share it. With another girl. An air hostess.' She brightened once more. 'But she's away right now. The flight she's on doesn't get into Larnaca until around three.'

Collier glanced at his wristwatch. 'That gives us plenty of time,' he reassured her.

The girl nodded happily. 'More than enough,' she whispered. 'And anyway, I have to be up early and I don't think I'd get any sleep at all if you stayed all night.'

Oh, you're so right, thought Collier, and he kissed her.

The Kitson Neve site was wrapped in darkness and deserted. Preece parked his Mercedes close to the narrow trench partly filled with rubble, got out and looked around. The gate had been no problem for Preece, he had a key. And he had counted on the nightwatchman, Filios, deserting his post and slipping down to the village for a few glasses of *zivenia* and a game or two of *tavli*. After all, he did exactly the same thing every other night around this time so why not tonight.

Preece moved to the back of the car and opened the boot. Morrison's body lay huddled inside, swathed in a large sheet of polythene.

My God, he's a weight, thought Preece as, with some difficulty and breathing heavily, he humped the body out of the car and dragged it across to the trench. Rolling the cocooned corpse into the rubble was easy enough.

Preece checked his watch. He had a good twenty minutes before the nightwatchman would stagger out of the *taverna* and begin to make his way back to the hut just inside the gate. And what had to be done now wouldn't take that long.

The engine of the bulldozer coughed into life on the first press of the ignition button. Preece lowered the scoop and drove the dozer forward and into the pile of rubble still to be tipped into the trench.

As Morrison stared up into the night with sightless eyes the stones and pieces of masonry cascaded down on to the polythene wrapped bundle. And then it was completely covered, buried beneath three feet of debris. And Preece knew that shortly after the men on the site reported for work that day the body would have another covering, the cement which was due to be poured into the trench as foundation for a wall.

As he clambered down from the bulldozer Preece smiled quietly to himself. Such a fitting burial place, he thought. Morrison wouldn't be working on the building any longer but he still had a contribution to make; he'd be helping to support it.

And he found the idea so amusing that, as he moved back to his car, he laughed out loud.

Less than an hour later, the Luger in his hand, he let himself into the Collier apartment in Paphos with the key which he had found on Morrison's body. He stood just inside the front door and peered into the darkness, listening. Then he moved quickly across to the partly open door of the bedroom and carefully edged his way round it, the automatic at the ready.

The bed was empty and undisturbed. There was no one at home. Collier's probably screwing the arse off that girl I introduced him to on the yacht, speculated Preece. And why not? I wouldn't have minded crumpling the sheets with her myself. Still, good luck to him. And lucky for me in a way that he managed to pull her. Makes things easier.

Methodically and carefully Preece began to search, first in the bedroom and then in the sitting room. He didn't find the briefcase he was looking for but he did find the key which Charalambos had hidden behind the books on the shelf by the fireplace.

Tossing it in his hand and gazing at it thoughtfully, Preece smiled. Of course! He wasn't going to leave it lying around with Morrison still on the prowl, was he, he reasoned. And a left luggage locker at the airport. What better place was there?

Well, David, he mused, I hope you're getting all you hoped for from Miss Newcombe. And then some. Because it's going to be one of the most expensive fucks in history.

And again he laughed.

CHAPTER TWENTY-SEVEN

Maria walked slowly and hesitantly into the police station and stared nervously around the bare and uninviting hallway. The desk sergeant looked up at her enquiringly.

'Yes. What do you want?'

'I want to speak to someone.'

As the desk sergeant leaned forward across the counter to her, Sergeant Karaolis came through the doors and began to make his way over to the stairs.

'Well,' said the desk sergeant expectantly.

'No. To Chief Inspector Mitsides. Is he here?'

At the mention of Mitsides' name Karaolis paused and looked at Maria with interest. Then he crossed slowly to the counter and gave a brief nod to the desk sergeant who responded in the same way before turning his attention back to Maria.

'Maybe. Maybe not,' he replied. 'But he is a very busy man. You have something to report?'

But Maria was not to be deflected. Stubbornly she stood her ground.

'I want to talk to the Chief Inspector.'

The girl's insistence intrigued Karaolis and he studied her closely. 'Why?' he asked.

Maria looked at him briefly and then turned back to the desk sergeant.

'I am worried about a friend of mine. I think something may have happened to him.'

The sergeant shook his head. 'You think?' he sighed as he reached for a report form. 'So tell me about it.'

Maria was obstinate. 'Chief Inspector Mitsides.'

Karaolis grinned and winked at the desk sergeant. 'Choosey, eh? Why him in particular?'

'Because he is the boss here, no?' Maria answered with simple logic. 'And because my friend mentioned his name to me.'

The detective had been amused by her determination but now he was interested and wanted to hear more.

'This friend of yours. Who is he?'

'He is an Englishman. His name is Morrison. Eric Morrison.'

The smile left Karaolis' face as the full import of what she had said struck him. 'I think you had better come with me,' he said.

Chief Inspector Mitsides smiled sympathetically at Maria. He had tried to put her at her ease while making a note of her name and address and listening to her rather vague story. Now he began to question her more closely.

'What do you mean, he's disappeared? He's run off and left you, is that it?'

Maria, who had been sitting fidgeting nervously with her handkerchief, bridled a little at this.

'No, he wouldn't do that.'

'Why not?'

'He loves me,' said Maria with conviction.

Mitsides and Karaolis exchanged doubtful looks. Then the Chief Inspector went on with his questioning.

'You haven't seen him since last night you say?'

'No.'

Mitsides shrugged dismissively. 'Well that's not long.'

'But he said he would be back. In three or four hours at the most.'

'Where did he say he was going?'

Maria hesitated and then she said evasively, 'To see someone. On business.'

'Where?'

'I don't know. He didn't tell me.'

'And this business. What was it about?'

Maria shifted uneasily in her chair. 'To do with his work I suppose.'

Mitsides got up from his chair and walked across to the window. His voice was friendly as he offered Maria the obvious explanation.

'So after he had finished his business he had a few drinks.'

'Maybe met a girl even,' Karaolis added quietly.

Maria shot him an angry look. The detective sergeant grinned.

'Anyway he went on the town and stayed out all night,' continued Mitsides. 'Nothing unusual in that. It happens all the time.'

'Men!' sighed Karaolis. 'You know what they're like.'

This time Maria ignored him. 'No, you don't understand.' She became slightly hysterical. 'He wouldn't stay out. Not last night anyway. He would have come straight back. Like he said he was going to.'

'What makes you so sure?' demanded the Chief Inspector.

For a long time Maria did not answer. Mitsides waited patiently, watching her as she rolled and unrolled the handkerchief in her hands. At last she looked up at him and blurted out.

'Because he was afraid.'

Mitsides frowned and glanced across at his sergeant.

'Afraid! Of what?'

Maria squirmed. 'Of being seen,' she almost whispered.

'But he went out. Last night,' exclaimed Mitsides.

'He had to. I told you. On business. It was important.' Maria spoke impatiently but almost at once she was anxious again. 'But he wouldn't have stayed away any longer than he had to. That's why I took him to the house of my cousin. So that he would be safe.'

'Safe from what?' asked Mitsides sharply.

Maria was on the brink of tears. How could she answer without implicating herself and Antonis? And if Morrison were alive and well he would be furious with her for going to the police. But then if something had happened to him she wanted revenge on whoever was responsible. She looked up at the Chief Inspector as a tear began to roll down her cheek.

'Someone has tried to kill him. Twice.'

Both Mitsides and Karaolis looked startled at this. The Chief Inspector moved back to his desk, sat down and leaned forwards across it.

'He told you this?' he demanded.

'Yes.'

'Who tried to kill him? And why?' The questions came quickly and sharply.

Maria shrugged helplessly. 'I don't know. And I don't think that Eric knows either.'

The detective studied her closely. 'Twice you say?'

Maria nodded. 'Yes,' she confirmed. 'Once when he was on his own and before that when he was with a man called David Collier.'

Mitsides sat back in his chair to absorb this last surprise. He frowned deeply.

Martin Preece was not at all surprised when he opened the luggage locker and found the briefcase in it. He was overjoyed though when, in the privacy of his Mercedes in the airport car park, he opened the case and found that the money was still in it. Neat bundles of Swiss francs.

And, enjoying such a promising start to the day, he hummed contentedly throughout most of the long drive back to the Kitson Neve site.

CHAPTER TWENTY-EIGHT

Collier's expression was hardly welcoming when he opened the front door and found Chief Inspector Mitsides standing on the step.

'Good afternoon, Mr Collier,' said Mitsides politely.

'Chief Inspector,' replied Collier unenthusiastically.

The detective walked in uninvited and Collier scowled at him. 'Yes. Now why didn't I think of that? Come in.'

'Thank you,' was the formal reply.

'Bit of a switch this. You coming to see me. Decided to deport me, have you?' demanded Collier surlily.

Mitsides came straight to the point. 'I am looking for Eric Morrison,' he said.

'Well! Well!' exclaimed Collier snidely. 'Welcome to the club.'

Mitsides started to wander about the room, his eyes taking in everything in it. Collier watched him.

'Why the sudden interest? When I wanted you to talk to him . . .'

The Chief Inspector cut him off. 'He has disappeared.'

'He's on leave. Don't you remember,' enquired Collier sarcastically.

Mitsides nodded. 'Up in the mountains. With his girl-friend,' he agreed. 'But yesterday evening he drove off somewhere and she hasn't seen him since. She is worried about him.'

'With good cause I'd say,' retorted Collier.

'Yes, perhaps.'

Collier made no attempt to hide his surprise as the Chief Inspector went on.

'She confirmed your story. About the shooting incident at Trimiklini. Morrison told her about it.'

Relief and delight chased one another across Collier's face. He moved eagerly towards Mitsides.

'Then you believe me! You finally believe me!'

The Chief Inspector regarded him levelly. 'About that. Yes,' he said quietly.

Collier's excitement turned instantly into dejection.

'But not about the money. The woman, Helene. Charalambos the barman. Basileos. That I was attacked. And Barry was murdered. You still don't believe in all that.'

Mitsides ignored his outburst and, to Collier's bewilderment, changed direction completely.

'Where were you last night, Mr Collier?'

'At a party.'

'Can you prove that?'

'Of course.' Collier was annoyed by the apparent irrelevance of the questions.

'What time did you leave?'

'I don't know. Around midnight.'

'And you came straight back here?'

'Yes,' snapped Collier. And then remembered and corrected himself. 'Well no, not straight back here. There was this girl. I . . .' He broke off and then went on angrily. 'Look, why the cross examination? I don't know where Morrison is any more than you do. I wish I did. I haven't seen him since . . .' Collier faltered and Mitsides prompted him.

'Since the day you had the fight with him?'

'How did you know about that?' challenged Collier.

'It was reported to me. By the police here in Paphos.'

Collier nodded resignedly. 'Of course,' he said sourly.

'What was the fight about?'

'Oh no, Chief Inspector!' Collier laughed bitterly. 'If you can't accept the other things I've told you there's no way you'd believe what that was all about.'

'Tell me,' suggested Mitsides, a hint of an order in his voice.

Collier plumped himself down in a chair. After all, why not? He had nothing to lose.

'All right. I came back here to the apartment and found Morrison with the briefcase. The one with the money in it. The one the mysterious woman I invented gave me. The one that was stolen from me in the attack I imagined. You know. That fairy story of mine. So, cue for laughter.'

The Chief Inspector looked at him with absolute seriousness. 'Go on,' he said quietly.

Collier was taken aback by Mitsides reaction. He frowned and studied the man intently but he could detect not even the trace of a smile.

'Look,' he said, 'what's the point?'

'I'm listening, aren't I?'

Collier sighed and then went on with his story.

'Well, Morrison claimed he found the briefcase in the bedroom.'

'And he didn't?' queried Mitsides.

'I suppose he must have,' admitted Collier grudgingly. 'But if he did I don't know who the hell put it there. It certainly wasn't me.'

'So?'

'So I tried to persuade him that the only thing to do was to take it to you. But he wouldn't go along with that. He shoved me out of the way and . . . well, the next thing is we're throwing punches at each other out in the street. Then the law moved in and broke it up.'

'And what happened to the briefcase?' asked the detective.

'Yes, well now we come to the bit you're not going to swallow. When the fight started it was lying there. On the floor. Open. But when I came back up here with one of your lot it had gone.'

'Morrison took it,' suggested the Chief Inspector.

'No. He pulled out empty-handed. I saw him go.'

'Then who did?'

Despair returned to Collier once more. 'I don't know.'

'So why didn't you tell me about this at the time?'

'You've got to be joking!' Collier exploded. 'After everything else that had happened! After you having as good as told me, less than an hour before, that I was crazy! Oh yes, sure! You'd have really gone for a story like that, wouldn't you?'

He jumped to his feet and faced Mitsides defiantly. 'You don't believe it now, do you? God knows what your reaction would've been then. My guess is that you'd have had me committed. You might do yet for all I know.'

Mitsides took no notice of his indignation. 'Do you mind if I look around?' he asked.

'I don't suppose I can stop you,' said Collier sulkily.

The Chief Inspector's tone was instantly icy and crushing. 'Oh yes, Mr Collier. Easily. Cyprus is not a police state. All you have to say is that you *do* mind.'

'And you'll get a search warrant.' Collier continued to sulk.

'Possibly,' conceded Mitsides. 'But that comes under the heading of legality. And your rights would still be fully protected. We believe in legality and justice. We learned about them from the British. Even though, sometimes, they forgot about them themselves.'

Collier accepted the rebuke. 'Go ahead.'

The Chief Inspector bowed his thanks and then walked through into the bedroom, closely followed by a curious Collier.

'What are you looking for anyway?'

Mitsides began to search through the wardrobe.

'Morrison and your brother were friends. There might be something here which could give me a lead as to his whereabouts.'

'I don't think so.'

'Then again I might find a briefcase.'

Collier frowned and then shook his head despairingly. 'I see. Well you're wasting your time. Tell me something, Chief Inspector. Why should I lie?'

Mitsides turned to him with a slight smile.

'*One thing is certain, that Life flies, One thing is certain, and the rest is lies,*' he quoted. Then he closed the door of the wardrobe and crossed to the door, catching Collier's puzzled look as he did so. 'Omar Khayyam. The Fitzgerald translation. As a philosophical proposition it is, hopefully, fallacious. But, nevertheless, it is one on which all police work is founded. Excuse me.'

He moved past Collier, walked through the living room

and into the kitchen. Again Collier followed him and watched him from the doorway.

As the detective checked the cupboards he began questioning Collier again.

'So you didn't see Morrison last night?'

'No. I've told you. Not since that day.'

'I ask that because we have found the pick-up truck he was driving.' He crossed back to the doorway and confronted Collier. 'It was here in Paphos. Parked in a street not more than three hundred yards from this apartment.'

Collier looked puzzled as he followed Mitsides back into the living room.

'What else did his girlfriend tell you?' he asked.

'Very little. Much less than she knows. I am certain of that. But about what . . .' He shrugged.

'Then make her talk,' said Collier angrily.

'What do you suggest, Mr Collier. A rubber truncheon?'

'No, of course not.'

Mitsides crossed to the desk and opened the top drawer. 'We will keep her under observation.'

He picked up Barry Collier's diary from the drawer and flipped through the pages. 'And the woman, Helene? Have you seen her again?'

'Yes.'

A flicker of interest crossed the Chief Inspector's face which went unnoticed by Collier. Then he replaced the diary in the drawer and picked up Barry's wallet and began to look through it.

'Where?'

'Here. Three nights ago.'

Mitsides had found the photograph of the hieroglyphics and he gazed at it with interest before continuing his questioning.

'At your invitation?'

Collier waxed sarcastic. 'Of course. I put an ad in the personal columns of the newspaper. Helene, longing to see you again, David.'

'What did she want?' He began a cursory examinination of the other drawers.

'You're interested in conversations with a phantom?' Collier mocked, and then, as the Chief Inspector opened his mouth to speak, checked him with a gesture.

'No. Don't tell me. You've got a quotation to cover that too. Okay. She wanted to go over the old, familiar ground. To explain why the Alfa Romeo wasn't where I left it when I took you back there. How it was that Charalambos was behind the bar of the Curium Palace that night and not the regular barman. And why the three of them ran off from the monastery the way they did.'

'And did she convince you?'

Collier qualified his affirmative nod. 'Well, more or less.'

'And what else did she say?'

'She insisted that Barry was murdered.'

'I see. And this time did she suggest any possible motive?'

'No.'

Mitsides started to move away from the desk but then paused as if worried about something. He turned back to the desk, opened the top drawer again and took out Barry Collier's wallet. He extracted the photograph of the hieroglyphics, crossed to Collier and showed it to him.

'What is this?'

'I've no idea. Some kind of carving,' replied Collier without interest.

'Your brother took this photograph?'

'I imagine so.'

'Where?'

'I haven't the foggiest.' Collier could not see why the Chief Inspector should be interested.

'May I have it?' Mitsides asked politely.

Collier frowned. 'Why? Do you think it's important?'

'I don't imagine so.' The Chief Inspector smiled disarmingly. 'Not for a moment. But I'm interested in such things. May I?'

Collier shrugged. 'Why not?'

'Thank you,' said Mitsides gratefully. He slipped the photograph into his pocket, handed the wallet to Collier and began to cross to the front door.

'You see,' said Collier. 'No briefcase.'

'No,' acknowledged the Chief Inspector as he opened the front door.

'Is that it then?' Collier sounded a little disappointed.

'Well for now, anyway. But until I give you the word you won't leave Cyprus, will you?'

Collier gave a wry laugh and shook his head in disbelief. 'The last time we met you couldn't wait to see the back of me.'

'I have changed my mind,' said Mitsides calmly.

'Really! There's hope yet then. You might even end up by believing me,' said Collier cynically.

The Chief Inspector studied him for a moment. 'Wolf! Wolf!' he said cryptically.

Collier looked nonplussed. 'I'm sorry, I don't understand.'

'The boy who cried wolf,' Mitsides explained. 'You cried wolf twice. But the third time you didn't.'

'What's the significance in that?' asked Collier, still at a loss.

'Either that you learned a lesson,' replied the Chief Inspector. 'Or I was wrong perhaps. And there are wolves about.'

Eugene Hellman, with a caddy in attendance, was teeing off as Travis and Olsen approached from the clubhouse.

Their employer ignored them and they waited patiently while he studied the fairway and practised his swing.

'Well?' he demanded at last and still without looking at them.

'They've been there for a couple of days,' confirmed Travis. 'Morrison and the girl.'

'And now?'

Olsen shook his head. 'No one. Just a kid pumping gas.'

Travis took up the report again. 'He says Morrison wasn't there when he turned up for work this morning.'

Carefully Hellman addressed the ball.

'And the girl took the first bus into Limassol,' said Olsen. 'She told him she was going to the police.'

There was the slightest pause in Hellman's swing but then

he drove off with a powerful stroke and watched the flight of the ball carefully.

'Look at that,' he exclaimed quietly, pleased with himself. 'Right down the middle.'

He handed his driver to the caddy and, for the first time, looked at the two men. 'And you know the secret? Always keep your eye on the ball.' He paused and studied them closely. 'And watch out for the way the wind's blowing.'

CHAPTER TWENTY-NINE

The fisherman hauled on the mooring line and slowly drew his boat into the quayside while Preece waited to board, tapping his foot impatiently and nervously biting his lower lip.

The visit of Chief Inspector Mitsides to the site that afternoon had worried him. The detective had been polite, overly polite even, but he had insisted on going over, in detail, the story which Preece had told about having seen and spoken to Eric Morrison on the afternoon of the alleged shooting incident at Trimiklini; an invention which had been necessary both to discredit David Collier's story and, if that failed, to divert any suspicion away from the fact that it was he who had tried to kill the two men that day.

Preece had been easy enough in his mind about that because, with Morrison dead and buried, there was no one now to prove him a liar. All he had to do was to stick to his story, but as Mitsides, apparently satisfied, was about to return to his car, he had dropped the bombshell which had really disturbed Preece.

'May I ask, Chief Inspector,' Preece had enquired. 'This double checking of yours? Has there been some kind of new development?'

The detective had nodded. 'Yes,' he had replied gravely. 'Previously my interest in Morrison was merely academic. But this morning his girlfriend, who it appears had been hiding him in the mountains for some reason or other, reported him as missing. And that is now the subject of an official enquiry.'

And as he had watched Mitsides drive away Preece had begun to sweat. Just how much had Morrison told this woman of his? And then again how forthcoming had she been when she reported his disappearance? Obviously nothing she had said had implicated him in any way, or the Chief Inspector would surely have taken him in for questioning then and there. But it was on the cards that she had perhaps deliberately withheld much which she had learned from her lover either to launch herself into a new career as a blackmailer or else to cut herself in on the deal for what would have been his share. Was she just biding her time?

These and other questions had tormented Preece ever since Mitsides had called on him but the only firm conclusion he had come to was that with the police now digging into Morrison's disappearance and with this unknown woman as a further possible threat in the background he was clearly at risk. And he'd also realised that if he were to make the kind of money he was after then he could no longer hide in the shadows. The time had come to make his play.

The fisherman held the boat in against the quay and Preece stepped down into it.

Eugene Hellman, stereo headphones muffing his ears, was sitting in one of the armchairs in his stateroom lost in the beauty of Mozart's Flute Concerto in D Minor when Travis entered and stood mouthing at him in the open doorway.

Hellman sighed and removed the headphones. 'What is it?' he enquired testily.

'Sorry to disturb you, Mr Hellman, but there's someone come on board who insists on seeing you.'

Hellman frowned. 'Oh! Who?'

Before Travis could reply he was brushed aside by Martin Preece as, shaking himself free from the grip which Olsen had on his arm, he stepped into the room. Preece was carrying a briefcase in one hand and a brown manilla envelope in the other and Hellman took note of the smug, self-confident expression on his visitor's face.

'Preece. Martin Preece,' he announced. 'You remember me. I was at your party. Good evening, Mr Hellman.'

Hellman looked surprised but he smiled pleasantly. 'Of course I remember you, Mr Preece.' He switched off the cassette player, laid the headphones down beside it and stood up. 'What can I do for you?'

Preece advanced further into the room. 'Spare me a little of your time.'

'Of course.'

Preece shot a meaningful look at Travis and Olsen. 'In private?'

A wary expression came into Hellman's eyes and he hesitated. But then he nodded. 'Very well.' With a wave he dismissed the two men standing just inside the doorway. 'It's okay.'

As they turned to leave Preece glanced across at Travis and grinned. 'Cashed in that lottery ticket yet, have you?' he jeered.

And Travis was still gazing back at the Englishman through narrowed, threatening eyes when Olsen closed the door behind them.

'So Mr Preece, how can I . . . ?' began Hellman.

Rudely Preece interrupted him. 'Thank you. I'll have a large scotch and very little soda.'

He put the briefcase and the envelope down on the desk and then crossed to the drinks table. Hellman frowned. He did not like the man's manner nor his tone of voice. 'Help yourself,' he said stiffly.

'Thanks. Something for you?'

Hellman restrained himself. 'No. Not right now,' he replied quietly.

The Englishman poured himself a treble whisky and then turned and raised his glass mockingly. 'Cheers.' He took a sip from the glass and relished it. 'Good scotch, this.'

'Thank you. You're a connoisseur of course,' Hellman's sarcasm was wasted on Preece who merely smiled and nodded.

'Like yourself.' He pulled a wry face. 'But sadly I have champagne tastes on beer money. You know how it is.' He looked around the stateroom and smiled again. 'But that was a stupid thing to say, wasn't it?' He gestured to the luxurious fixtures and furniture. 'Because you don't, do you?'

Hellman studied him closely. 'I get the feeling that this is not a social call,' he said coldly.

'Business.' Preece again raised his glass. 'And pleasure. We have to have a chat, you and I.'

'About what?'

'Oh, this and that.'

Slowly Hellman crossed to his desk. Quite apart from his insolent bad manners there was an edge of hysteria to his visitor's bonhomie and banter which disquieted him and which he found strangely menacing. This was not a meeting which he was anxious to prolong. Casually he put out a hand to the bell push on the desk.

Preece read his mind and suddenly he was no longer smiling. Or acting. The tone he adopted was now business-like and domineering. 'Like antiquities,' he said darkly. 'Around ten million dollars' worth.'

Hellman hesitated, his finger on the button. Then he turned and, frowning, fixed Preece with a stare.

'You're wasting your time looking for Morrison, you know,' Preece continued. 'You won't find him. No one will. Ever. And it was never Morrison you had to deal with anyway. Or Barry Collier. It's me.' He crossed to the desk and picked up the envelope. 'I'm the one who wrote to you.'

'You wrote to me?' said Hellman with an air of innocence.

'No more games, Hellman,' snapped Preece. 'No more hide and seek. It's time we talked money.'

The American hedged. 'I receive so many letters.'

'This one wasn't signed. Remember?' Preece put down his glass and opened the envelope. 'And along with it you got a set of photographs. Like these.'

He tipped a dozen or so enlarged colour prints on to the desk. The photographs were all of ancient artefacts worked in gold, silver and precious stones, fabulous in their beauty.

Hellman gathered up the prints and studied them closely. Then he unlocked one of the desk drawers and brought out from it another set of pictures and compared them. They matched perfectly.

'Satisfied?' asked Preece.

Hellman looked up at him and nodded. 'Tell me,' he asked. 'Just as a matter of interest. How did you find all this?'

'We were doing a seismic survey. Using small explosive

charges. One of them caused a rock fall. And when the dust cleared, bingo. There was the way in.'

'And Collier and Morrison?'

'Just happened to be there. Worker ants. Nothing more. You didn't really think that either of them had enough imagination or brains to set up this kind of operation, did you?' He scowled. 'They were just greedy little men. In a hurry. And easily satisfied. But now you're dealing with me. Direct.'

He set the briefcase flat on the desk, opened it and then swiveled it round so that Hellman could see the money in it.

'And as far as I am concerned this money you gave Barry Collier is just a deposit. A down payment. You're going to have to come up with a hell of a lot more if you and I are going to do business. I'm not even going to start listening until you're into seven figures.'

Hellman gave him a look of genuine surprise. 'I'm sorry, but I don't understand,' he said. 'You are clearly suffering under a misapprehension, Mr Preece. I never paid Barry Collier a cent. For anything.'

Preece was taken aback at first but his expression quickly turned to one of suspicion.

'It's the truth,' Hellman assured him. He picked up one of the photographs which showed a symbolic death mask of the goddess Aphrodite. Set into the eye sockets were two perfectly matched light blue sapphires. He held the photograph out to Preece.

'When Collier approached me he had one of those sapphires with him. He asked me if I would be interested in purchasing it. Along with its twin. I told him that I would and he said that he would return with the two stones the next night. But, sadly, the following day he met with an unfortunate . . .' He paused briefly to make his point. '. . . accident? I never saw him again.' He pointed to the briefcase. 'So you see, that money isn't mine.'

'But Morrison told me . . .' Preece protested. The American cut him short.

'Maybe. But I assure you. He was mistaken.'

All the cocky self-confidence fell away from Preece as he

tried to come to terms with this totally unexpected turn of events. His expression was one of complete bewilderment.

'Then where did Collier get it from?' he asked floundering.

'It's obvious, isn't it?' said Hellman blandly. 'Another buyer.'

'Another buyer!' Preece exclaimed, shocked. 'Who?'

Hellman shrugged. 'I've no idea.'

Preece thought hard and then he exclaimed, 'The woman!'

Now it was Hellman's turn to be puzzled. 'What woman?'

'The one who was at your little get together last night. Wearing the necklace. Or is she part of your set-up?'

The American looked at Preece blankly. 'I don't know what you're talking about. What necklace?'

'The necklace that was lifted along with the sapphires,' snapped Preece, picking up the photograph from the desk and showing it to Hellman. 'That necklace.'

Puzzled and confused, Hellman studied the picture. 'A woman wearing this was here last night?' he said quietly.

Preece scowled again. 'Yes. It was her who pointed me in the direction of Morrison.'

'What's her name?' demanded Hellman.

'We didn't introduce ourselves. It was only a brief meeting. But informative,' muttered Preece. He searched Hellman's face intently. 'Are you saying that she's not tied in with you?'

'In no way. I told you. I bought nothing from Collier, or Morrison.'

Preece nodded thoughtfully. 'Well then she has to be the competition. Or part of it at least.' He shot another look at the American. 'And you had no idea she was on board?'

'None.'

'But she must have been invited.'

'Not necessarily. But even if she was,' Hellman shrugged. 'With so many people. And if you don't know her name.' Looking thoughtful, he crossed to the drinks table and poured himself a scotch on the rocks. He glanced at Preece. 'What was she like?'

'Beautiful.'

The American shook his head and sighed. 'That description could fit several of the women who were here. Depending on your taste.'

'No. I mean really beautiful. Outstanding.' Preece was emphatic. 'A collector's item.'

Hellman sipped his drink and then gave a wry smile. 'I'm sorry I missed her,' he murmured.

Preece, whose mind had been racing, moved in quickly towards him. 'Collier,' he snarled. 'The brother.'

'What about him?'

'Well, he went to the police with some cock and bull story about a beautiful woman he met in the bar of the Curium Palace Hotel.'

The American showed no surprise. 'Yes. Helene.'

Preece frowned. 'You know about that?'

'Yes.'

'How?' demanded Preece warily.

'David Collier told me when he came to see me,' said Hellman. Then, seeing that Preece still didn't understand, he added, 'To ask for my help. In finding Morrison.'

'And you agreed?' asked Preece suspiciously.

'Naturally. In my own interest. Because from what Collier said it seemed that Morrison was the man I had to deal with.'

'Well you were wrong, weren't you?' sneered Preece. 'But don't you see,' he went on, warming to his theory. 'Maybe Collier wasn't having the police on. Not entirely anyway. Maybe it wasn't all fantasy and the bit about the woman was true. And maybe this Helene of his and the woman I spoke to last night are one and the same person. He might even have brought her to the party.'

'No. He came alone.'

'All right,' said Preece. 'But it's still a possibility, isn't it?'

Hellman crossed back to his desk and stared down at the money in the briefcase. He nodded. 'A possibility. Anyway this woman, whoever she is, she bought the sapphires from Barry Collier. Is that what you're suggesting?'

Preece nodded. 'She had the necklace so it's obvious, isn't it?'

The American picked up one of the bundles of notes and riffled it. 'If she did she cheated him,' he said.

Preece laughed scathingly. 'And you wouldn't have done?'

Hellman swung round on him. 'No, Mr Preece. I wouldn't have,' he replied icily. 'My offer would have been a fair one. As always.' He tossed the bundle of notes back into the briefcase and then moved round behind the desk and sat down. 'And the necklace. She got that from Morrison?'

Preece nodded again. 'For free. An even bigger cheat.'

The American studied him and sipped his drink. 'She seems like a great person to do business with,' he said quietly. 'A dangerous one too.'

'Dangerous?' Preece frowned, unable to follow Hellman's reasoning.

Hellman shrugged. 'Well you said it yourself. She pointed you at Morrison.'

'Locked me right on to him.'

'Why?' enquired Hellman blandly.

The question thoroughly confused Preece. He had been so eager to settle with Morrison that he had never once questioned the woman's motives. The American watched Preece closely as his face showed first bewilderment and then growing fear and near panic. Hellman pressed home the point.

'You never asked yourself that? What did she have to gain? There's only one answer, isn't there? As far as she was concerned Morrison had outlived his usefulness. And if she was finished with him it had to be because he had already told her everything she needed to know. Maybe even drawn a map for her. Pinpointed the location.'

Preece's face took on an ugly, frightening expression. He slammed his glass down on the desk and started for the door.

'Yes, good idea,' encouraged Hellman. 'You check, Mr Preece. Because you never know. The cupboard might be bare.'

In the doorway Preece rounded on Hellman. 'If you're thinking of putting your two heavies on my tail, forget it,' he warned. 'For their sakes and yours. You'd have to pay the funeral expenses.'

The American ignored the threat. 'Even if someone hasn't got there ahead of you,' he goaded. 'The lady. Helene or whoever. She's still a threat.'

'We can take care of her,' said Preece confidently.

Hellman stood up and shook his head. 'Oh no, Mr Preece. This is your problem. For you to solve the way you see fit. I am not an executioner. I have a different function.' He smiled quietly at a private joke. 'I am merely a receiver. Admittedly I have a somewhat unsavoury reputation. But I don't kill. It's an unbreakable rule.'

'I see,' said Preece contemptuously. 'But dealing with killers. I don't imagine you have any scruples about that.'

'None at all,' Hellman assured him and still smiling. 'I do it all the time.'

Preece nodded. 'Okay. So I'll handle it alone. I've gone solo this far. Just be ready to pay out when the time comes.'

'I will be,' said the American quietly. 'To whoever delivers the goods.'

Preece scowled and turned to leave but Hellman checked him. 'Haven't you forgotten something?'

Angrily the Englishman swung round to face him again and Hellman indicated the briefcase on his desk. 'Your bonus, David Collier's pension.'

Grimacing, Preece strode angrily over to the desk, grabbed up the briefcase and turned on his heel again. Quickly he moved back to the door, opened it and stepped out on to the deck.

Hellman watched him go and his expression was one of distaste.

CHAPTER THIRTY

Chief Inspector Mitsides sat at his desk, an empty coffee cup in front of him, and stared at the photograph of the hieroglyphics. What did they mean? Where were they from? In his time he judged that he must have visited just about every archaeological site on the island but he could not recall having seen this particular inscription anywhere. And not in any of the museums either.

And it wasn't as if the inscription wasn't eye-catching, something that would pass unnoticed. The characters, for instance, were unique and bore little resemblance to any form of Greek script. Minoan perhaps, he thought, but then dismissed the idea for these were letters more than symbols and there was something about them which, although unintelligible, in a strange way said something to him. This writing, even if it hadn't originated in Cyprus, was somehow closely associated with the island. He felt it; he knew it. And then he remembered the tablets written in an unknown language which had been found on the island and had been dated as originating somewhere between 1000 and 800 BC. And yet if this carving was plainly on public view anywhere why hadn't he seen it? Of course it could be in some private museum, he supposed, but there weren't that many and he'd been in most of them too. And from what he knew of Barry Collier he didn't seem to have been the kind of man to have spent much time in a museum of any kind. So why had he taken a photograph of it in the first place? A passing curiosity, an interest maybe? A wasted frame of film to test his camera? Yes, those were both possibilities but where had he seen it? And, having taken a picture of it, why had he kept it in his wallet along with snapshots of naked girlfriends. It didn't make sense and it didn't fit in with Barry Collier's character. Unless?

Mitsides turned the photograph this way and that, examining it from every angle but he could find nothing in the inscription whichever way he looked at it which could even vaguely be taken as sexually suggestive. And yet the man had kept it in his wallet. Why? And where had the picture been taken?

The Chief Inspector frowned. He was undoubtedly wasting his time even bothering to pose such questions, but there was something about the inscription which had nagged at him from the first moment he had seen the snapshot. He sighed. I'm getting old, he thought, and giving way to fancies. And fancies I can't even put my finger on at that. But still he could not dismiss from his mind the impression that in some way the hieroglyphics were important and that, even as he studied the carving, it was saying something to him. But what?

Frowning, he slipped the photograph into his pocket and stood up. As he opened the door of the office Detective Sergeant Karaolis was about to enter.

Karaolis pulled up sharply and looked at his chief, surprised. What's the old man doing coming in this early, he thought, and he frowned. Something must be up.

He smiled. '*Kalimera.*'

'*Kalimera,*' replied Mitsides absently and with a nod.

'Have you been in long?'

'An hour or so.' The Chief Inspector sounded vague, as if his mind were elsewhere.

Karaolis gave him a quizzical look. 'There is something troubling you?' he asked.

'Probably nothing. But just the same.' Mitsides shrugged. 'I'm going to Nicosia. I'll see you later.' And with that he moved quickly out of the office and down the corridor.

'Damn! Why don't they answer?' Collier slammed down the telephone and glanced at his watch. Someone should be there by now, he thought.

He had rung the number twice before but had got no reply. 'So what does one do on Cyprus when the electricity's on the blink and the people who should fix it don't answer the telephone?' he despaired out loud.

Hopefully he crossed to the light switch and tried it again.

Nothing. A blown fuse. That had been his immediate thought when he had gone into the kitchen first thing to make some coffee for his breakfast, only to find that the electric kettle wouldn't work. And it had been the same with the toaster, the lights, the radio, everything. And he'd searched but he couldn't find a fuse box anywhere.

He looked at his watch again. Dear God, what time do electricians start work in this country anyway? Where are they all? And then as he reached irritably for the telephone again, his question was answered by distant music and the sound of excited chatter of voices in the street outside.

Quickly he crossed to the front door and opened it.

People were spilling out from the houses and apartments opposite and on either side, men, women and children all in their Sunday best, some in traditional costume and all moving in the direction of the music being played, slightly discordantly, by a brass band.

A woman who he recognised as the one who had greeted him on the day that he first came to the house looked up and saw him standing at the top of the steps. She smiled and waved.

He called out to her. 'What is it? What's happening?'

She pulled a face and then laughed. 'What is happening!' she shouted back. 'It is carnival. That is what is happening. It is a holiday.'

And then she was drawn into the throng and swept away down the street. And standing there, looking down on the crowd, Collier was immediately caught up in the carnival atmosphere.

Well, there'll be no electricians on call today, he thought ruefully. Then, infected by the gaiety of the scene, he shrugged and smiled. 'Well, if you can't beat the system,' he muttered. And, turning back into the house, he crossed to one of the cupboards and took from it a black, leather camera holdall which was part of his brother's legacy to him.

Barry had been a very keen photographer and he had earned the kind of money to indulge his hobby. There were two expensive cameras in the holdall, a Mamiya and an

Olympus OM2, as well as several lenses, an electronic flash and various other attachments.

No stranger to cameras himself, David dismissed the Mamiya as too bulky for what he had in mind and took out the Olympus, checked that there was film in it and then removed the standard lens and replaced it with a zoom. Slipping a couple of spare rolls of film into his pocket, he put the holdall back into the cupboard and made for the front door again.

Paphos was *en fete*; the streets and squares decorated with bunting and packed with townspeople and outsiders from the villages on the coast and deep in the interior, all attracted by the delights of the carnival and all intent on having a good time.

Collier wandered among the stalls selling all kinds of local produce and assorted foods and sweetmeats, pausing at some of the numerous booths distributing free wine and stopping to watch the many kinds of entertainers entrancing the crowd. Martin Preece, who had seen him leave the house, followed him, taking considerable pains to keep out of sight.

The band, having marched round the town, now took up a position in the square outside the Post Office. Here the carnival was at its most picturesque and Collier was delighted both with the scope which the scene presented for photography and with the silken smoothness and ease of handling of the Olympus. Eating an orange presented to him by one of the pretty girls who were distributing them among the crowd, Collier found, somewhat to his surprise, that he was enjoying himself.

He wandered away from the Post Office, down a narrow street and into another, only slightly smaller square. Preece was not far behind him.

The square was alive with activity and excitement. A pig was being roasted on a spit, large audiences were gathered around a group of folk singers and dancers and a troupe of actors who were playing out the traditional Cypriot festival theatrics known as *chattismata* to the laughter and applause of the spectators. Among the dozens of street vendors one man, decked out with whirling, multi coloured, stick windmills and other novelties and clutching the strings of a mass of balloons which floated and bobbed above his head, was doing a roaring trade.

Taking up a vantage point on some steps, Collier raised the Olympus and aimed at the man and his young and eager customers. And then, as he was focussing the zoom lens, a figure stepped in between him and his subject. It was a man who, out of focus, was unrecognisable, but he was clearly looking toward Collier. Instead of drifting through the viewfinder along with the other passersby he stood his ground and made no effort to move out of the way.

Frowning, Collier zoomed in on the intruder and reacted with a start. It was Charalambos. The man was smiling and regarding him with unabashed interest.

Collier lowered the camera and, moving off the steps, edged his way through the crowd to where Charalambos waited to greet him.

Martin Preece watched as the two men came face to face.

'Well! Well!' said Collier. 'If it isn't Charalambos, the helpful barman.'

Charalambos' smile widened. 'You are surprised to see me, Mr Collier?'

Collier nodded. 'Yes, you could say that. But then you've been a constant surprise to me since our first meeting.' This seemed to please the man even more. 'Not working at the Curium Palace today?' jibed Collier.

Charalambos' smile faded and he assumed a pained expression. 'But Helene told me that she had explained . . .' he began in a hurt tone.

'Yes, she did,' interrupted Collier. 'She explained some things. More or less. But if you were to come with me now and talk to Chief Inspector Mitsides . . .'

'But I cannot,' replied Charalambos with a helpless shrug. 'You know that.'

'Yes. But I don't know why.'

The man gave him a reproachful look. 'No questions. Not today.' Then he smiled again and put a hand on Collier's arm. 'Today it is festival,' he reminded him.

'Maybe so. But just the same . . .'

Charalambos shook his head and raised a hand to silence him. 'No. Soon,' he said. 'I promise you. Soon all your questions will be answered. But today we enjoy ourselves, eh?' He made a movement as if to guide the Englishman further into the crowd but Collier did not budge. 'Come, come,' pleaded his new-found companion. He gestured to the people around him. 'See! You are in good company. People with troubles. All kinds of trouble. But now they celebrate. As you must also.' His eyes bored into Collier's. 'While you can.' Once more he gently urged the Englishman further into the crowd. And this time Collier, even if a little grudgingly, went with him.

'And what exactly are we celebrating?' he asked, as they made their way across the square.

Charalambos grinned broadly. 'Life, my friend. Life.' He led Collier through the happy throng and over towards one of the wine stalls.

Collier searched among the crowd around them looking hopefully for another familiar face. 'Are you alone?' he asked.

Charalambos laughed. 'On this day, here in Paphos, no one is alone.'

'No, what I meant is . . . Well, did you come to the festival with anyone?'

Charalambos shot a wicked, mischievous look at him. 'Who did you have in mind?' he asked.

Collier shrugged. 'Basileos perhaps,' he lied.

'Helene for instance,' countered Charalambos with a grin, reading his mind.

They broke out of the crowd milling around in the centre of the square and approached the wine stall and there, flanked by two very attractive and clearly devoted girls and grasping a jug of wine in both hands, was Basileos himself.

He was wearing exactly the same clothes as he had been when Collier had first met him and the hilt of the hunting knife still protruded from the top of one of his boots. But on festival days he clearly left his rifle and ammunition at home. Wherever that may be, thought Collier.

Basileos drained the jug of its contents without once

taking it from his lips. Tossing it into the hands of a passing and bewildered reveller, he turned with a smile to face the two men. And he showed no surprise whatever at seeing the Englishman.

Putting an arm around each of the girls, he advanced on them.

'Greetings, Englishman!' Basileos boomed expansively and warmly.

Collier regarded him warily. 'So what do you know?' he sighed. 'Another friend. If that's the right word. Basileos the philosopher. And poacher too from what I've been told.'

Basileos roared with laughter. He tightened his affectionate grip on the two girls, glanced at each of them in turn and then looked at Collier again. 'My children,' he announced. 'This is a man who did not drink. Until he met me. But who has always liked women.' He winked. 'And enjoyed them. Eh, Englishman?'

Charalambos, who had stood watching the reunion with a faint smile on his lips, now moved towards the wine stall.

'This must be a very special occasion for you,' said Collier drily, his eyes still on Basileos. 'All this wine around. And for free.' He glanced meaningfully at the girls and then added, 'And you are obviously planning on lighting some more small flames in the darkness.'

'You remember!' Basileos roared, delighted.

'I remember.'

The bearded man let out another great bellow of laughter. 'Good. You are learning, Englishman. You are learning.'

'Perhaps. But not enough. So will you add to my knowledge and tell me some things I need to know?' said Collier.

Basileos stopped smiling and regarded Collier solemnly. 'I will tell you only this,' he replied quietly. 'Take what pleasure and what happiness you can find. And wherever you find them. Time is your one true enemy, friend. Time.' Then he smiled broadly once more and raised his voice which took a jocular tone again. 'So do not waste it.' He hugged his two companions to him. 'Come my little ones. Before all the barrels run dry.'

Then, with his arms still around the girls, he moved off and as he did so he began to sing the same song with which he had entertained Collier on their long climb up into the mountains. The trio were quickly swallowed up by the crowd.

Frowning slightly, Collier reached into his pocket and took from it the folded handkerchief which he had found in the armchair after Helene's night time visit to him. He gazed at it thoughtfully and he was still gazing at it when Charalambos returned from the stall carrying two glasses of wine.

Quickly Collier put the handkerchief back into his pocket but Charalambos had seen it and he smiled quietly to himself. He handed one of the glasses to Collier. '*Yassas,*' he said, raising his drink.

Collier lifted his glass in acknowledgement and they drank.

'Helene. She interests you?' enquired Charalambos, his eyes on the Englishman.

Collier was discomforted both by Charalambos' gaze and by his question. He looked away from him. 'She's a very attractive woman,' he said dismissively.

Charalambos nodded. 'Yes, isn't she?'

Collier took another sip from his glass and then looked back at Charalambos again. 'How well did she know my brother?' he enquired casually.

'Very well. Even the secrets of his heart,' replied Charalambos and, seeing the expression which came on to Collier's face, he asked, 'That bothers you?'

'No. Why should it?' snapped Collier, embarrassed. He drained his glass in one swallow and then, lowered it, gazed out into the crowd and as he did so he saw her.

She was standing in the centre of the square and, like a river breaking round a rock, the crowd flowed and eddied around her, isolating her in an island of emptiness.

She was looking even more beautiful than usual. There was a very special air about her. She was dressed simply but elegantly. The wind was moving her hair slightly and she was looking across at Collier and smiling.

Fascinated, Collier held her gaze, both startled and pleased but, at the same time, hesitant.

Charalambos did not even glance in her direction. It was as if he had been aware of her presence all the time. He studied the Englishman's face, then smiled and reached across and took his glass from him.

'Perhaps she knows other secrets too,' he said quietly. Collier shot a look at him. 'Go to her,' he urged. 'This is your day. And hers. Share it. Because tomorrow . . .' He shrugged. 'Well, who can tell?'

Still Collier hesitated. He looked across at Helene again. She had not moved and she was clearly waiting for him.

Collier glanced back at Charalambos who nodded. Slowly the Englishman stepped away from him and into the square.

Martin Preece, standing out of sight, followed his progress with his eyes and as he drew level with Helene, Preece recognised her and smiled. His patience had been rewarded. As he had hoped, Collier had led him to his next victim.

Still smiling gently, Helene looked up into Collier's face. 'Hello,' she said simply.

'If I turn round and then look back again, will you still be here?' asked Collier, his eyes on hers.

Helene nodded.

Collier put it to the test. When he turned round once more she was still there. He smiled. 'Well that's an improvement. And if you don't run out on me again, when the day is over and we say goodbye, what then?'

'You may have learned something,' said Helene.

Collier opened his mouth to speak again but she reached out and laid a finger on his lips and added, 'But only if you don't ask any questions.'

Collier shrugged resignedly and nodded. Then, side by side, they started to walk across the square while those milling around them, as naturally as they had created it, began to refill the space which was made for their meeting.

Charalambos watched them go and then, slowly he shifted his gaze and he was instantly on target.

Martin Preece, unaware that he was being watched, was

edging his way through the promenading merrymakers in pursuit.

Charalambos nodded, smiled to himself and raised his glass in a mocking salute.

'Professor Stylianou can see you now, Chief Inspector,' said the woman. And she led him towards the office.

'Thank you,' said Mitsides.

He had spent the time he had been waiting wandering around the museum studying some of the exhibits, and he did not feel that it had been wasted for, in his philosophy, moments spent with beauty were to be treasured and not regretted.

Professor Stylianou, a white haired man in his middle to late sixties, stood up behind his desk as the Chief Inspector crossed the room. He put out a hand to the detective. 'Chief Inspector Mitsides,' he said with a warm, welcoming smile.

Mitsides shook hands with him. 'I'm sorry if I'm disturbing you, Professor.'

'Not at all,' Stylianou assured him, indicating a chair. 'Please sit down.' The policeman did so and Stylianou settled himself back down at the desk again. 'So what can I, an archaeologist, do for the police?' he asked.

Mitsides took the photograph of the hieroglyphics out of his pocket and handed it to him. 'Does this mean anything to you?' he enquired. 'And, if it does, where on Cyprus will I find it?'

Stylianou picked up his spectacles, put them on and studied the photograph. His face took on an expression first of disbelief and then of mounting excitement. He shot a look at Mitsides and then, opening a drawer, took out a magnifying glass and peered at the photograph once more, examining the hieroglyphics keenly and apparently making some sense of them. Then he lifted his head again and gazed in wonderment at the detective.

'Where indeed, Chief Inspector,' he breathed. 'I only wish I could tell you.'

CHAPTER THIRTY-ONE

Collier and Helene spent the rest of the day together enjoying the sights, sounds and smells around them and enjoying each other's company even more. They listened to the singers, watched the dancers, sampled more of the wines and bought sticks of *souvlakia* from one of the stalls and sat on the sea wall down by the harbour and nibbled at the small pieces of charcoal grilled lamb, laughing and juggling the hot meat on their tongues.

And Martin Preece was never more than twenty yards behind them.

It was then, as they stood up from the wall again, that Collier said, 'Do you realise, apart from your name, I know absolutely nothing about you. Not even where you live.'

Helene smiled. 'I was born here in Paphos,' she replied gaily. 'This is my island.' And then, taking him by the hand and like an excited child, she led him into the midst of the raucous funfair which had been set up on the quay and which was in full swing and reaping a rich harvest.

They rode the roundabouts, hung suspended for a while high above the harbour on the Big Wheel and duelled with one another on the Dodgems. And Collier tried to win a doll for Helene on the coconut shy but failed at each attempt.

Late in the afternoon they stood on a jetty and watched two local youths sitting astride parallel, greased wooden poles suspended above the sea and jousting with long bamboo lances tipped with mop heads.

They laughed and applauded as the loser of the bout was toppled from his perch and then they and the other people around them were splashed with sea water by the indignant small boys, loyal supporters of the vanquished contestant, who were crowded into the boats moored to the jetty below them.

Little of the water landed on Helene but Collier was well sprinkled with it. Smiling and unthinking, he reached into his pocket, pulled out her handkerchief and dabbed his face with it. Helene took the handkerchief from him to finish the job and immediately recognised it. She looked up into his eyes and for a moment they held one another's gaze. Then she smiled, looked away from him, refolded the handkerchief and slipped it back into his pocket.

'Come,' she said, putting her arm through his.

'Where are we going?' he asked.

'To another place. Another time.'

Karaolis had not dared to speak since Mitsides had returned from his visit to Nicosia loaded down with three heavy books and had immediately buried himself in one of them. The Chief Inspector had given no explanation as to why he had gone to the capital and throughout the rest of the day he had been totally absorbed in reading. He hadn't even paused for lunch and it was Karaolis who had sent out for a bottle of beer and the two cheese pastries for him. And Mitsides had been too preoccupied even to thank him when they had been delivered. But nevertheless, reaching out over the top of the book he had been reading at the time, he had drunk the beer and eaten the food.

For more than two hours now his attention had been riveted on a leather bound volume the title of which the sergeant, sitting across from him, could see, gold blocked on the spine; *Cyprus: History, Myths and Legends* by H. R. C. Hudson.

At last Mitsides closed the book, looked up from it and gazed thoughtfully into space for a time. Then, with an air of resolution, he stood up, crossed to the window and stretched.

'I want to have another word with Eric Morrison's girlfriend, Maria Thalassinos,' he said. 'Pick her up and bring her in.'

Martin Preece opened the boot of his Mercedes and took out of it a rifle fitted with a telescopic sight. He didn't need to check that the gun was loaded for he had made sure of that when he had set out for Paphos early in the morning.

Helene had driven Collier out of the town and then along a narrow track which led to some spectacular columned and colonnaded ruins of the Hellenistic period set in a natural amphitheatre overlooking the sea. They were there now, strolling together among the relics of a nobler but no less barbaric civilisation. And from the ridge of the grassy slope beneath which Preece had parked they presented even an unpractised marksman with an almost ideal field of fire and two perfect targets. And Preece had had plenty of practice with a rifle recently.

He peered around cautiously to recheck that there was no one else about and then, satisfied and keeping low, he clambered up the slope and looked down into the basin beyond which the sun, a burnished blood red shield, was low in the sky.

The couple were moving slowly, side by side, between the ruins of two rows of Doric columns. Lying on the grass, Preece raised the rifle to his shoulder, took aim through the sight and zeroed it in on Helene's head, forward of and a little below her left ear. He was counting on Collier being paralysed with both shock and fear when she fell and also on the Englishman turning to her so that, in those few seconds before he dropped on his knees beside her, the second bullet, tearing through flesh and shattering bone, would hit him squarely in the heart.

Preece's finger tightened on the trigger and at that moment he sensed that someone was standing over him. He froze and tensed his muscles. But it's not possible, the thought flashed through his mind. There was no one in sight. And then, too late, he remembered the small stone hut some distance up the track from where he had parked the Mercedes.

Slowly he began to turn his head but the only thing he even glimpsed before the butt of a rifle crashed on to the back of his head was a pair of leather boots from the top of one of which protruded the hilt of a hunting knife.

Basileos looked down at the unconscious man and shook his head. 'No,' he said quietly. And then added with a trace of a smile on his lips, 'Not yet, my friend. Not yet.'

He stooped and, seemingly without effort, swung Preece into a fireman's lift across his shoulders. Then, with both rifles in his free hand, he carried him back down the slope and across to the hut.

Tossing his burden inside he closed the stout wooden door and barred it with a thick baulk of timber.

Then, with the two rifles slung on one shoulder and singing happily, he strode off across the wasteland bordering the other side of the track.

'This is what I wanted to show you,' said Helene, as they strolled down the avenue of ruined columns.

Collier gazed around and nodded. 'It's beautiful,' he said.

'It is a jewel,' she assured him gravely. 'What you have seen since you came here from England, what you saw today, well that is Cyprus as it is now. The Cyprus of the twentieth century. A small island in a vast sea.'

Collier looked at her. 'Your island,' he reminded her quietly.

Helene nodded. 'Yes. My island. My home. Which I love very much. And which is always in my heart. Wherever else I may be. But once it was different. Once my island was one of the anchors of the world. The garden of civilisation.' For a moment she was lost in thought as she added almost in a whisper, 'Long ago. Long ago.' Then she smiled brightly and took his arm. 'I will tell you something. When I was young I came to this place alone . . .' She broke off and frowned as Collier suddenly pulled up sharply and cocked his head slightly to one side, a perplexed and intent look on his face.

The sound came to him in waves, faintly but each one just a little louder than the last. It was like that of a hundred distant flutes accompanied by a host of tinkling cymbals and all carried on a gentle breeze. But it isn't music, is it, he thought. They're voices, aren't they? Yes, they're voices. And he strained to catch what they were saying.

Helene gazed at him. It was as though he were in a trance. 'David?' she said quietly. And then, when he didn't respond, she tried again and louder this time. 'David?'

Collier pulled himself back from wherever he had been like someone coming out of hypnosis.

'What is it?' Helene enquired anxiously.

He stared at her for a few seconds and then he shook his head. 'Nothing. It's just that for a moment I thought I heard . . .' He broke off and again he shook his head in bewilderment.

'What?'

'Voices,' replied Collier, frowning.

Helene laughed lightly. 'Oh! And what did they say?' she asked.

Feeling more than a little foolish, Collier dismissed the matter. 'It's not important, is it? And, anyway, I don't remember.' And he didn't. 'Besides, there weren't any voices, were there?' he continued. And yet he had heard something. He was certain of that. 'Did you hear anything?'

Helene shook her head. 'No.'

Collier grinned. 'There you are. You see. Probably the wind.'

'But there isn't any,' she said quietly.

'Imagination then,' he insisted, looking at her and laughing the incident from his mind. 'Echoes, perhaps.' Then he took her hand and drew her in towards him a little. 'Tell me something,' he asked, and he was no longer laughing. 'Why did you bring me here?'

Helene studied him. 'So that you might learn something of our history. See it. Feel it.' She smiled. 'Hear it even.'

'And is that the only reason?'

She held his enquiring gaze and shook her head. 'No. I wanted us to be alone. Is that not what you wanted too?'

Collier frowned. He did indeed want that. Very much. But there was a barrier and Barry's face floated into his thoughts.

'Your friend, Bambos, tells me that you knew Barry very well. "Even the secrets of his heart". That's how he put it.'

Helene nodded solemnly. 'And he was telling the truth,' she said. 'I did know your brother very well. Especially the secrets of his heart. But we were never lovers if that makes a difference.'

Collier saw the truth in her eyes and he smiled. Barry was no longer between them. 'Of course it does,' he said. And it would have done from the very beginning, but more than ever today.

She came willingly into his arms and their bodies flowed together into one as they kissed and the setting sun bronzed them as though they were statues.

CHAPTER THIRTY-TWO

Even before he opened his eyes and found the empty space beside him in the bed, Collier knew that Helene had gone. And in a way he was glad. Their night together had been one of magic with a spell-like quality to it which he doubted would have survived the light of day and the commonplace of breakfast.

They had driven back from the ruins and shopped for food and wine among the street stalls of the festival which by then, under a canopy of fairy lights, was fast building in tempo and excitement towards its midnight climax of bonfires and fireworks.

From such simple things as they had bought Helene had prepared a meal that had surprised him and, with the electricity still not working, they had eaten it by candlelight and to the accompaniment of a group of musicians playing yearning, romantic melodies in the street outside. And the leader of the group had had a virtuoso touch with a harmonica, the like of which Collier had never heard before.

They had kissed and kissed again and then Helene had taken him by the hand and led him into the bedroom. And then . . . ? And then . . . ?

Propped up on his elbows and staring at the pillow beside him, savouring the honeyed fragrance of her hair which lingered on it, Collier frowned. And then . . . ? His frown deepened. He could not remember.

That what had happened had been like nothing he had ever experienced or was ever likely to experience; that, before they had, at last, fallen asleep in each other's arms, it had been a night of rapture, tenderness and passion such as was beyond imagination. That they had been as one as yet undreamt of musical instrument, played on and playing with joy and soaring from one *glissando* to the next; these things he knew and that knowledge, that certainty, cloaked him with peace and happiness. But of the style, the moment and the exact nature of the physical intimacy of their love-making he could remember nothing, nothing at all. Not one single detail. And the more he tried so the more the euphoria which suffused him ebbed, threatening to desert him altogether and only sweeping back over him again the moment he gave up the effort. And, for now, he was content to live with that. And with the words of the note which she had left for him on the bedside table; *we will meet again*, it read. Later he would remember everything without breaking the spell. He felt sure of that.

Lovingly he stroked the pillow beside him, then he got out of bed, slipped on his dressing gown and padded through into the kitchen. And, as he pushed open the door, he saw the wide pool of water beneath the refrigerator and the rivulets from it which had trickled across the floor. Puzzled and tiptoeing over to the fridge he opened the door. The interior light did not come on. Then he realised. With the electricity cut off for more than twenty-four hours the wretched thing had defrosted itself.

Cursing under his breath, he took out the milk and the butter that were in the refrigerator and sniffed them and recoiled from the rancid smell.

Moving over to the sink, he poured the milk away and dumped the butter in the wastebin.

Returning to the refrigerator, he spread a towel over the puddle beneath it and then removed the rest of the food and put it on the table.

Carrying the two ice trays which were awash and dripping over to the sink, he tipped the water and the floating fragments of ice from them.

He was about to move away again when, glancing down into the sink, he saw something. Lying amid the water which was draining away down the plughole were two flashing, glittering lights. Curious, he reached into the sink and picked up a pair of perfectly matched, flawless, light blue sapphires each the size of an almond. Awestruck and bewildered, he held them between his fingers, one in each hand, and examined them.

The stones caught the light. They were breathtakingly lovely, vibrant, living things.

Collier gazed at the gems, hypnotised.

The policewoman shepherded Maria into the office and sat her down on a chair while Mitsides, a cup of coffee in his hand, turned from the window and looked at her.

Maria's face was strained, her expression anxious. Her hair was unkempt and she had clearly slept in her clothes. If she had slept at all, thought the detective. She stared sullenly at him.

Mitsides glanced at the policewoman. 'How is she this morning?' he enquired. The WPC shrugged. 'Well then,' he went on, turning his attention to Maria. 'You have had a night in a cell to think about it. What do you have to say now?'

'I don't know what you want from me,' Maria muttered defiantly.

'Honesty.'

She flared. 'Are you saying that I am not honest?' she challenged.

With a quiet smile but a slightly reassuring gesture, Mitsides put his coffee cup down on his desk and crossed to her. 'Frankness then,' he said.

'I have already told you . . .'

'Only what you wanted to.'

Maria stared down at the floor. 'I don't know what you mean,' she mumbled.

Mitsides nodded. 'I think you do,' he insisted. 'The day before yesterday when you came to me I believe there were some details which you left out of your story. So now I want you to repeat *everything* Eric Morrison told you. Everything.'

Maria gave him a sulky, rebellious look. The Chief Inspector studied her and sighed. 'No? You still have nothing to add?' He shrugged. 'Very well then. I can wait. And we have plenty of accommodation.' He gestured to the policewoman and then turned from Maria dismissively.

The WPC closed in on the girl, put a hand on her arm and began to raise her from the chair.

Maria shook herself free and then, with a deep sigh of resignation, capitulated. She nodded. 'Treasure,' she said surlily. 'He said that they had found treasure. In a cave.'

This was what Mitsides had been waiting for. Confirmation of his suspicions. He swung round on her again. 'Where?'

'I don't know.'

The detective gave her a hard, disbelieving look. 'If you hold anything back from me now . . .' he warned icily.

'I don't know. And that's the truth,' she protested. 'Eric did not tell me where.'

And the Chief Inspector was in no doubt that she was telling the truth about that at least. 'How did they find it then?' he probed. 'And when?'

'Luck. Eric told me they stumbled on it. Just like that. Some time ago.'

'And they? Who are they?'

Maria shrugged. 'Eric. And Barry Collier.'

Mitsides crossed slowly to the window and gazed thoughtfully out of it. 'Go on,' he prompted.

'That's all,' sniffed the girl. 'Except that Barry Collier had sold two of the jewels which were in the cave for fifty thousand pounds.'

'Who to?'

'Eric said he never knew who the buyer was. And that before Barry Collier could tell him he was murdered.'

Mitsides spun round at the window. He was frowning. 'Morrison told you that Collier was murdered?' he asked quietly.

Again Maria shrugged. 'Well he said his death was not an accident.'

'As I accepted it to be,' sighed Mitsides angrily and cursing himself for his stupidity. And then a thought struck him. 'As perhaps too many deaths have been accepted as accidents.' He moved quickly over to one of the filing cabinets, opened a drawer and took from it a bulky file.

'He also said that twice someone had tried to kill him,' volunteered Maria. 'Once when he was with Barry Collier's brother. But I told you that when I came to you about him.'

Mitsides, leafing through the file, nodded. 'Anything else?'

Maria scowled. 'Only that they would have made a fortune from the treasure that they found.' The thought of what was now lost to her forever did not please her.

'They . . . They . . . They . . .' whispered the detective on a rising note of excitement, turning over the reports of the accidental deaths on the Kitson Neve site and the suicide of Alexis Eliades. Attached to each report was a photograph of the man concerned. 'All working together. And on a construction site.' He looked up and for a moment gazed abstractedly into space. 'Interesting,' he mused. Then, decisively, he closed the file and dropped it back into the drawer and made quickly for the door of the office. 'Lock her up,' he ordered over his shoulder.

Outraged, Maria jumped to her feet. 'But I did nothing,' she whined.

Mitsides paused briefly in the doorway to look back at her. 'Precisely,' he agreed. 'You did nothing. And sometimes that in itself is a crime.' He saw the bewildered, incensed scowl that came on to her face and shrugged sympathetically. 'I know,' he sighed. 'There's no justice in this world, is there?'

And then he was gone and Maria heard him hurrying down the corridor.

David Collier stood on the stage of the Curium Theatre and gazed out over the sea to where only a few minutes earlier Eugene Hellman's yacht had dropped anchor.

Behind him the tiers of stone seats rose like a high, semicircular cliff. Here, in this open air amphitheatre, Romans had once gloated over gladiatorial combat and before that, Greeks had sat entranced by the plays of Aeschylus and Euripides.

Collier turned as Hellman, escorted by Travis and Olsen, came into sight above the topmost row of seats to his right.

The American stood for a moment gazing down at the lone figure on the stage way beneath him. He had been puzzled when Collier had telephoned and intrigued by the urgency in his voice. And he had been even more intrigued by his odd choice of meeting place. And when he had questioned Collier about it the Englishman had clearly found it difficult to explain why it had to be at that particular location. It was almost as if it were some strange whim. 'It's private there' had been the only reason he had been able to come up with.

And Hellman hadn't pressed him further. It was a pleasant day and a gentle cruise along the coast from Limassol to the theatre had not been without its appeal. What had he got to lose anyway? Indeed there had been something in Collier's tone which had suggested that the excursion would be positively to his advantage. But, nevertheless, he had brought Travis and Olsen across with him in the motorboat. Just in case.

Slowly, tier by tier, the three men made their way down towards the stage but then, when they were still six rows off from it, Travis and Olsen stopped. As their employer continued his descent and crossed to Collier, they took up positions from which they could provide cover and, if necessary, almost immediate support.

'Well here I am, David,' smiled Hellman. 'So what did you want to see me about?'

'These,' replied Collier flatly. He reached into the pocket of his jacket and when he pulled his hand out again and opened it the two sapphires were lying in his palm. The jewels sparkled brilliantly in the sunlight.

Hellman reacted with a look of amazement which quickly turned to an expression of more than just curious interest. He stared covetously at the gems and stretched out a hand towards them but Collier drew them back sharply out of reach. The American looked up into his face and gave him a warm, reassuring smile.

'Do you know what these are?' asked Collier.

Hellman nodded. 'Yes,' he said quietly, fixing Collier with a gaze. 'They are sapphires. They are known as the Eyes of Love. Stolen from the death mask in the tomb of Aphrodite.'

'Who by?'

Hellman hesitated. But then he shrugged. This was not the time to consider anyone's feelings. 'Your brother.'

Collier nodded sadly. He had known all along that this had to be the answer but now it had been confirmed.

'And I'll give you a million dollars for them,' said Hellman. 'Cash.'

It was a staggering offer. A sum which Collier, who still measured his monthly salary in hundreds, could not fully comprehend. But he did realise the implications behind it. 'You're not surprised. And you know all about them. You've known about them all along, haven't you?' he accused.

Hellman was unperturbed. 'Of their existence. Of the existence of the tomb, yes. Their whereabouts and the location of the tomb,' he shook his head, 'unfortunately I've never been in possession of that information.' He smiled. 'In business of this kind people tend to be very untrusting.'

Collier was not amused. 'And you want to buy them?'

'Naturally,' confirmed Hellman. 'And all the other artefacts. That's why I came to Cyprus. Your brother and I had already entered into negotiations over those sapphires before he was killed.' Collier reacted with a start. The American nodded. 'Yes,' he went on, 'I think I can safely confirm that Barry's death was no accident. But that is hardly a surprise to you, is it?'

As a frightening possibility occurred to him, Collier scowled belligerently. He clenched his fists. 'Did you . . . ?' he snarled, and stepped in close to the American.

From their vantage points Travis and Olsen saw this sudden threatening movement and they both reached for their shoulder holsters.

Hellman shook his head. 'For what possible reason?' he argued. 'I've told you, Barry and I had come to an amicable arrangement.'

Collier studied the American's face searchingly and he could see that his disclaimer was genuine. Then he remembered the briefcase and nodded. 'Of course,' he sighed. 'You'd given him a deposit, hadn't you. The fifty thousand pounds.'

Hellman shook his head. 'No. He didn't get that from me.'

'From where then?' demanded Collier, more than somewhat taken aback.

'It would appear that I have competition. But not from a buyer I would recommend anyone to do business with. Someone totally dishonest and entirely without scruples.'

'Well whoever it was paid over the money didn't get the sapphires, did they?'

'Obviously not,' agreed Hellman. 'Tell me. Where did you find them?'

'They were in one of the ice trays in the refrigerator in Barry's apartment.'

'How apt.' Hellman smiled. 'Frozen assets. Literally.' He shook his head ruefully. 'And right under our noses. Very amusing.' His smile took on an edge. 'I must speak to my associates about that,' he said softly.

'You had them looking for these?' demanded Collier.

'Well, I wouldn't have been unhappy if they had found them,' replied Hellman. 'But principally they were trying to get a lead on the location of the tomb itself. I take it that you still can't be of any help on that score.'

'I don't know anything about a tomb,' muttered Collier. 'But if Morrison was in on the robbery with Barry he must . . .' He broke off as another realisation struck him. Disappointed and inwardly cursing his own stupidity, he regarded the American scathingly. 'But of course, that's the only reason you agreed to help me find him, isn't it?' He nodded towards Travis and Olsen whose hands were by their sides once more. 'And your bloodhounds still haven't been able to track him down, eh? A pity. For both of us. Although if they had I don't suppose you would have let me get close to him.'

'Morrison's dead,' Hellman said quietly. And then he drove the point home. 'Murdered.'

'Who by?' Collier's voice trembled a little.

'The same person who killed your brother,' said Hellman.

Collier exploded into vengeful anger. 'Give me a name. I want a name.'

Hellman shook his head. 'I'm sorry, David. You only have the sapphires and I may yet have to do business with the killer. However distasteful that may be to me. But I like you.' He saw the expression that came on to Collier's face. 'No, I really do,' he assured him. 'So I'll tell you what. When it's all over. When everything's tied up. Well then I'll give you the name you want. As a bonus. That's a promise. And what you do then.' He shrugged. 'Well that's up to you.' Then he returned to the theme dearest to him. 'So what do you say? One million dollars. In cash. Or, if you prefer, a certified cheque drawn on just about any bank in the world and you can take the money in the currency of your choice. Swiss francs, German marks, yen. Roubles even.'

Collier opened his hand again and stared down at the sapphires. 'But they don't belong to me,' he said hesitantly.

'Sure they do,' Hellman cajoled. 'They're part of Barry's legacy to you, aren't they? Okay, so maybe, technically, he stole them. But when you come down to it, who from? Who's the loser? Not some insurance company, even. It's not like he broke into Tiffany's, is it? He got those out of a hole in the ground somewhere. Some place no one's been into for more than a thousand years. A place no one even knew was there. Those sapphires. They're sort of, well, lost property. And finders keepers, eh? So Barry found them. And suddenly you got lucky. You're standing at the end of the rainbow, boy.'

Collier looked up at him unbelievingly. 'A million dollars,' he whispered.

Hellman misunderstood him. 'It's a fair price,' he said. 'You won't find anyone who'll top it. So what do you say? Is it a deal?'

CHAPTER THIRTY-THREE

Collier hesitated. He gazed down at the sapphires once more.

'Set you up for life that kind of money,' tempted Hellman. 'And, as I said. As a bonus, later on, I'll give you that name you want.'

'I . . .' faltered Collier, looking up at him. And then he heard it again, the strange, silvery musical sound which had transfixed him while he was strolling among the ruins with Helene – faintly at first, but then as a loud, insistent but melodic fugue which filled and echoed in his mind.

Hellman saw the sudden trancelike, inward-looking gaze which came on to the Englishman's face and it disturbed him. Then Collier nodded absently as though answering another voice and his eyes focussed in on the American again but there was something of a faraway look in his eyes and when he spoke his voice had taken on a gentle and authoritative tone which had not been there before. It was as if in a single moment he had achieved a certainty and an objective which were unassailable and in which he had found peace. And his happiness showed in his face. But there was resolve there too and quiet determination.

'Well?' snapped Hellman irritably and more than a little discomforted.

Collier shook his head. 'I'm sorry,' he said simply. 'But you are wrong. These sapphires are not mine to sell. Nor were they Barry's.' Then, smiling politely, he turned from the American and slowly began to move away from him.

Hellman grabbed at his arm and checked him. 'What do you mean?' he demanded angrily. 'Where are you going? What are you going to do with them?'

Collier looked at him and again he smiled. 'I'm taking them back where they belong,' he explained, as though talking to a petulant child.

The American's frown deepened into a troubled, dangerous scowl and as, effortlessly, Collier pulled his arm free from his grasp and started to walk away again, he raised his hand and signalled to Travis and Olsen.

The two men made a movement to intercept Collier but they had only taken a single, lunging step when a bullet struck the stonework an inch from the toe of Travis' right shoe and the whine of the ricochet merged with the crack of a rifle.

While Collier continued on his way across the stage, seemingly oblivious of the sound and without as much as a glance over his shoulder, Travis froze. And so did Olsen. And then, slowly, they turned and followed the gaze of their employer who was now staring up towards the rear of the amphitheatre.

Basileos was standing at the edge of the walkway above the highest tier of seats, his rifle levelled and unwavering.

Slowly and with deep sighs of frustration, Travis and Olsen reluctantly half raised their hands, keeping them well clear of their jackets.

Hellman gazed up at the figure with the rifle and he frowned. Even in half silhouette there was something familiar about the man. Then the American became aware of further movement to his left and he turned his head and looked across the stage.

Helene and Charalambos were standing, statue like, in one of the aisles half way up the tiers of seats, waiting to greet Collier who was crossing the orchestra area towards them. Helene's expression was impassive and her eyes were on Hellman, as were Charalambos'. But on his lips was the trace of a sardonic smile.

And even at that distance Hellman recognised them both. And he knew then for certain who the man with the rifle was.

His anger gave way to wry amusement. He grinned and shook his head in genuine admiration. He was beaten and he knew it. He also knew now how it was that his every move in the game which he had been playing had been so successfully frustrated.

'Well! Well!' he chuckled quietly. 'Of course. I should

have known.' And then he laughed, greatly enjoying the joke. 'Helene! How apt.'

Collier climbed the steps and came face to face with Helene. He looked at her questioningly but with a distant expression still in his eyes.

Helene nodded. 'We will take you to where you want to go,' she said softly, her voice blending with the music still reverberating in his head.

Then, with a farewell glance at Hellman, she turned and led the way up the steps. And, while Charalambos followed, Basileos, his rifle at the ready and with his eyes fixed on the three men below him, moved slowly round the walkway to complete Collier's escort. The four of them disappeared from view through the main entrance.

Travis and Olsen skipped and hopped down through six rows of seats and then ran across to their employer who, still smiling, was staring up at the spot where Helene and the others had last been visible.

'Shall we go after them?' suggested Travis a little hesitantly.

'There was nothing we could do,' said Olsen, anticipating a tirade of scornful abuse.

But to both men's surprise Hellman wasn't angry; merely resigned. He looked at Olsen and then at Travis and his smile became almost pitying. He shook his head. 'Against *them*!' he sighed. 'Of course not. Up against them *you* never stood a chance.'

And then, with a brisk decisive movement, he walked back the way they had come and to where the motorboat would be waiting.

Collier and Helene got into the back of the red Alfetta and, with Basileos sitting beside him drinking deeply and contentedly from a bottle of wine, Charalambos switched on the engine.

The Alfa Romeo pulled away and quickly gathered speed.

The shepherd herded his small flock of sheep around the midnight blue Mercedes parked on the track. As he passed the car he peered into it. It was empty. He looked around but there was no one in sight. He shrugged. Then, as he drew near to the stone hut, someone or something began bellowing and beating on the door from inside it. He pulled up sharply and stared at the hut, puzzled and a little afraid. Cautiously he approached the door and listened. The thumping and bellowing continued.

Now very fearful of what might be inside, the shepherd hesitated and backed away a little. But then, summoning up all his courage, he moved in on the door again and lifted the baulk of timber which was barring it.

Dropping the stout length of wood, he stepped back in alarm as the door was pulled inward savagely and a man, a foreigner from the looks of him, unshaven and his face contorted with rage, burst out into the sunlight.

Pausing only to glance briefly at the shepherd, his eyes staring and mouth open, Preece ran for the Mercedes.

The track was too narrow to turn in so he slammed into reverse and the car's rear wheels spun wildly in the soft ground. Then they bit and the Mercedes backed down the track erratically and skidded onto the road.

The shepherd, peering around the corner of the wall behind which he had taken refuge, was deeply concerned. 'I am an old fool,' he muttered. 'And I shall say nothing of this. For like Pandora, and out of curiosity I think perhaps I have released an evil on the world.'

And as Preece drove the Mercedes at a furious and reckless speed along the coast road, so Chief Inspector Mitsides was searching his office on the Kitson Neve site. It was the Englishman's story that he had seen Morrison on the afternoon of the shooting at Trimiklini and which Maria Thalassinos had finally proved to have been a lie which had brought him there.

And although Preece had been clever and worked on the trees in the forest principle, Mitsides at last found what he was looking for. In the drawer of one of the filing cabinets, among the hundreds of prints and negatives recording every detail of the various buildings of the desalination plant and power station at every stage of construction were other negatives, other prints; coloured enlargements of fabulously beautiful and precious artefacts, treasure which held the detective spellbound for some time. And treasure the like of which he knew had never been excavated anywhere on Cyprus, legally anyway.

The photographs themselves were, he felt certain, evidence enough for him to apply for a warrant for the arrest of Martin Preece. But with the Englishman in gaol the jigsaw would still not be complete and it could be that, despite rigorous questioning, despite a prison sentence even, Preece would hold on to the most vital piece of all, the location of the tomb.

And then it came to Mitsides. It was the only possible answer. The tomb was unlikely to be on the site itself; the entire area was now covered in concrete and besides it was far too public and seldom unattended. No. Preece and the others had to have stumbled on it during the earlier survey work.

The detective crossed to the large scale map hanging on the wall and examined it.

The Alfetta bumped and bucketed over the scrubland and then stopped. Collier followed Helene, Charalambos and Basileos out of the car.

With Charalambos in the lead and Basileos, his rifle in the crook of his left arm, bringing up the rear, they moved off across the cliff top in the direction of the sea. They neared a narrow headland in the centre of which was a wide and deep depression bordered by outcrops of large boulders and thickets of scrub and stunted trees.

They scrambled down into the hollow and crossed to its far side. They reached a wall of rock, its base strewn with rubble, which was partly screened by thorn bushes and other vegetation.

Charalambos pulled aside some of the foliage to reveal a narrow vertical fissure.

The crack was no more than six feet high and just about wide enough for a well built man, turning sideways, to squeeze into it.

While Basileos stood guard, his eyes scanning the ridge

above them, Charalambos took a candle from his pocket and lit it. Then he looked at Helene, who nodded. He edged his way into the fissure and Helene indicated to Collier that he should follow.

Frowning a little and with that distant, faraway look in his eyes, still in the grip of the compelling sound, he hesitated. Helene smiled at him. 'Come,' she said gently. 'We are there.' She moved past him and slipped through the crack in the rock. Collier followed her.

Basileos rearranged the foliage to cover the fissure once more and then clambered out of the depression and took up a position among some of the boulders on the crest of it, hidden from sight but with a good view of the entrance to the tomb.

Resting his rifle against a rock, he settled himself comfortably, pulled out the bottle of wine from inside his battledress blouse and raising it to his lips drank from it. Lowering the bottle again, he belched loudly.

CHAPTER THIRTY-FOUR

With the candle as their only illumination, Charalambos guided Helene and Collier along a narrow ramp-like ledge hewn out of the rock, which curved down into the depths far below sea level.

At the foot of the ramp Charalambos ran on ahead and dodging, darting, twisting and turning like a will o' the wisp he lit several ornate torches which were set into holders in the walls of a vast cavern. And as each torch was touched by the flame of the candle and flared up, so more and more of the magnificence and splendour of the tomb was revealed, until it was awash with brilliance and colour.

The walls of the chamber, constructed out of great blocks of stone, were covered with painted frescoes depicting idyllic, Elysian pastoral scenes and looking as fresh as they must have done on the day when the artists completed them. Resting in silver-lined niches in the stonework were many beautifully decorated vases, plates, amphora and priceless votive offerings of all kinds. Carved into one wall and dominating the chamber was the hieroglyphic inscription which Barry Collier had photographed.

Standing in the centre of the cavern, resting on a catafalque, was a painted, stone sarcophagus. On top of it was a lifesize figure of Aphrodite made of solid gold. The figure was intricately worked to show every fold in the goddess's funeral robes and the head was covered by a death mask, highly stylised rather than representational, resting on a gold pillow.

The eye sockets of the mask were empty.

Standing around the catafalque were four statues representing Aphrodite's attendant nymphs. They, too, were made of gold and ornamented with precious stones and they stood as though weeping, mourning the death of a loved one.

Collier gazed about in spellbound, rapturous wonderment

as the scene was revealed. Around him the flaming torches sent shadows chasing across the vaulted walls, shadows which were lost in the darkness which lowered over the resplendence of gold and jewelled tribute and glowing painted homage.

Blowing out the candle and then slipping it back into his pocket, Charalambos turned to his companions. Collier and Helene exchanged looks. Again she smiled at him. And then, with the Englishman on one side of her and Charalambos on the other, she slowly and solemnly approached the catafalque.

As they did so, high above them, Basileos saw Martin Preece come into view on the opposite side of the depression from where he had hidden himself. The Englishman had a Luger automatic in his hand and as he slithered down into the hollow and crossed to the wall of rock Basileos smiled but made no attempt to reach for his rifle.

Preece looked around carefully and then, pulling aside the foliage covering the fissure, squeezed his way into it and out of sight.

Basileos, his eyes fixed on the opening, nodded. 'Yes, now!' he whispered softly, grim faced. 'Now!'

Gazing down at the death mask Collier opened his hand and looked at the two sapphires lying in it. Their lustre added extra brilliance to the tomb. Carefully he replaced the jewels in the empty eye sockets and then looked up at Helene and smiled. She smiled back at him and nodded. Then she glanced across at Charalambos who drew from his pocket the gold necklace and handed it to her.

Helene put the necklace back around the neck of the figure of the goddess and arranged it carefully.

'Very cosy.'

The voice came from the darkness at the foot of the ramp behind them. And suddenly Collier, as if waking from a dream and for the first time fully aware of his surroundings and what was going on, spun round and reacted with a look of alarm as Preece stepped into the light, covering them with the Luger.

Very slowly Helene also turned to face the Englishman

and Charalambos looked across at him. But neither of them showed any sign of surprise or concern.

'Preece!' exclaimed Collier.

'None other. Hello, David. Cutting yourself a slice of the cake, eh? And if it isn't the beautiful and talkative Helene.' Preece shifted his gaze a little. 'And you must be Charalambos. Right?'

He moved in a little closer to the catafalque, saw the sapphires and the necklace and, confused, frowned. 'What are you doing? A place for everything and everything in its place. I don't understand.' He shrugged. 'Still, none of my business. And thanks. Back to square one. Much tidier for me. And more profitable.' He grinned at Helene. 'So Morrison did let you into our little secret before I got to him.' Then he frowned again and shot a look at Collier. 'Or had you known about this place all along?'

'The name,' breathed Collier vehemently. 'The name of the man who killed my brother. The name Hellman wouldn't give me.'

Preece looked surprised. 'Really! Ah, but then he's a businessman, isn't he?' he reasoned. 'He likes to keep his options open. And very wise of him too. As things have turned out.' Slowly and deliberately he swung the Luger on to Collier and took aim. 'Sorry about this,' he said with a mock apologetic smile.

And as his finger tightened on the trigger Charalambos let out a wild, savage cry. Surprised and alarmed, Preece took two steps backward and swung the automatic round on him. Collier could see from the look on Charalambos' face what he had in mind.

'No! Don't!' he shouted.

But the man took no notice. He lunged at Preece and as he did so Collier grabbed Helene and, shielding her with his body, retreated with her to the far side of the chamber.

Charalambos, arms outstretched, was almost on Preece when he fired and the chamber echoed with the shot.

The bullet struck Charalambos in the chest and he was blown backward under the impact of it. Preece watched him, expecting him to fall, but he did not. Instead, his eyes fixed on the Englishman, he stood swaying on his feet and then, already bleeding badly, lunged at him yet again.

Preece fired once more. This time at point blank range. And again the force of the bullet hurled Charalambos back violently and he crashed against the sarcophagus.

Crouching in the shadows, Collier watched, sickened and aghast, and he was surprised at how calm and seemingly unmoved Helene was by the scene before them.

His eyes still on Preece and now bleeding profusely from both his wounds, Charalambos, supported by the sarcophagus, first smiled and then, quietly at first, began to laugh.

Preece stared at him, confused, disbelieving and increasingly afraid.

Charalambos' laughter grew louder and louder. He seemed vastly, incredibly amused. And then, suddenly, he stopped laughing and coughed. His eyes began to glaze and blood trickled from the corners of his mouth. His legs buckled and slowly he slid down the side of the sarcophagus and in doing so, under the weight of his body, the catafalque supporting the sarcophagus and the prone figure of Aphrodite moved two or three inches, as though on runners. Charalambos sank into a sitting position on the floor and then, his eyes staring vacantly, he toppled to one side.

And, as his head struck the floor, the chamber was filled with the clanking and rumbling of pulleys, counter-weights and ratchets and somewhere beyond the great stone blocks of the walls an ancient mechanism, triggered by the movement of the catafalque, swung into action.

And the sound built and built until the whole chamber was reverberating with it. Terrified, Preece turned wildly in a circle, staring at the walls, trying to identify the sound and locate its source.

Equally disturbed, Collier shot a look of deep concern at Helene. Her face was expressionless. 'The trap,' she said calmly. And then, in answer to Collier's questioning frown, she added, 'the trap built by the faithful against thieves.' And at that moment, to Collier's horror, the trap was sprung.

On either side of the chamber a great block of stone set in

the face of each wall began to rise. And as they did so sea water burst into the tomb, first as a narrow, horizontal, pressurised blade-like jet and then, as the stone sluice gates rose higher and higher, as two overwhelming, ear shattering, thundering, spuming bores.

Terrified and panic stricken, Preece turned and ran for the base of the ramp but, trapped between both inrushes of water, he was struck by them, swept off his feet, smashed against the catafalque and then sucked under and engulfed.

The tomb flooded rapidly and Collier and Helene were knocked down by the mass of water which continued to surge through the twin sluices. Now, as the chamber was inundated, Collier knew that to stand any chance of staying alive they must swim, but Helene showed little if any inclination to fight for her life. It was as if she had accepted the inevitability of death.

Desperately Collier made a grab for her and supported her. 'Swim,' he shouted furiously. 'For God's sake, swim.' But Helene made no attempt to strike out on her own. And the only explanation Collier could come up with was a terrifying one. She can't swim, he thought. She doesn't know how to.

Slipping one arm around her waist and thrashing about with his free arm, he just managed to keep both their heads clear of the water, but then they were drawn into a vast, whirling vortex and spun around in it.

Martin Preece, spreadeagled and lying face downward, was swept past them.

The noise was almost unbearable and the water was rising with incredible speed. The chamber was three quarters filled. The flaming torches had long been extinguished and the only illumination now was from the eerie, boiling phosphorescence of the sea.

With a supreme effort Collier managed to free Helene and himself from the grip of the whirlpool and, kicking and flailing, he reached the ledge by which they had made their way down into the tomb.

Near to exhaustion and with one hand still gripping Helene, he hauled himself on to the ledge just clear of the water and then, lying on his stomach, reached down with his other hand to pull her up alongside him.

But even as he did so, to his horror, Helene began to slip from his grasp and he hadn't the strength left in him to prevent it. He let out an anguished cry. 'No! No!' And then she was gone, sucked down into the depths of the water and Collier found no consolation in the fact that as she disappeared from his sight her expression was strangely calm. It seemed for a moment that there was even a faint smile on her lips. All he knew was that she was lost to him forever. He cried out again. 'Helene!' And the echo of his despair was lost in the tumult around him.

Stunned, he lay on the ramp, the rising water plucking at him fiercely. Only the instinct for survival overcame grief and fatigue. He struggled to his feet and, with the sea beginning to surge in on the higher level, he staggered up the ramp.

Around him the walls of the chamber were shuddering and beginning to crack under the enormous pressure exerted on them by the explosive flood. Showers of rock and earth and stones were falling from the roof. Gasping for breath and close to collapse, Collier scrabbled his way towards the surface and out at last into the open air.

Basileos, his rifle over his shoulder, was standing close to the fissure in the rock wall which, like the floor of the depression, was in the grip of a great earth tremor. Accompanying the tremor and coming from below ground, was a rolling, menacing rumble.

Runnels of stones and small rocks began to crash down the sides of the hollow. The larger boulders standing on the crest above were swaying dangerously. But Basileos appeared unconcerned by the ominous sounds and the movements around him.

As Collier, his clothes soaked with sea water, his face drawn and streaked with mud, hauled himself back through the crack, Basileos took the folded blanket from his shoulder, shook it out and wrapped it around him.

Collier, in a state of shock, focussed his eyes on him.

'They're dead,' he said flatly. 'Helene. Charalambos. They're both dead.'

There was absolutely no reaction from Basileos to this news.

The earth was trembling even more violently now. Basileos looked around at the stones and rocks which were beginning to cascade with greater force into the hollow. 'Come. You cannot stay here,' he said quietly.

Collier gazed at him piteously. 'Charalambos saved my life. And Helene . . .' He winced at the memory. 'I tried. I tried. But I couldn't. I . . .' He broke off and lowered his eyes and shook his head miserably. Still he evoked no reaction from Basileos.

'Quickly.' This time when the man spoke it was a command.

Putting an arm around Collier's shoulders, he guided him away from the fissure and across the depression. Such was the strength of the earth tremor now that the two men had difficulty in keeping their feet and the runnels of earth, stones and rocks had become torrents. The air was filled with dust and the roaring sound beneath them had become even more threatening. Two or three of the larger boulders swaying on the crest of the depression toppled over and crashed down into it.

'Up there,' ordered Basileos, pushing the Englishman ahead of him. And when, at last, they reached the higher ground, he guided him over to a stunted tree some distance away from the hollow and sat him down at the base of it. And, at that moment, the ground in and immediately around the depression caved in and the two men, shaken by the subsidence, were caught up in a swirling cloud of dust as hundreds of tons of rock collapsed inward while mud, sea water and boulders bubbled up to meet them.

Five minutes later absolute stillness hung over the area. The earth trembled no more, the air was clear of dust and what had once been the hollow was now a tumulus of disordered rocks and gently sifting soil. The tomb was completely sealed.

Collier sat transfixed, his eyes on the aftermath of the

subsidence. 'I tried,' he whispered. Basileos glanced down at him and then crossed to where the hollow had once been as if making a final check. Satisfied, he nodded. Then he turned and started to move briskly away in the direction from which they had approached the headland.

Collier was suddenly aware that his companion was leaving him. Frowning, he turned to gaze after him. 'Basileos!' he called. 'Wait! Where are you going?' But the man's stride did not falter and he did not look back.

'It is done, Englishman,' he shouted over his shoulder. 'It is done.'

Desperately Collier struggled to get to his feet to go after him but he didn't have the strength. With a great sigh, he sank back again into a sitting position with his back against the tree trunk.

And it was there that, an hour later, Chief Inspector Mitsides found him.

CHAPTER THIRTY-FIVE

Eugene Hellman stood by the rail of the sundeck and gazed across at the coast, lost in thought.

A gentle but chill offshore breeze struck him and he shivered and came out of his reverie.

He looked up at the sky and then turned and moved back into the stateroom where he crossed to his desk and sat down at it.

Lying on the desk, in a neat pile, were the coloured photographs of the various artefacts in the tomb. Hellman picked them up and flipped through them and then, with a sigh, he tore them in two and dropped them into the waste bin.

The papers on his desk fluttered momentarily as another chill breeze eddied in through the open glass doors. Again Hellman shivered and he got up and closed the doors to the deck. Then, crossing back to his desk once more, he pressed the bell push.

Reaching down, he opened one of the bottom drawers of the desk and took out a handsomely framed photograph of a strikingly attractive woman, her black hair styled in an almost classical Greek manner. He was still staring at the picture when there was a tap on the door and it opened and Travis entered.

Hellman looked across at him and then set the photograph upright on the desk. 'There's nothing here for me now,' he said. 'So no point in hanging about. Besides, it's getting late.' He glanced at the photograph. 'Soon she'll be coming back to me again.' Travis, his eyes on the picture, nodded. 'And I wouldn't want to keep her waiting,' continued Hellman. 'So let's get under way. We're going home.'

'Right,' replied Travis, with a note of relief in his voice. Then he turned and left the stateroom, closing the door quietly behind him.

Hellman sank into the chair behind his desk, turned the

photograph to him, looked into the woman's eyes and smiled warmly.

The fisherman hauling in his nets some way off the yacht's port side heard the sound of the anchor being raised and saw the wake beginning to build under its stern as the propellers slowly edged it forward.

The yacht swung hard to starboard and it was then that, for the first time, the man in the caique saw the name painted on its transom; *Kore*.

Whoever owns that beauty, he thought, has to be a Greek. For only to a Greek is the queen of the underworld known as Kore. He spat into the sea and crossed himself. Foreigners called her Persephone.

Collier, morosely sipping a glass of brandy, sat wrapped in a blanket that smelled of antiseptic which a constable had brought up from the cells.

The police doctor had examined him and pronounced that, apart from exhaustion and some minor cuts and bruises, there was nothing physically wrong with him. He had not commented on the Englishman's emotional state because no one had asked him to. Besides, that was obvious and only time would heal that.

One by one Mitsides took the accident report forms from the Kitson Neve file and laid them on the desk in front of Collier.

'Peter Miller. Electrocuted. Verdict accidental death.' The Chief Inspector's tone was brisk and businesslike as he went through the roll call. 'Edward Willet. Fell from the gantry of a crane. Verdict accidental death.' Collier stared dully at the photographs of the dead men. 'Jack Ransome. He was killed during some rock blasting. Alexis Eliades, one of the Cypriots employed on the site. Until now it was believed that he committed suicide. And Eliades, like the others, was a member of the team which carried out the first survey under Preece.'

And then, attached to the last report was a photograph of his brother and Collier pre-empted the detective's obituary.

'Barry Collier,' he interjected bitterly. 'Killed when the

Landrover he was driving went over a cliff. Verdict accidental death.'

Mitsides accepted the rebuke gracefully.

Collier took another sip from his glass and then, his eyes still on Barry's photograph, he sighed. 'Eight murders. The friendly Mr Preece racked up quite a score, didn't he?'

'Eight?' queried Mitsides.

'Barry. The others. And Morrison.'

The detective nodded reflectively. 'Probably.'

Collier was in no doubt. 'Charalambos certainly,' he continued. 'In cold blood. And, indirectly,' he winced at the memory, 'Helene.'

Mitsides gathered the reports together into a neat pile. 'He has paid for his crimes,' he said quietly. 'With his own life.'

Collier drained the rest of the brandy. 'Tell them that,' he suggested with a nod at the reports, bitterness flooding back into his voice once more. 'And Bambos and Helene. I don't think they'd find much consolation in it.'

'There seldom is any consolation in justice,' the Chief Inspector assured him gently. 'Of any kind. Or even satisfaction. Just some sort of balance.'

The telephone rang. Mitsides picked it up. 'Mitsides . . .' He nodded. 'I see. Very well. Thank you.' He replaced the receiver and Collier glanced up at him. 'The American, Hellman,' he explained. 'His yacht has sailed and is already out of Cypriot territorial waters.' He shrugged. 'Not that I think we would have had enough evidence to charge him with anything.'

'What about Basileos?'

'We are looking for him.'

'I'd say he's up in the mountains,' said Collier. 'But then I suppose he could be anywhere.'

Mitsides looked thoughtful. He nodded. 'Yes, he could.'

The Englishman shook his head. He just couldn't make it out. 'Why did he just walk away like that?' he asked.

'He did not wish to become involved with the police. Neither he nor his friends. Remember?'

'But why?'

The Chief Inspector shrugged. 'A mystery within a mystery.'

'There's the car,' suggested Collier, but without enthusiasm. 'Helene's Alfa Romeo. The registration might give you a lead to him.'

Mitsides shook his head. 'We've already checked on that. It's not registered and the number plates are false.' Collier frowned. 'Yes,' agreed the policeman. 'Another question mark.'

The door of the office opened and Sergeant Karaolis came into the room carrying the Englishman's clothes which had been dried out in front of an electric fire in the basement. He put the bundle down on the desk.

Collier reached out and picked up the report lying on the top of the pile and gazed into his brother's face. Then he burst out savagely, 'Nine people dead.' He slammed his glass down. 'And for what?'

And it was not until that afternoon when he was back again at the scene of the subsidence and standing alongside Professor Stylianou and the Chief Inspector that anyone really answered his question.

'The Tomb of Aphrodite,' said Stylianou. 'One of the richest archaeological treasures in the world.'

But Collier wasn't really listening. His eyes were fixed on the mound of rocks and boulders which now filled the hollow and his thoughts were elsewhere.

'And sadly lost to us forever,' continued Stylianou with a sigh.

Mitsides looked at him and frowned. 'But surely you will excavate, Professor!'

Stylianou shook his head. 'I doubt it. We will, of course, take advice. But in my opinion it would be too difficult. And very dangerous. Look.' Gingerly he stepped forward a little and tapped the ground gently with his foot. There was an immediate minor landslide.

The Professor moved back quickly. 'The ground is unsafe. And with the pressure of water in the chamber any attempt at excavation and I think the whole headland would collapse into the sea.' He sighed again. 'A pity. No, more than that.

A tragedy. A great loss for mankind. Still, Aphrodite will rest in peace. Beneath the sea. From where she came and where she belongs I suppose. Nevertheless, a great loss.' He drifted into a world of his own. 'What a find the tomb would have been,' he whispered. 'More exciting even than Schliemann's discovery of Troy. Just think how much it might have added to our knowledge. One of the great burial chambers of the Ptolemaic Period. And of greater historical interest than the pyramids.' He came out of his reverie and smiled ruefully at the Chief Inspector. 'Imagine the work that must have been put into it all those centuries ago.'

'But why?' asked Mitsides. 'I mean, why a tomb for a goddess?'

The Professor warmed to his specialist subject. 'Because, when the Hellenistic civilisation was in decline and barbarism and other religions threatened this area of the Mediterranean, the people, in their despair, believed that the old gods must be dead, so they buried effigies of them. And as Cyprus was the birthplace of Aphrodite it was only fitting that her tomb should also be on the island.' He shrugged. 'Of course they were wrong to believe what they did. The gods were not dead. They had merely deserted them. And if they had really thought about it they would have realised that. All gods and goddesses are immortal. They cannot die.' He gazed out over the infilled hollow once more and shook his head sadly. 'A tragedy.' He looked at Collier. 'From the photographs, it has to have been magnificent.'

Collier nodded. 'Yes. It was,' he said flatly.

'And you saw it! With your own eyes! You are a very privileged person, Mr Collier.'

Slowly Collier turned his head and gazed at the archaeologist. 'Perhaps. But I'll tell you something, Professor. It wasn't worth the admission fee.'

And then he turned on his heel and walked away up over the cliff to his car, to drive back to Paphos.

The long stemmed rose, fresh and fragrant, was lying on the pillow of the still unmade bed, the pillow which had been Helene's.

Frowning, Collier picked it up and gazed at it. Had it

been there when he woke up that morning? Possibly. But if so he didn't remember it. He shrugged. But then there was so much he couldn't remember, wasn't there? And too much that he could.

He savoured the scent of the rose and then stretched out his hand and touched the pillow on which it had been lying.

CHAPTER THIRTY-SIX

The lawyer was leaving the house as Mitsides drove up to it. The two men exchanged brief pleasantries and then the Chief Inspector climbed the steps to the front door.

David Collier was standing just inside the sitting room gazing absently around it. On the floor beside him was the luggage he had brought with him to Cyprus and his brother's camera holdall. He turned to Mitsides.

'All settled?' enquired the detective.

'Yes. I've left everything in Mr Michaelides' hands as you suggested. He has full power of attorney,' Collier said listlessly.

Mitsides nodded in approval. 'He's a good lawyer. He'll not cheat you.' He smiled encouragingly. 'But now that it's all over, why don't you stay a little longer?'

The Englishman's reply was unequivocal. 'No. For what?' Then his voice lost some of its sullen edge. 'Anyway I have to get back to London. I've a living to earn.'

'What time is your flight?'

'Three thirty,' said Collier. And then he added out of politeness. 'It's good of you to drive me to the airport.'

'Not at all. The least I could do.' The Chief Inspector reached for Collier's suitcase. 'Well, if you're ready then.'

The Englishman nodded. Then, after one last lingering look around the room, he picked up his briefcase and the camera holdall and followed Mitsides out of the front door.

As they drove out of the town Collier asked, 'Any new developments?'

Mitsides shook his head. 'No. We still haven't found Basileos.'

'And the briefcase with the money in it?'

'Not a trace of it. Anywhere.'

'Maybe it's finally vanished for good.'

The detective nodded. 'Possibly.' And then he added mysteriously, 'It's purpose accomplished.' Collier frowned and gave him a puzzled look. 'I have a feeling that the money was merely a catalyst,' Mitsides explained. 'A means to an end. A trigger to set in motion an inevitable train of events. An intriguing case,' he said thoughtfully, his attention on the road ahead. 'For instance, the woman, Helene. Charalambos. Basileos. They went to such lengths. Acted so deviously. But what was their interest? They were clearly not looking for profit from the tomb. They gained nothing.'

'Two of them died,' Collier reflected grimly, the memory still a fresh and open wound.

'Exactly. But to achieve what? And Basileos has disappeared without a trace. Why? He has nothing to fear. He has done nothing illegal.'

The Englishman shook his head and sighed. 'As you said, so many questions.'

'And here's another,' Mitsides went on. 'Hellman offered you a million dollars for those sapphires. Now that's a great deal of money. A temptation for anyone. And one I don't think many people could have resisted.' He grinned. 'Me included. But you did. You refused his offer and took the jewels back to the tomb. Why?'

Collier had puzzled deeply over this question himself during the past forty-eight hours. 'I don't know,' he admitted lamely.

'Perhaps because you couldn't help yourself,' suggested the detective quietly. And Collier was about to follow this up when Mitsides glanced across at him and smiled. 'Do you mind if we make a slight detour?' he asked. 'There's something I'd like to show you. It won't take long. And we have the time.'

Collier shrugged.

A mile or so further along the highway the Chief Inspector swung the car on to a minor road and a few minutes later parked it close to the well-preserved and partly restored ruins of an ancient temple.

Mitsides got out of the car and Collier followed him. He looked around, puzzled. 'Come,' said Mitsides. And he led the way in among the ruins.

'What are we doing here?' Collier asked.

The Chief Inspector smiled. 'Humour me. Please,' he begged, as he guided his companion into the centre of a group of five lifesize standing statues and then paused beside the plinth of one of them and looked up at it thoughtfully.

Collier followed his gaze.

The face of the statue was worn by time and weathered by the elements but it was still recognisable.

Frowning, Collier looked away from the statue and across at Mitsides who met his gaze. 'Apollo,' he said.

The Englishman shrugged. 'That has some significance?'

Mitsides smiled. 'Apollo! No, I think not.' He indicated the statue standing alongside the god of the sun. 'Nor Hermes.' And then, from his pocket, he drew the photograph of the hieroglyphics which had been in Barry's wallet. He handed it to Collier. 'This belongs to you,' he said.

Collier studied the photograph and shook his head sadly. 'I saw these carvings in the tomb. I told you, didn't I?'

Mitsides nodded. 'Do you know what they say?' he enquired. Collier looked at him blankly. 'Professor Stylianou translated them for me,' the detective explained. 'It is a warning. If you like, a threat. The inscription makes it plain that the tomb is dedicated to Aphrodite and that it is under the protection of the goddess herself. With Dionysus and Pan as co-guardians. And it goes on to say that violation of the tomb would be sacrilege and would bring down on the offender or offenders the full wrath and vengeance of these three divinities.'

Collier frowned deeply and looked at the photograph again.

'Well the tomb was violated, wasn't it?' Mitsides went on. 'And five of those who were guilty of that sacrilege, including your brother, paid the ultimate penalty for their crime. Preece killed them. As I think there can be little doubt that he also killed Morrison. But that would still have left the gods unsatisfied. The vengeance of the gods would not have been complete.'

Collier gaped at him. The Chief Inspector was undeterred. 'Preece had also to be destroyed,' he elaborated. 'And, at the same time, those artefacts already stolen from the tomb, or which they had allowed to be used as bait, had to be returned to it and then its future as a hallowed place, undefiled and undisturbed, had to be ensured. And to achieve those ends what would have amused those three more than, as in ancient times, to use some poor unsuspecting mortal?'

By now Collier was seriously beginning to question Mitsides' sanity. 'Oh come on now!' he burst out. 'This has got to be some kind of joke. Either that or . . .' He decided against bluntly stating the alternative. 'You're not seriously suggesting . . .' Again he broke off as, very deliberately, the Chief Inspector looked away from him and gazed at something above and beyond his right shoulder.

Frowning again, Collier turned and looked up.

He gasped, and reacted with a look of shock and then of incredulity at what he saw.

The face of the first of the three statues standing in a semi-circle behind him was undoubtedly that of Charalambos.

Mitsides was watching him closely. 'Pan. The mischief maker,' he said.

Slowly Collier, his eyes still on its face, crossed to the statue. 'It's Charalambos!' he exclaimed in amazement. And then he swung round on Mitsides. 'It's him, I tell you!' he insisted. 'It's Charalambos!'

The detective was regarding him dispassionately. Astounded and with growing excitement, Collier turned back to look at the second statue.

There was no question about it. It was Basileos.

'Dionysus. God of wine.' And Mitsides made it sound like a formal introduction.

'Basileos!' breathed Collier and then, faintly, he began to smile. 'Basileos,' he repeated affectionately.

Quickly he moved to the base of the third statue but this time he hesitated, hardly daring to look up at it.

'The goddess of love and beauty. Aphrodite,' said Mitsides quietly.

Slowly, fearfully, Collier lifted his head to look at the statue and then, bewildered but overjoyed, he smiled again.

Aphrodite was the twin of Helene and for an instant she was again in his arms and he was kissing her. He spun round to face the detective again and his expression was one of confused wonderment. 'It's them!' he marvelled. 'Charalambos. Basileos. Helene. It's them!'

The Chief Inspector smiled quietly. 'A positive identification, Mr Collier?' he asked.

Collier nodded. Then he frowned. 'But it isn't possible, is it?'

Mitsides shrugged. 'There are some who would say it was. But I am a man of the twentieth century. And a police officer. I deal in facts. Evidence. And there are no facts, no evidence to support such a theory. But I am also a Cypriot and this is a magic island. So I put it to you as a possibility. But nothing more.' He looked at his watch. 'We must go.'

Collier's face fell. He would have liked to have stayed longer. Here among his friends.

'The past, Mr Collier, whichever way you look at it.' Mitsides reminded him. 'Two thousand years or three days. It makes no difference. It is still the past. And today and the future are waiting for you. And these are only statues.'

He moved briskly away, heading for his car and, very reluctantly, Collier followed him. But more than once he looked back over his shoulder.

Collier and Mitsides came out of the terminal building side by side and walked across the tarmac towards the other passengers already boarding a Boeing 727 of Cyprus Airways.

Collier was carrying his briefcase and he had the camera holdall slung over his shoulder. Accompanied by the Chief Inspector he had had no difficulty in passing through Customs and Immigration and, for the first time in his life, he'd had the satisfaction of seeing his suitcase handled almost reverently by the baggage handlers behind the check-in counter.

A few yards off from the aircraft Mitsides stopped, turned and put out his hands. 'Goodbye,' he said.

Collier shook hands with him. 'Goodbye. And thank you.'

'For what?'

'The detour.'

Mitsides smiled. 'Perhaps one day you will return to Cyprus,' he said.

'Perhaps.'

'I hope so.'

Collier shrugged. 'We'll see.'

'You should,' Mitsides advised him, and there was a twinkle in his eye. 'Because who knows what you might find waiting for you.'

Collier smiled and then, with a farewell nod, he walked on towards the aircraft.

The detective watched him go and when Collier was almost at the foot of the boarding steps he turned and looked back at him. 'Has it occurred to you,' he shouted. 'That if they were using me then they were also using you.'

Mitsides laughed. 'Of course,' he shouted in reply. 'But isn't that the destiny of us all? To be the plaything of the gods. Why else were we put on this earth?' He waved. '*Kalo taksithi*.'

Collier waved back and then, jostled by the other passengers, he climbed the steps.

The air hostess checked his boarding card and then led him to an aisle seat.

The aircraft was packed and the seats next to Collier were occupied by a middle-aged Cypriot woman and her husband.

With some difficulty he stowed his briefcase and the camera holdall under his seat and the seat in front of him and then settled himself down and fastened his seat belt.

As the aircraft began to taxi the woman sitting beside him began to cross herself several times and Collier remembered the flight out from London and prayed that this time it would be different.

The Boeing turned on to the runway, paused and then thundered forward, took off and climbed.

The 'no smoking' and 'fasten seat belt' signs were extinguished and Collier reclined his seat and stared up into space and was soon lost in thought.

And he had a lot to think about. Of course what Mitsides had put forward as a possibility when they were standing amidst the ruins of the temple was preposterous, and the likeness on the faces of the three statues could only have been a trick played on his subconscious by the brilliant Cypriot light. He had seen what he wanted to see. Nevertheless, for a while at least, he had derived some comfort from the theory and from the illusion.

It was the voice of the air hostess which brought him out of his reverie.

'Excuse me, sir.'

Collier looked up and focussed on her. She was standing beside him and leaning forward slightly.

'I'm sorry, sir,' she said with a smile and she pointed at something in the aisle. 'But this must go under your seat.'

Puzzled, Collier gazed at her blankly. 'I beg your pardon?'

The air hostess's smile faded a little and she sighed. 'This can't stand in the aisle, sir,' she said firmly. And she reached down, picked up a briefcase and put it into Collier's lap. And before he could protest or disclaim ownership she moved off.

Collier looked at the briefcase and then started. He had seen it before. Once at night in a deserted village and then again in the house in Paphos when he had fought Eric Morrison for possession of it. And then it had disappeared. Unbelievingly Collier unfastened the catches and lifted the lid slightly, but wide enough for him to catch a glimpse of the bundles of Swiss francs that it contained.

Hastily he slammed the lid shut again and shot a worried look at the couple sitting alongside him. And he was reassured to find that they were both peering out of the window.

Dumbfounded, he got to his feet and, clutching the briefcase, hurried for the privacy of one of the lavatories.

Safely locked inside it, he opened the briefcase again. All the money was there, the whole fifty thousand pounds. Just as it had been when Helene had first handed it to him. But now there was something else.

Lying across the bundles of notes was a long stemmed, fresh and fragrant red rose, only recently plucked.

Collier picked up the flower and gazed at it.

The Boeing 727 banked lazily on to a new heading and Collier began to laugh. And as he did so he knew for certain that somewhere the gods were also laughing. And not at him, with him.

THRILLERS

0352	Star	
	Georges Arnaud	
397012	**WAGES OF FEAR**	75p ♦
	David Axton	
395184	**PRISON OF ICE**	85p
	Paul Boncarrère	
396474	**ULTIMATUM**	75p
	William F. Buckley Jr.	
396962	**SAVING THE QUEEN**	60p*
	Richard Butler	
396059	**WHERE ALL THE GIRLS ARE SWEETER**	60p
	Henry Denker	
300523	**A PLACE FOR THE MIGHTY**	75p*
	Burt Hirschfeld	
398582	**FATHER PIG**	60p*
395176	**SECRETS**	85p*
398590	**MOMENT OF POWER**	75p*
398604	**BEHOLD ZION**	85p*
	Tony Kenrick	
396253	**THE SEVEN DAY SOLDIERS**	60p
	Hugh C. McDonald	
396849	**THE HOUR OF THE BLUE FOX**	60p*
	Graham Masterton	
395982	**PLAGUE**	75p
396911	**FIREFLASH 5**	60p
	Michael Maguire	
395818	**SCRATCHPROOF**	70p
397853	**SLAUGHTER HORSE** (also see Tandem Thrillers)	70p
	Lawrence Sanders	
300078	**THE FIRST DEADLY SIN**	95p

† For sale in Britain and Ireland only.
* Not for sale in Canada.
♦ Film & T.V. tie-ins.

THRILLERS

0426 Universal/Tandem

	Nick Carter	
183584	**ASSASSIN: CODE NAME VULTURE**	60p*
173635	**BERLIN**	50p*
174437	**CAMBODIA**	50p*
174275	**THE CHINESE PAYMASTER**	60p*
173554	**THE COBRA KILL**	50p*
128028	**CODE NAME WEREWOLF**	60p*
174003	**THE DEATH STRAIN**	50p*
173988	**THE DEFECTOR**	50p*
174518	**HOOD OF DEATH**	50p*
173201	**THE HUMAN TIME BOMB**	50p*
180836	**ICE TRAP TERROR**	60p*
18470X	**THE JERUSALEM FILE**	60p*
180917	**MASSACRE IN MILAN**	60p*
173716	**THE MIND KILLERS**	50p*
173120	**THE LIVING DEATH**	50p*
176898	**THE MAN WHO SOLD DEATH**	50p*
180089	**THE N3 CONSPIRACY**	50p*
179889	**THE PEKING DOSSIER**	50p*
180674	**THE SIGN OF THE COBRA**	60p*
184467	**SIX BLOODY SUMMER DAYS**	60p*
176545	**THE KATMANDU CONTRACT**	60p*
181042	**VATICAN VENDETTA**	50p*
184114	**THE Z DOCUMENT**	60p*
	David Chandler	
183908	**THE GANGSTERS**	95p*
	John Gardner	
184548	**THE LIQUIDATOR**	60p
	Michael Maguire	
172914	**SHOT SILK** (also see Star Thrillers)	70p

† For sale in Britain and Ireland only.
* Not for sale in Canada.
♦ Film & T.V. tie-ins.